THE BLUEGRASS BATTLEGROUND

CLIFFORD'S WAR

THE BLUEGRASS BATTLEGROUND

CLIFFORD'S WAR

J. DENISON REED

Charleston, SC
www.PalmettoPublishing.com

Clifford's War

First Edition

Hardcover ISBN: 978-1-7371640-0-5
Paperback ISBN: 978-1-7371640-2-9
eBook ISBN: 978-1-7371640-1-2

To Jessica, my wife, who was my sounding board, inspiration, and support throughout the entire process. I wouldn't have finished this without you.

Contents

Chapter One

With **bloody fingers** and cracked fingernails, he pries at the loose screw on the wooden table. Bound at the wrists with old frayed rope, his chances to free himself depend on getting something sharp to poke at the knot to loosen it. He has no memory of how he found himself strapped here.

He continues to pick and pluck at the screw. His vision, still blurred by the blow to his head, is blinded by the sun peering in through the slatted holes in the ceiling. The rot and decay of the surrounding structure lead him to believe that he's in a building, possibly abandoned for decades.

This feeling is familiar.

His memory slips back to when he was a POW in Afghanistan. He can hear screams, but cannot make out words. With a jolt, the memory slips away into nothingness, bringing him back to the task at hand.

Blood is pooling around the screw and his wrists are becoming raw as he tugs on the ropes. The blood starts to lubricate the screw as it drips down into the hole, making it slippery and more difficult to grasp with his torn fingertips. With the plucking and tugging, he is slowly pulling and twisting the screw out of the splintered wood. One final tug and he pulls the screw free. He holds it in the palm of his hand and lets out a sigh of contentment. After a moment, he begins to poke at the knot near his wrists.

Suddenly he hears a crack, what sounded like a plank falling, and feels a little give in the wooden table where he is strapped. The leather straps across his chest and abdomen seem to tighten and pull down onto him as the loose plank falls to the floor. He stops picking at the rope as the table cracks again and becomes unstable. He palms the screw tightly, shifts his body weight, and the table starts to slowly rock head to toe, back and forth, freely. After a third crack, the table's legs near his head give way and break under his weight. With his legs pointed toward the tattered and hole-filled ceiling, the blood is starting to rush to his head. He closes his eyes briefly as his head begins to spin from the force of gravity of the leaning table. He begins to pick at the rope again and the knot becomes loose enough to slip his hand out.

Freed, he swings his hand across his naked body and tries to reach the other knot on his left hand. Picking and prying at the knot, the rope is turning red, stained from his blood. He pulls on the rope to create enough slack to loosen the knot. With relief, he cheers as his other hand slips out of the tight confinement.

Sweat is rolling up his back as he's removing the buckle of the large leather strap holding him to the table. He swings his body up with one grunting situp. His abs are sore and bruised and it feels as if he was hit in the stomach with a wrecking ball. He falls back down on his back with heavy panting breath. He swallows a bunch of air and muscles his way back up, grasping the sides of the table for added leverage. He unties the knots, freeing his legs, and stumbles off the table and onto his stomach.

The wooden floor creaks and seems to cry in pain with the stress of his weight as he makes his way to his feet.

He slowly shuffles across the floor, trying to avoid getting a loose nail, splinter, or a shard of glass in his bare feet.

He winces in pain as he touches his head. It feels as if he was struck by something.

He tries to remember the events that brought him here, but everything is fragmented. The memory of Afghanistan continues to haunt him as he struggles to remember the last twelve hours.

The muted screams become clearer as the mangled man, lying next to the smoking wreckage of a humvee, is calling out his name. "DEE!" the soldier is painfully screaming in fear.

"1-2-3-4-5, Clifford Dee is still alive," he says to himself as he closes his eyes.

This is the same technique he used as a POW in Afghanistan to help reassure himself.

Clifford swings open a solid oak door to a joining hall. He turns behind him to see that he was in the sanctuary of an old abandoned church. The table he was strapped to, was an old altar of some sort. There is a stained-glass window of what he believes to be Saint Peter at the gates in the back by the pulpit. It's hard to tell due to it being partially smashed and broken. Clifford turns away from the sanctuary and heads into the darkened hall. Beams of light are streaming across the darkness as he makes his way to the illuminated doorway in front of him.

Pushing through the doorway, he feels a burning in his blue-green eyes as they attempt to adjust to the blinding daylight.

Looking around he comes to realize that this church is in the center of the woods.

Clifford laughs to himself, "I think this is how horror movies start out."

He spots a dirt road through the trees that look just large enough for a car to pass.

Clifford, standing naked in the sunlight, realizes that he must find something to protect his body and more importantly, his feet if he's going to journey back to civilization. He stumbles back into the church looking for anything to use as clothing. Clifford finds a cracked wooden cupboard that has a tattered burlap sack inside. As he pulls on the sack, he is startled by a rat scurrying by.

"JESUS CHRIST!" he exclaims as he jumps back with the sack in his hand.

From behind the sack, there is a worn hand-painting of the crucified son of God. Clifford says to himself, "Literally," as he makes out the picture.

The sack opening is big enough to fit his legs and waist into. He rips a large piece from the bottom, so he can use it for pants. Clifford walks over to the broken table where he painfully awoke earlier. He wraps the ripped portion of the sack around a large shard of glass, to use as a handle, and starts shaving rope off the ties that previously bound his hands and feet. After he cuts off several pieces of rope, he slips his naked legs into the sack and pulls it up around his waist. "This is really going to chafe my dick," he mutters to himself in discontent.

He wraps a piece of rope around his waist and rolls the top of the sack down onto it. He ties a knot into the rope, using it as a belt to keep the sack around his waist.

Clifford picks up the leather strap that once buckled him to the table. He uses the glass knife to saw it into pieces for the bottoms of his feet. He uses the remaining burlap to wrap his feet all the way to his ankle and secures it with the last bit of frayed rope, making the worst pair of shoes he's ever worn.

He isn't going to be able to play basketball wearing them, but they might be able to protect the bottom of his feet long enough until he finds something better.

Clifford picks up his make-shift glass knife and looks at the reflection of his face and has a brief flashback.

Coming to in the backseat of a car, hands tied behind his back and a gag in his mouth. He glanced into the rear-view mirror where he could see the driver.

They make eye contact.

Darius said, "Look who's awake."

Marcus looked over his shoulder, "Not for long," As he punched him directly in the side of the head with a shiny pair of brass knuckles.

End memory.

Clifford was hunting Darius and Marcus Tye. The notorious Tye brothers. They were hitmen hired to take out family members of local "Connected Men," to send messages. The media, unaware of the mob connections, are calling them, "Spree Killers." A mistake was made, and Clifford's employer, Mr. Bandoni, was affected. While contracted to kill the daughter of the head of the O'Connell family, Brenden Bandoni, one of Mr. Bandoni's rising stars and nephew, was asleep in her bed. Everyone says he put up a good fight to defend her, but no one really knows if that was the case, as both were killed.

Clifford doesn't know the politics of this situation, but with no families protecting them, Bandoni was given the green light to have them taken out. Bandoni decided to go outside the family and hired Clifford to do so.

Back outside in his makeshift shorts and shoes, Clifford is walking with more confidence that he will not catch his feet on anything sharp. The ropes and burlap are slight agonizing torture to the tops of his feet, but worth the pain knowing that the bottoms are well protected. While making his way down the dirt road through the trees, Clifford looks around to notice the sun toward his back. "I'm heading East," he says to himself trying to understand his bearing.

After about an hour of walking down the narrow car path through the woods, Clifford hears a car.

He darts off the path and crouches behind a small shrub. His heart is racing as he knows that he's too weak to fight off someone's grandmother, let alone the two psychopaths that already got the drop on him once. The car slowed to cross a few of the bigger dips and rivets of the stony path. He can hear music playing as it passes the tiny shrub that is concealing him. Clifford, peering through the bush, looks inside the car to see that it was, in fact, the brothers.

Clifford remembers following them to an apartment building.

They pull up and both jump out and head inside. Clifford stops across the street and waits. After a few minutes, Darius exits alone and walks up the street, away from his car. Watching and wondering where Marcus is, Clifford decided to follow Darius. He walked up toward their car and peered inside. "Clifford Dee?" He heard from behind him. Standing before him, Marcus said, "Stacey says, 'Hello'." The last thing Clifford saw was the sun glimmering off of the pipe before it struck him on his head.

Clifford realizes in about 20 minutes they'll be disappointed to find an empty church and will probably come looking for him soon after. He waits until the car is out of sight and starts walking at twice the pace. The sun is starting to set behind him and the air is getting colder.

He can see a crossroad off in the distance. The intersection is paved, but the road which continues east turns to gravel. At the intersection, he hears a car approaching from the north. Knowing that The Tye Brothers had no way of doubling back to come from that direction, he wanders to the side of the road and waves his hands. A small sedan approaches and passes him, doing about sixty miles per hour. He continues to wave his hands at the car. The driver of the car, noticing that Clifford is basically naked in the middle of the road, decides to stop.

Clifford sees the brake lights and the car quickly coming to a stop and cheers, "Yes! Thank you!" he blurts out as he drops to his knees in exhaustion. The driver begins to back up slowly and throws the car in park as it gets close to Clifford, climbing back onto his feet.

A beautiful young woman steps out of the car and slowly walks toward Clifford.

"Are you okay, sir?" was the sweetest sounding question he has heard all week.

"I need a hospital, please," Clifford says as his legs start to give out. His feet are sore and worn and his burlap shorts are in shreds. "Do you have any water?" He questions as he is severely dehydrated.

She opens the backseat door of her sedan and helps Clifford into the car.

"What's your name?" she asks.

"Kyle," he responds, "My name is Kyle Somers."

Wincing outwardly over his lie which she assumes is due to pain and exhaustion.

"Well, Kyle Somers, you're lucky I found you," She says as she closes the door. "I will get you some help."

He closes his eyes and the rhythmic sound of the rubber on asphalt lulls him to sleep.

Chapter Two

Clifford jolts awake in a hospital bed. The room is filled with the faint sound of breathing machines and of various other health monitors. He can smell antiseptic and artificial bubble gum scented cleaner. Clifford's eyes painfully adjust to the light of the room. His vision is blurred and hazy. He looks over to see an I.V. attached to his arm. His fingers, head, and feet are neatly wrapped in gauze and tape.

A young male nurse walks up to Clifford, "Easy fellah, you're safe here. Kyle, right? Do you remember what happened to you?"

With a puzzled look on his face, Clifford looks at the nurse, "How did I get here?" He asks.

"You were brought in last night. Ashlea found you in the middle of the road on her way into work. Do you have any recollection of what happened?" The nurse questions.

"No," Clifford lies. He wanted to continue keeping things very close to the vest for now; play it safe.

"Okay, sir," He says, "You need a bit more rest. You got quite a few bumps and bruises, oh, and a huge lump on your noggin. Lucky you didn't need any stitches if you ask me," He continues, "So, you just sit there and recover, okay? We got ya."

Clifford just nodded along to this barrage of information the nurse was throwing at him.

"Oh, my name is James, by the way, and I'll be here for a few more hours and will check in on you periodically. We got you on a drip, just a bit of Caldolor. Ibuprofen, for you non-medical types," He continues with a smile and light chuckle.

"You are going to be A-O.K. Just sit tight," He says, flicking his wrist. He pats Clifford on the leg and turns tail and walks over to the next patient.

Clifford lays his head back and lets out a huge sigh. The flash of light from the TV in the corner of the room catches his eye. The volume is muted, but it is clear they're talking politics, something that Clifford despises. He starts to look away when he notices the ticker at the bottom of the screen.

"...Several bodies found in the trees outside a nature preserve have local police questioning if these are even more victims of The Tye Brothers...."

Clifford has a laser focus now on the ticker.

"...Police continue to investigate and welcome tips from anyone that may have more information...."

Clifford remembers doing research. He isn't one to just take a thick envelope and start hunting. He knew The Tye Brothers' style and they wouldn't be this dumb.

Clifford wasn't shocked that Eustachio Innocenzo Bandoni, the head of the Italian family in this area, didn't trust his top guy to take care of The Tye Brothers. Liam Stacey was probably the only one dumb enough to dump bodies in the open like that. He was sloppy. How he was Bandoni's number one was beyond Clifford.

"I want The Tye Brothers DEAD! I don't care how, but you get them this week and you get the rest of your money."

Clifford took the envelope off the desk and shoved it inside his jacket pocket. "Consider it done," He confirmed.

"I got word that they are leaving town. Don't Fuck this thing up, or it is your ass. IF THEY FUCKING DISAPPEAR, YOU WILL TOO. Hai capito?!"

Clifford nodded, "Understand completely Mr. Bandoni."

"These God-damned assholes deserve everything that is coming to them for killing my nephew," Bandoni said as he handed him a picture of The Tye Brothers.

"Like I said, consider it done!" Clifford responds.

Clifford sat wondering how he was going to get back on the scent of The Tye Brothers. Nurse James waves at Clifford with a smile and nods as he turns to walk out of the room.

"Odd fellow," Clifford says to himself. He looks back to the TV to see if he could catch the time. It is 10:28 am.

He has a feeling that the police will want to talk to him about the murders since he was found on that same stretch of road. Clifford knew that he has to get out now, or else he'll lose much-needed time while being held by the police for questioning.

With one swift tug, he pulls out the I.V. needle and tosses it on the floor. He swings his legs over the side of the bed and stands up. Clifford's knees give out and he flops back onto the hospital bed, grasping the edge to keep from hitting the floor. He pulls himself back up to his feet and sits on the edge of the bed until he gets his bearings.

Clifford pushes himself off the bed and onto his neatly wrapped feet. The bandages offer very little traction. He slips across the floor as though he is on an ice-skating rink with no skates.

He thinks to himself that the first thing he needs to do is find a change of clothing. Walking out of a hospital in a gown would probably raise a few questions and enough people have already seen his ass.

Clifford made his way out to the hallway where another staff member waves over to him after seeing him leave the room. "Can I help you, sir?" She asks.

"Oh, I need to stretch my legs. They're starting to hurt, just laying there," Clifford responds.

"Okay, just don't go too far," She says as she returns to her sudoku.

He steps into another room, which was empty. No patient, or bed, for that matter.

He figures they must have wheeled the entire bed out of the room to take the patient out for tests or surgery.

Clifford looks inside the small closet and finds a shirt and pants folded neatly in a plastic bag. He takes off his hospital robe and begins to dress in his newly found clothes.

The pants are a bit too big, but that was okay. Better than being too small. He uses a piece of gauze from his hand wrap and ties two of the belt loops on the pants together, and makes the pants fit perfectly. He throws the oversized shirt on and glances down to see a pair of slip-on loafers on the floor.

Walking out of the room, Clifford sees James talking to two police officers near the room where he was supposed to be, "resting up." He has a feeling they came to question him about where he was found. He doesn't have time for that.

Clifford walks in the other direction and heads toward the elevator. The slip-on loafers are about a size and a half too big which almost fit perfectly over his neatly bandaged feet. He sees a hospital diagram and heads toward it. Looking it over for a few moments trying to plan his great escape, he notices that there is a skywalk to the parking garage from the maternity ward.

Clifford walks back over to the hallway near the elevators and frantically presses the elevator button. He jumps into the first open elevator, and as the doors begin to close, he hits six for the maternity floor. The doors shut, and he is slowly lifted, watching the numbers light up as it hits each floor.

three...four...five...Ding.

The doors open on the fifth floor and a nurse walks in, with her head down, buried in a chart. She turns to the number panel and half-reaches as she notices that six was already pressed.

She lifts her head and looks over at Clifford.

"Kyle Somers?" She questions after doing a double-take.

"Uh," Clifford stammers.

"There is no way you are well enough to leave just yet," The nurse states. Clifford looks at her in deep confusion as a fuzzy recent memory enters his mind.

"What is your name?" she asks. "Kyle," he responded, "My name is Kyle Somers". "Well Kyle Somers, you are lucky I found you," She said as she was closing the door. "I will get you some help."

The elevator takes a small eternity to go from floor five to floor six. Clifford stands there in disbelief as the woman that found him in shambles on the side of the road is standing just before him. "You found me last night, didn't you? So, you're Ashlea?"

"Uh, yeah," she says, "Ashlea Davis. I'm a nurse in maternity, but I never gave you my name," She continues in slight confusion.

"I have psychic powers," Clifford says with a smile. "Nah, I'm kidding. A nurse downstairs mentioned your name."

With a ding, they hit the sixth floor, and the elevator doors open. Clifford says, "I'm just out and about for a stroll. It was getting stuffy in my room."

Walking out of the elevator, Ashlea begins to look at him a bit more confused. "Where did you get those clothes?" She asks.

Clifford stammers a bit before saying, "My sister came by and dropped them off. She grabbed some from my donation pile. I lost a bit of weight this year."

Ashlea nods "Okay. How're you feeling?" She asks. "You were a bit out of it last night. You really should still be resting. It's only been about," glancing at her watch, "ten hours since I brought you in."

They begin walking together, slowly, while continuing their conversation. Clifford is still trying to think of some way to excuse himself from her company without tripping any alarms in her head. Clifford stops for a second, looks around, and brushes off the question. "Yeah well…"

"Well, come on now, and let's go back to your room," She returns sternly. Clifford stands there a bit reluctant to move. "I can't go back to my room, I have to…"

Ashlea, growing tired with him says, "What's going on, Kyle? Be honest with me."

Clifford winces inwardly, remembering the fake name he gave her the night before. He knows there is no straight-forward way to get out of this situation. He looks her in the face and says, "Ashlea, thank you so much for stopping last night. Thank you for saving my life. Thanks for the ride here, and thank you for everything, but I have to go. I can't tell you why."

Ashlea grabs his arm as he starts to pull away from her. "Hey, wait a second!" She says concerned. "You can't just leave!"

Letting out a deep sigh, "I can't stay any longer. I gotta be somewhere. Please let me go," Clifford says, pleading with her. She loosens her grip on Clifford's arm and says, "Okay look, if you want to go, there is nothing we can do to stop you. That's your decision."

Clifford responds, "Thank you. I knew you'd understand."

Over the PA system, Ashlea hears her name, realizing she is being paged to a room. She looks over to Clifford and says, "Okay, I have to go, but promise me you will get some rest. You need it."

"Okay sure, I will get rest," Clifford says.

Knowing that the police are most likely going to be look-ing for him, he can't just go and sign a form and walk on out. They would turn him over to the authorities as soon as he pops his head into the office.

Clifford walks back into the elevator as Ashlea looks on.

He steps out onto the first floor and starts walking back in the direction of his room.

He could hear Nurse James defending himself from a distance.

"I'm sorry, officer. No one told me that he was supposed to be held for police questioning. He was just found on the side of the road last night. We called it in."

One of the officers snaps back, "We notified the hospital that we wanted him held for questions."

Clifford hides in an empty room for a moment to listen to the extent of the conversation.

James starts to raise his pinched nasal voice, "Well, it didn't get down to me and I am the head nurse on duty in this section. Don't get mad at me."

Shaking his head, the officer continues to barrage James with sly comments.

"Excuse me." The nurse at the desk tries cutting in during this massive finger-pointing but, like a third-party politician in a presidential election, she is being ignored by everyone.

"James!" She says with more gusto to only be ignored again.

Now louder than everyone in the area, she blurts out, "Are you looking for Kyle Somers!? Ashlea from maternity saw him upstairs and wants to know if he made it back down yet."

One of the officers asks, "What? Upstairs, why would he be upstairs?"

She continues. "I have no idea. Well, there is an exit to the garage up there."

15

The other officer says, "Yeah, we need him to answer a few questions before he tries to leave." The officer turns to his partner, "Get their statement, I'll look for Mr. Somers."

The cop runs past the room Clifford is listening from. He pokes his head out of the room and sees James and the other nurse talking to the other cop. Across the hall, he sees a sign pointing to the ER.

Clifford heads down the long hallway and pushes through double doors. He can hear more police officers talking as if they were starting to lock down the hospital to search for him. Keeping his head down he sneaks past a few of the cops and turns down another hallway toward the ER. He bumps into an officer who looks him up and down.

"Dee? Is that you?" The officer asks.

Clifford's eyes widen, "Oh, Hey-ya, Billy. How's your sister?" He asks.

"She's good, getting married next week. What are you doing here?" He asks.

Clifford raises his bandaged hand, "Yeah, it's a work-related injury. I'm good."

Billy laughs, "Dogs bite you know. You sleuth types should know that."

Clifford smiles and says, "Okay, well gotta go."

"Yeah, sure," Billy says. "We gotta guy to find. We think he's got some info about those Tye sumbitches."

Clifford waves as they pass each other and says, "Sounds like fun."

Billy gives two thumbs up as he rounds the corner.

There are pros and cons with taking cases that involve the police.

Clifford continues down the hallway into the ER and out the large sliding door. More police are pulling up as he walks down the street and gets onto a bus.

Chapter Three

It's late afternoon by the time Clifford makes it back to his place. It's an extremely nice two and a half bathroom, 2 bedroom condo, in the upscale part of town. He got a pretty good deal on the property because there was a homicide there two days before another client was going to close on it with the bank. The young buyers were devastated when they discovered the body during the final walk-through. It was tragic for them, but, when Clifford heard that the buyers were backing out, he seized the opportunity and was able to scoop up this gem for nearly half the price.

He also works out of his place, so it's good that it has two entrances. Converting the main suite into an office, the primary entrance opens to what was the original "Living Room," but is now a small waiting room with a fireplace.

He replaced the wall that the secondary bedroom shared with the living room with privacy glass paneling. This was made into his office, and it looked better than most corporate offices. Just past the office was a fully equipped kitchen with real wood floors, updated molding, granite countertops, and top-of-the-line appliances.

This looks to be a pretty decent-sized place, even not knowing there was a false wall separating his business side from his private side.

His private entrance was on a side hall which was away from the main elevator lobby.

If someone didn't know any better, they would have thought it was a separate apartment.

At the end of the hall are a door on one side and a stairwell leading to the garage. Next to this stairwell was a huge window with a planter filled with live plants to increase the ambiance of the hallway.

Clifford waves to a black man in a wheelchair as he walks past the front of the park. The man nods back at him as he rolls by. He strolls over to the back entrance of the condo and walks over to the planter. He pushes up a portion of the conifer and digs his hands into the rear left corner of the soil. He pulls up a large amount of moss, and then dirt. With one more scoop, he pulls up a latex balloon with two keys and a wad of money inside.

He replaces the dirt and moss and pats it down, trying to make it look undisturbed.

Clifford tears open the balloon and fishes out one of the keys. He walks over to his door and unlocks it. Entering his condo, he lets out a huge sigh of relief. He is exhausted. The small cuts on his feet reopened and started bleeding into the gauze, causing a squishy, sticky feeling as he walked.

This side entrance opens into a small hallway, with a closet on one side, and a small powder room on the other side. He bypasses the powder room and heads into his bedroom area.

Tossing the keys and the balloon filled with cash into a small bowl sitting on an antique wood side table, Clifford limps into the bedroom and flops onto the bed, kicking off the stranger's large shoes on his feet.

Although they were much better than leather straps, they were terribly uncomfortable, and he was ready to put something onto his feet that would quiet those barking dogs. Plucking at the gauze with his swollen fingers became more of a challenge than Clifford realized it would. He finally gave up and slid the loafers back on, so he could walk without getting blood on the floor.

He shuffles into the bathroom and sits on the closed toilet seat. The marble floor was a whole lot easier to clean than the wood in his bedroom. Clifford, again, kicks off the loafers and sets his bloody feet on the floor. He stands up and rifles through a drawer on the side of his sink and pulls out a pair of small scissors that he uses to trim his nose hair. He begins cutting at the gauze. He removes most of it when, all of a sudden, he hears something that causes some alarm.

Clifford has a silent alarm for his office area. When someone trips the alarm, all lights in front of the false wall will turn off so it doesn't cast light from the other room into the office. Then, red lights would kick on in the bedroom and a light squeal would go off for 30 seconds. It was the squeal that Clifford heard.

He finishes cutting through the last piece of gauze and sets the scissors down. His feet were not as bad as he thought they would be. Just a little blood, a few small contusions, and pain. He walks on his tip-toes and limps into the other room. Next to his bedroom area, there are a set of monitors. Clifford clicks them on.

The monitors are a collection of closed-circuit cameras he has set up in his office. One of them looks directly at the empty space where his 2008 Mustang Bullitt used to sit in the garage. He still has no recollection of where his baby is and what The Tye Brothers may have done with it. Next to that empty space is his Jeep Wrangler.

Looking back into his office, he sees the door swing open. Whoever it was can really pick a lock. He has two deadbolts on his office door and they picked through them like professional shoppers in a bargain bin. Clifford immediately identifies the two locksmiths as The Tye Brothers. It's likely that they found his ID after they went through the pockets of the pants they stole from him.

They dig into their case file which Clifford left sitting on his desk. Most of it is just notes and scribbles. The majority of the information is on his laptop, which is encrypted. Clifford knew that there is nothing he could do right now, as he is still a bit too weak. Besides, he wouldn't want to mess up his office.

Clifford reaches over and turns on the warning alarm in the hopes of scaring off his visitors.

"WARNING, YOU HAVE JUST ACTIVATED THE ALARM SYSTEM. THE POLICE ARE ON THEIR WAY."

This belts loudly over a PA system in his office. The alarm system did not actually alert the authorities, but The Tye Brothers didn't know that, nor did they want to chance it.

Quickly wrapping it up, The Tye Brothers grab the entire folder and start toward the door. Marcus Tye stops for a moment and then returns to Clifford's office.

He pulls out the shredded paper from the shredder and dumps a pile of it onto his desk.

He pulls out a matchbook, strikes a single match, and drops it onto the shredded mess. This caused a fire to swirl up and start burning out of control. Marcus folds the matchbook and attempts to toss it into the fire, but it skids past the flames and across Clifford's desk.

Darius looks over toward his brother with his hands akimbo. "Come on man, that wasn't necessary!" He says as Marcus meets him at the door.

"Fuck that guy. I hope it burns to the ground," Marcus says and they walk out of Clifford's office.

Lucky for Clifford, there was no accelerant to embellish the flames. The paper fire went out just as quickly as it was lit.

Clifford opens the false wall and limps into his office. The room was filled with a giant plume of smoke, leaving a giant pile of ash on his desk. He heads into the kitchen and grabs his mini fire extinguisher to put out the smoldering paperwork on his desk.

Clifford let out a groan as the building fire alarm went off. The plume of smoke billowed out of his office and into the hall where the building fire alarm sniffed it out. This is the last thing that Clifford needs. He doesn't want the attention of the authorities on him, or on The Tye Brothers. He picks up the matchbook that Marcus tossed across the desk and shoves it into his pocket. He scoops the smothered ash from his desk into his trashcan and walks it over to the kitchen, then heads to the front door of his office.

His younger neighbor from across the hall runs out of her apartment, seeing the plume of smoke rolling into the hallway, she covers her mouth and nose and walks in Clifford's door.

"Clifford, oh my God! Is everything okay?" She asks, with major concern.

Coughing, Clifford says, "Hey, Sara. Yeah, it's all good." as he meets her at the door and ushers her into the hallway. "No real damage. Just some vandals broke in and set some papers on fire. I was able to put it out pretty easily. I think it might have been some kids or something."

"That's good. Well, I mean, the putting it out part. The fire part sucks," Sara says.

She turns and points to the red and white flashing lights silhouetted on the wall in the lobby. "Looks like the Fire Department's already here. That was pretty quick."

Clifford places a hand on her shoulder, "Could you do me a huge favor?"

She nods, "Of course, whatever you need."

The firefighters were making their way up the stairs leading to the apartments and Sara belts out "It's okay! It's okay! The fire's out!"

The firemen start removing their masks. One of them walks over to the door and looks in. "What happened?" he questions, looking back at Sara.

"I'm a huge idiot, that's what," Sara says. "I was cooking for my neighbor. He just got out of the hospital. So I left the burner on and went to go talk to him."

The firefighters give each other a sardonic look. A bouncy girl in her mid-twenties burning dinner wasn't something unfamiliar to them.

"Oh, I know, right. I'm terrible," Sara continues as she notices the glances they gave each other, "So anyways, I didn't realize it was on and so when I came back, I set my paper towel roll onto it and it caught on fire."

"Really?" The fireman says in disbelief.

"Swear to Jesus. I am so dumb," Sara says.

"Okay, was there any damage?" One of the firemen asks.

"Nope, except for my paper towels," Sara says with a little laugh.

The firemen take a quick look around the hall and say, "Okay, It doesn't seem like any damage was done, we will walk around the parameter and do a quick check and be on our way."

Sara smiles, "Thanks! And sorry y'all had to come out here for my silly mistake."

"It's part of the job, Ma'am," He says as he turns away.

Sara walks over to the edge of the stairs and watches the firemen having a conversation. She sees her downstairs neighbors Jamie and Simon out looking around. The firemen are asking Jamie a question when Simon walks up to talk to Sara.

"Hey," Sara says to Simon.

Simon looks around. "So, I heard you talking to the firefighters. You were cooking?" He says with a smile.

"Yeah, I was cooking," Sara says with a smirk.

"So, what *really* happened?" Simon inquires.

Sara says, "I think Dee had a few disgruntled clients or something."

Hearing the conversation through the door, Clifford pokes his head out. "Hey!" He says to get their attention.

"Dude, what's going on?" Simon asks.

Clifford quips back, "disgruntled clients."

"Fine, don't tell me, but that just means I can't help out, you know," Simon says.

"Oh," he continues, "Jaime and I are going to head over to Stubini's to get some grub, you guys wanna join? My treat."

Simon is a good neighbor. He's the closest thing to a best friend that Clifford has. He knows Clifford has his secrets, but he doesn't judge him.

Sara shakes her head, "Nah, thanks though. You guys go have a nice dinner."

Clifford, looking pathetic and exhausted, looks up then waves him on. "I'm pretty worn out and I'm pretty sure the stench rolling off me would clear out the restaurant."

Simon chuckles, "That was the plan. I wanted private dining!"

"Okay Jerk! Go have fun," Clifford says with a smile.

Sara turns to Clifford and says, "Go get some rest, I will make sure the fire department leaves."

Chapter Four

The firefighters do their inspection of the building and start to wrap things up. Sara is itching to find out more about what Clifford got into. He's pretty tight-lipped about his business, but only because he has to be. As the firetrucks pull away, Sara walks back to the stairway of the building when an unmarked police car pulls up and a plain-clothes cop steps out of the car.

"Excuse me, Miss?" The officer says.

Sara looks back and starts walking toward him. "Hey, Officer, I explained everything to the fire department. It's all good."

"I'm Detective DiPietro. You're Dee's neighbor, right? Sara? He's mentioned you."

"Oh, yeah Detective DiPietro. How are you?" Sara says.

"Please, call me Martin," He says. "I heard the call on the scanner and an officer told me he saw Dee in the hospital. I just wanted to swing by to see if everything's okay," Martin continued.

Sara smiles and says, "Hopefully he's asleep. I was trying to keep him resting by making something for him, but instead, I made a mess of things."

Martin smiles, "He's lucky to have friends like you. Let him know I stopped by and I'll catch up with him later." He winks at Sara as he climbs back into his car and drives off.

Martin is a rising homicide detective and a damn good ally to have in the city. He has asked Clifford on several occasions to help on cases and he has been a very trustworthy friend for him.

Sara stands there for a minute while watching the cruiser speed off. Across the street, she notices a 30-something-year-old black man in a wheelchair looking on. Once she notices him, he turns and wheels himself into the park. She thinks it's a bit strange, but decides it's better to just mind her own business. There has been enough excitement on the block for one evening and he's probably just curious.

Early the next morning, fresh from her morning jog, Sara spots Clifford grabbing a newspaper by his door. She waves and he replies, "Hey," and motions for her to come in. "Thanks again for handling all that yesterday. It was pretty huge," he says.

"Uh, no sweat. You've saved my butt several times. Let's not forget that stalker who didn't believe I was gay and kept bugging me," Sara reminds him.

"Yeah, that was fun," Clifford says, smiling as he's recalling it. "Oh!" Sara exclaims, "Detective DiPietro came by to check on you."

Letting out a huge yawn, Clifford says, "Did he want anything?"

"Just to see how you were doing. Said he heard you were in the hospital," Sara says.

"How did he know?" Clifford wonders out loud, "Oh right, Billy!" He says as he remembers his adventures in the hospital. "Another officer saw me," He says to Sara.

She folds her arms and sternly says, "So, since I did you a favor, are you going to let me know what you got yourself into?"

Acting like he was thinking for a second, Clifford says, "Hmmm... Nope!"

Sara says, "Come on! I'm gonna keep bugging you until you tell me."

Clifford again says, "Nope," as he starts eating some eggs he just cooked for breakfast.

Sara again persists. "Cliffooorrd!" She says, dragging out his given name that no one ever calls him by.

"Saraaaaaa!" He says back, "Have some eggs," He continues, trying to change the subject. Pushing the plate away she says, "Okay fine, don't tell me, but don't ask me for any favors anymore."

Clifford nods, "Fine with me," He says.

"What's fine with you?" Martin asks as he pushes open the door.

Clifford and Sara both look over. "I was just telling my neighbor that I'm going to stop doing her favors," Clifford says. "So, she says you came by yesterday?" He continues.

Martin steps into the foyer and says, "Yeah, I heard you were banged up a bit, heard the fire call on the radio, so I figured I'd swing by and see how my favorite PI was doing."

Sara walks over toward the door and says, "I will let you guys talk. I have to get ready for work anyway."

Clifford invites Martin to sit, but he refuses. "Nah, I'm on my way into the office as well. Just wanted to see how you were doing."

"So, how am I doing?" Clifford asks sarcastically, "I have to say. I think I need a longer vacation."

"You take vacations?" Martin asks with a smile. "So, your neighbor, Sara right?" He continues.

Clifford nods.

"She told me that the fire yesterday was her fault. You gonna tell me what really happened here, or are you letting her take the blame?" Martin asks. "Cuz it sure smells like smoke in here, but not in the hallway. Just saying."

"Man, you got a hell of a nose. I air freshened the shit out of this place, but, yeah, she insisted. She's a good kid. I acted as a big brother a few times and now she treats me as one."

Martin nods as Clifford continues, "She just wanted to help out so I could get some sleep. Nothing major, just a B&E, and two guys tried to destroy a file. I have it all backed up," Clifford explains.

"Oh, just a B&E, huh?" Martin asks. "And you were just in the hospital with a minor hand injury too, right?" He continues.

Clifford smiles at the questions. "Yeah, work hazards, I tell ya," He says with a smirk.

"Well, if you saw them," Martin says, "Maybe I can pull up some local camera feeds and we can find those little fuckers."

Clifford knew that he couldn't spend any time on this. "Nah, it's good. There really wasn't any damage other than a few papers. Like I said, I got soft copies of all that anyway. It's really all good."

Martin nods and looks around. "Don't be dumb, if you need help let me know."

Clifford's smile grows, "Of course. You'll be the first one I go to if I find myself in some trouble."

Martin shakes his head and says, "You say that, but I don't believe you," as he heads out the door. Clifford follows and asks, "Why don't you believe me?" a few steps into the hall, Martin turns around and says, "Because I know you."

Clifford closes the door, locks it, and finishes the last bite of eggs. He leaves the kitchen and slides open the hidden false wall next to the powder room that conceals his bedroom area. He walks over to the dresser and picks up the half-burnt pack of matches that The Tye Brothers left for him. On the back, it reads, "Dollhouse." He's heard of the place. It's a strip club out in the middle of nowhere. He never visited but heard they have several stages and private party rooms for executive types. This is the only clue he has on where The Tye Brothers could be, so he has to look into it, he has no choice.

Clifford studies the areas surrounding the club using online internet maps to find anything that could remotely resemble a "Hideout," but found nothing overly suspicious.

The club was a decent drive from town, but it went by very quickly driving against the morning traffic. Knowing that he most likely would not be able to make a return trip back to the office, he came prepared. In the back storage compartment of his Jeep, Clifford has a small arsenal. Remington .22 sniper rifle, his military-grade M14, a pump-action 12 gauge with buckshot, several handguns, and several tactical knives. He also made sure to bring his ghillie suit, a tacky club suit, several silent trip alarms, and a wad of cash. Two thousand dollars, to be exact.

Strapped to his leg was his .45 Taurus Judge. Strapped to his hip was his 9mm Bersa CC, two flip pocket knives, and a lockpick set. He's taking no chances this time around. The last time he underestimated The Tye Brothers, he found himself on a table, bleeding.

Clifford closes in on the club. It isn't open, but he can imagine the glow of the neon lights exploding through the trees. Clifford steps out of the car and gives the place a 'once-over.' The air surrounding the building feels warm and has a slight smell of cheap perfume and sweaty ass. Clifford starts checking for exits, entrances, windows; really any place a person could escape from. He does not want to kill them in the club, but he also doesn't want them to elude him either.

Clifford jumps back into his car and heads south. With most of the hotels in that direction, he figures it's best to start there and work his way north.

He spots a sign that reads, "Kentucky River BBQ 2 miles." This sparks a memory:

Jolted awake as the car hits a pothole, Clifford found himself bound and gagged in the back seat of The Tye brother's car. His body bouncing, he fell onto the floor. Under the seat, his eyes begin to focus on a napkin that says, in bold lettering, 'Kentucky River BBQ.'

Clifford shakes the memory from his mind and decides it was worth checking out.

Kentucky River BBQ looks like a quaint place, nestled up against the Kentucky River. It has outdoor seating and located in a small town with small mom and pop shops all within walking distance. The area looks like a place to take your grandmother on a day trip.

Clifford parks his car and decides to stretch his legs. He walks past the BBQ joint and down the cobblestone-lined strip. He finds a small café with nice outdoor seating where he can have a cup of joe and think for a bit. He walks up to the establishment and notices a group of four young women sitting inside. Two of them are wearing ball caps, one that says "DH" on the side. They were in loose t-shirts and workout pants. They had the memory of last night's makeup on their faces and some glitter on their skin. They certainly looked like strippers.

He steps inside and walks past their booth "G'morning, Ladies," He says with a nod to the group as he passes. The women look up but do not deviate from their conversation, pretty much blowing him off.

Clifford chooses a spot at the counter angled to the side of where the women are sitting. He wants to keep them in his peripheral vision and hopefully, maybe, spark up a conversation. He figures they're approached all the time given their looks. Girls with big tits, small waists, thick legs, and firm asses usually cause most men to think with their little heads. A sudden desire to strike up a conversation will set off warning alarms with these ladies for sure.

Clifford orders a cup of coffee and eggs, sunny side up with a side of toast.

"You new in town?" The waitress asks.

"Just passing through. Looking for a place to rest, really. Been driving all night," Clifford answers. The waitress pauses for a minute, "Well," she stands tapping her pencil on her order pad. "There's these cabins down the way. A couple miles or so. I believe you can rent one for just a night, but they are pretty pricey though."

Clifford smiles and says, "Cost isn't an issue, but I'll check to see if they have anything. Thanks."

He notices that the mention of having money causes one of the girls to perk up. She looks over to Clifford, "So you're looking for a place for the night?"

The waitress rolls her eyes, "Your eggs are gonna be up in a minute," She says in disgust as she turns and walks away.

"Thanks," Clifford says to the waitress as he turns to continue talking to the stripper, "Yeah, just for the day so I can shower and get a bit of shuteye."

"There's a decent enough motel just north of here. It's not great, but it's a place," She says to Clifford.

He figures she's familiar with it seeing as it's near the club. It could also be where The Tye Brothers are staying. He knows it's worth looking into.

"Sure, do you have the address?" Clifford asks.

"Well, not really, but it's down the road from this club, called, 'The Doll House.' You could check it out," She says, offering up much more information than Clifford hoped.

"Check out the motel or the club?" Clifford asks with a smile.

"Both," She returns quickly with a laugh.

Laughing, Clifford says, "Sure, sounds like a fun night. Where is this place?"

She scribbles an address on a napkin and hands it to Clifford.

"This is the club, I'll be there tonight, ask for me, Coco."

Clifford looks at the note.

"Thanks, and for the motel?" He asks.

"If you go up that way to Old Richmond Road to Grimes, you'll pass it on your left 'bout a mile before you reach the club. It's called Old Grimes Lodge."

"Got it," Clifford says, "Thanks. I'm John, by the way. See you tonight?"

"Yeah, tonight. John," Coco says.

As she turns back to her company at the booth he overhears one of her companions call her a slut. "What? He's cute!" she whispers back.

The waitress walks in with Clifford's food and sets it down in front of him in a less than gentle way. "You know that saying, about waking up with fleas?" She asks as she sets the food down.

He looks back at Coco as she throws a snarky look at the waitress.

Clifford looks back at the waitress and says, "C'mon, That's not nice."

Pointing her pencil in the stripper's direction, "Neither are they, just be careful," The waitress says. "They have chewed up and spit out more men than I can count," She continues as she walks away.

Clifford looks over his shoulder at Coco, "I guess she isn't getting a tip?" he jokingly asks.

"Let's go, ladies." Another girl at the table suggests.

As they shuffle out of the café. "See you tonight," Coco yells out reaching for the door.

He nods.

Clifford sits and finishes his coffee and eggs. He looks back at the waitress who has the look of disapproval.

He doesn't care.

He follows Coco's directions and finds the motel easily. It stands out like a sore thumb because of its name "Old Grimes" which described it perfectly. It's old, beaten down, and it looks grimy. It also looks like there are more than a few rooms available. He slowly pulls into the parking lot, and to his surprise, notices a very familiar car.

Conveniently, The Tye Brothers are staying at the Old Grimes Lodge.

Clifford drives past their car and toward the office. He slips into a spot and quickly heads inside. A clerk, dusting shelves, stands with a coffee in his hand. He looks over his shoulder when Clifford walks in. He quickly sets his coffee and duster down and walks over to the counter.

"Welcome to Old Grimes Lodge, how can I be of assistance?" The man looks beaten and battered by life. He's probably in his forties, but his worn face makes him look like he's already enjoying his senior citizen's discounts. Clifford looks around at the décor in the retro-looking office, then retrains his focus on the gentleman at the counter.

"I need a room, just for one night," Clifford says.

"Just one night?" Questions the man. "If you check in now, I have to charge you for last night too. It's still pretty early."

"What, really?" Clifford asks.

"Check-in is supposed to be after 2 pm. It's not even 8:30 yet," The clerk says.

Clifford asks, "You don't have hourly rooms?"

The clerk scowls, "This ain't no fuck shack!" He belts. "At least it's not supposed to be," he continued in a quieter tone.

"Okay, fine, I just need some rest," Clifford says with affirmation.

"Sorry for the outburst. This used to be a really nice place," the clerk says.

Clifford nods. "Looks it!"

"Okay, well do you have any preferences? We have a few rooms in the front along the road and several in the back along the tree-line, if you prefer that."

Clifford ponders for just a moment and finally decides on a room in the back by the trees.

The outdated lodge still used real keys. It's very impressive how clean the room looks on the inside. It's not the worst room that Clifford has stayed in. It's an end unit with the window on the side pointing toward the road, which was very good. He'll be able to keep an eye on who's coming and going.

While settling into the room, he hears the sound of a car starting. Moments later he sees The Tye Brothers heading out toward the way he just came from. Hoping that they didn't decide to leave a day early, Clifford walks over toward the room their car was in front of to check it out.

The window has its blinds shut, so he has to try to break in. Using his lock-pick, he quickly opens the door and enters the room. He flips on the light and first sees the two messy twin beds with a small duffel bag of cash sitting on one of them.

Clifford's phone starts vibrating. He pulls his phone out of his jeans pocket. "Shit!" Clifford says under his breath as he pushes the answer button. "Hello, Mr. B," Clifford says as he brings the phone up to his ear.

"Just checking in on you since I have not heard from you in three days. Have you done it yet?"

Clifford politely says, "No, Mr. B., but I have located them, and it will be done tonight. I'll send you your verification that the job is complete."

"Good, good! I was starting to worry about you," Mr. Bandoni says in a joking manner.

"Oh, Mr. B. quick question," Clifford says. "Is Liam Stacey also on this job?"

After a second of silence, Bandoni with an irritated tone, quickly asks, "Why do you ask me this?"

Clifford stammers, "Well, I had a confrontation with one of the brothers and he mentioned Liam. I thought maybe you had him working the job, too."

"No, Stacey is not working any jobs right now. You know this," Bandoni says.

"Yeah, okay. I just wanted to confirm. Let me get back to work. I have a lot to do before tonight. Thanks for checking in," Clifford says as he is a bit annoyed.

Mr. Bandoni thinks for a moment about what Clifford told him. He picks his phone back up and places a call. "I want you to keep your eyes on Liam Stacey. Report back to me every one of his moves." Mr. Bandoni sets his phone back down and takes a sip of his coffee.

Continuing into the room, Clifford notices there are beer cans and cigarette butts strewn about. On the dresser sit two fake IDs and passports to match. For a moment, Clifford thinks about swiping them but knew that they would notice and would probably run. He sets them back down and walks over to the closet. Inside are two very nice suits and shoes to match. On the side, are two small empty suitcases. He can tell they're preparing to leave soon.

Clifford walks back to his room and grabs the keys to his jeep. He unlocks and opens the storage area and looks through his inventory. He pulls out a few GPS trackers and opens an app on his phone. He scans the code on the trackers and links them to the app. After a few minutes, he goes back to The Tye Brothers' room. He dumps the wads of cash onto the bed and slips one of the trackers in between the bills. He starts returning the cash to that bag when he hears a noise from out front.

He looks out of the peephole and sees The Tye Brother's car idling in front of the room, with Marcus walking toward the door. Clifford quickly locks the door and heads to the back of the room. He tries the windows in the back, but they do not open. "Shit!" He whispers to himself out of frustration as he can hear the key enter the lock.

Clifford stands frozen as the door is about to swing open. Out of pure desperation, he drops to the floor and scoots as close as possible to the bed near the back wall. Marcus Tye swings open the door and he shouts back to his brother, "Hey, Darius, I told you it was right here."

He scoops up the bag of cash and tosses it over to his brother.

"How did you forget an entire fucking bag?"

"Shut up, you didn't grab it either."

They continued to quarrel as they shut and locked the door.

Clifford lets out a sigh of disbelief that he was not spotted.

He jumps up and quickly walks to the door and presses his face against the peephole.

Darius pops the trunk, still berating his brother while Marcus takes a wad of cash from the bag.

"What the fuck are you doing with that?" Darius questions.

"It's for Cinnamon. I'm gonna get her to suck my dick tonight," Marcus says while provocatively raising his eyebrows.

"You have a problem, you know that?" Darius says slamming the trunk down. "What is it with you and cheap women anyway?"

"You see this wad? She ain't cheap." Marcus says getting into the passenger side of the car.

Clifford watches as they drive off to conduct whatever business they have. Clifford retreats to his room and spends the rest of the morning prepping, knowing he has to check out the club.

Chapter Five

Liam tosses on a blazer and pulls keys from his pocket. One of the guards asks, "Hey, where ya goin'?"

"Breakfast run, gonna get one of them jumbo breakfast burritos from Mama Rita's!" He shouts back as he jolts to his car.

The guard turns to one of Mr. Bandoni's men and says, "Follow him and report everything to Mr. B."

Mr. Bandoni's guy, Nick, stays far enough behind Liam to not seem suspicious. He sees Liam pulling off the main road onto a single-lane dirt road toward a small abandoned farm. Nick pulls to the side of the road and takes a cell phone picture of Liam's car driving toward the old barn. Nick can't drive down the dirt road without being noticed so he decides to drive to the next road over and see if he can see anything from there.

From the side road, he is able to see the barn through the trees. Nick pulls over, jumps out of his car, and walks through the thick strip of woods to get a closer look. He spots Liam getting out of his car. He slowly walks to the front and sits on the hood with his feet dangling. Nick snags another photo.

Nick hears the sound of another car coming up the dirt road. He hides behind an old fallen tree and watches as The Tye Brothers pull up. The car stops and Nick gets a few perfect pictures of the three men talking. He attaches the photos to a text message, "Liam meeting with Tye Bros," and sends it off.

With the full intention to kill the brothers, Liam reaches for a gun behind his back, but Nick's phone made a "text sent" confirmation tone that was not within the sounds of nature. The sound draws the attention of the men. When he meets Nick's eyes, Liam's heart starts to race as he knows how much trouble he's in.

Liam exclaims, "Aw shit!" as The Tye Brothers spring into action. Darius pulls two pistols from his back and begins firing toward Nick, who jumps up and darts away. Nick pulls a pistol from his side and blindly fires behind him toward where The Tye Brothers were standing. He takes cover behind a tree to hide just for a moment. Liam hops into his car and speeds away down the dirt road.

Marcus runs parallel to Darius toward the woodline and into the woods. Darius fires another shot at the tree Nick is hiding behind. Nick bolts from the tree towards the road, but Marcus jumps out in front of him. Nick drops his gun and begins to put both of his hands up, but Marcus decides to put a bullet between his eyes.

Chapter Six

Detective DiPietro is in his office halfway into his second cup of joe. He decides to take it upon himself to do some light research on Clifford's arsonists. He's able to obtain the tapes of some traffic cameras around Clifford's street.

Scouring the tapes for anything suspicious is the least he could do for his good friend. The only problem is the incident happened during a relatively busy time of day.

There are delivery trucks, residents, and local business owners coming and going.

Martin got to the point of the video where the firetrucks passed through the intersection. He slowly rewinds the video to look for anything suspicious.

The only thing he notices is a boxy car driving through the intersection next to Clifford's place and parking on the side of the road. He watches as the blurry figures of two gentlemen step out of the car and turn towards the building as if they were waiting to see it go up in flames.

Martin tries to zoom in, but they're too far away from the camera. Their license plate, as well as their faces, are too pixelated to identify.

As the firetrucks pass, the two gents get back into their car and drive away.

Unsure of who they are, he has a hunch that they were the two people Clifford saw.

Chapter Seven

As the sky is growing dark, Clifford drives up the street to the club. It's already starting to pick up. He circles his car around the back of the club and parks in the shadows. He walks up to the door and the hostess looks him up and down. "Oh, the café guy, right?" she says.

Clifford pauses for a moment, "Oh yeah, were you with Coco?"

"Yeah, she's in the back, changing. She's supposed to go on in a few," She says pointing towards the back of the club. "Thanks," Clifford says as he starts walking past her.

"Uhhh?!" she stops Clifford and points to the sign just to her left that reads: $25 cover.

"Oh. I'm sorry. Didn't see that," Clifford says as he pulls a wad of cash out of his pockets. He counts out five singles and pairs it with a twenty and hands it to her.

Her eyes open wide at the amount of cash Clifford pulled from his pocket. She says, "You're going to be popular tonight," as she takes the admission fee and hands him a card.

Her attitude instantly changes. There is a slight flirtatious tone to her voice when she speaks the typical scripted lines they have to say to new customers. "So, you get a free lap-dance with this card. Additional dances are $20 or $50 if you want the dance in the private room upstairs," She says leaning in closer. Clifford takes the card. "Thanks!" She shoots him a smile, "I'm done door duty in an hour so, see you inside?"

Clifford stuffed the card in his shirt pocket. "Maybe." He says, winking back at her.

He walks past the beaded curtain and his eyes begin to adjust from the bright lobby to the dark club. Surprisingly, it looks much bigger inside. Most men would walk in and start looking around at the tits and ass bouncing from pole to pole, but not Clifford. His former Army Ranger training kicks in, so he immediately finds himself searching for the entrances, exits, windows, and places to cover. His instincts have him paying attention to all these.

After that, he focuses on a great spot where he can scope for The Tye Brothers. It is away from the main stage where two strippers wearing only white t-shirts and white thongs are shooting each other with water guns, which expose their nipples and the perfect outlines of their camel-toes. It draws most of the attention in the room.

He sits down and continues to scan the room when his eye catches Coco.

He leaves his seat and wanders over to the stage she's dancing on. She smiles when she sees him and gives him a little wave. He sits down and she crawls over toward him.

"I see you made it!" She shouts to Clifford over the music. Clifford just winks.

She rolls over onto her back and spreads her legs in his face. She rolls over again, grabbing the pole, and flips her legs up, pulling herself up onto it using nothing but her legs.

An amazing acrobatic feat.

Clifford, smiling and enjoying the show, felt a sudden vibration in his pants.

It's his phone.

He pulls the phone out of his pocket to view the notification and notices that the silent alarm for The Tye Brothers room tripped twenty minutes ago.

"Shit!" he says to himself, knowing they will probably arrive here soon.

Clifford tosses a $20 bill onto the stage and waves at Coco. She gives him a strange look as if to ask where he's going. Clifford mouths the words, "I'll be back."

While he's quickly making his way up the steps to the main entrance, he sees Marcus Tye chatting up the hostess. He can't hear what they were saying because of the music, but he can tell he is being treated like a regular.

Clifford turns from the entrance and steps into the men's room. An attendant stands in the corner, so to avoid suspicion, Clifford walks over to a stall and pretends to pee.

He is keeping his eye on the door in hopes that the brothers don't walk in. After about 30 seconds, Clifford steps away from the urinal and it auto-flushes. The attendant holds out liquid soap and squirts some in Clifford's hands. As he's washing his hands, Clifford is still eyeing the door. The elderly attendant looks over his shoulder at the closed door and turns back to Clifford.

"Are you expecting someone, son?"

Clifford shakes his head "No, I just thought I saw someone I used to know. It's strange."

Handing him a towel, the attendant says, "Sometimes the past has a way to remind you that it's still there. Don't let your demons catch up to you, son. Cologne?"

"No, thank you. I'm good," Clifford says, handing the old man a $5 bill.

"Them girls don't like this cheap shit anyway," The attendant says with a chuckle, "Keep your head down."

The man had one thing right about Clifford. His past is filled with demons chasing him. He has to do his best to keep them in the past. Walking out of the men's room, Clifford notices the brothers sitting at the stage where he was once enjoying Coco's show, but her dance is over.

He starts to walk over to his corner but realizes someone else had taken his booth while he was in the bathroom. He starts looking around at other available spots that are out of direct eyesight of The Tye Brothers. Clifford walks over to the nearest empty booth and sits down, to avoid being noticed.

It isn't perfect, but he has a decent view of the Brothers from over his left shoulder.

About 30 feet in front of him, he has a bird's-eye view of another stage where a young black girl is twerking her lovely lady lumps to a bunch of guys tossing bills at her. Most people would be completely focused on that, but not Clifford. He keeps his eyes on The Tye Brothers.

Suddenly, a pretty thing with nice tits sits down across from him. Clifford glances over at her. "Hello?" He asks as she stares at him.

"Let's go in the back for a dance," She says.

Clifford looks back at The Tye Brothers and then back at her.

Not many men would turn away from her strawberry-blonde hair, nice perfect pair, and sporty frame. He didn't get a chance to look at her ass, but he only imagines that it was about as great as the rest of her. As much as he would love to have her crawling all over him in an intimate setting, he could not lose The Tye Brothers. At least not tonight.

"I'm sorry honey, not right now."

"It's on the house," She says.

Clifford looks back at her and sees a very stern look on her face. He knew that someone made him.

"Let's not make a scene, okay?" She says standing up holding out her hand.

Clifford stands up and takes a hold of her hand and she whisks him away into the backroom behind long beaded curtains and heads up a set of stairs toward the "Champaign Room."

On the way to the room, a jerk reaches over and grabs her firm round ass. She turns and punches him square and hard, like George Foreman. As the man falls back into his seat, two brawny men quickly scramble toward them and grab the man, escorting him out.

They continue to a small room where she frisks Clifford. He's glad he left his weapons in the car. She swipes a $50 bill from the wad of cash that was in his pocket, and hands him the rest of his cash and his phone, but not his wallet. She pushes him into a huge chair where they normally do the $50 dances. "Sit," She says.

Behind her, two more gentlemen appear. She hands them his wallet and walks away. Next to the larger gentlemen, a darker-skinned man appears, sharp-dressed, head to toe in white. He didn't seem much older than Clifford but was well into his 40's. Clifford eyes him up and down as he begins to speak. "Any reason you are more interested in two guys in the club rather than the fine pieces of ass we have provided for you?" the man in white says.

Before Clifford can open his mouth to talk, the man continues. "Before you speak, I want to make it perfectly clear that I love honest answers a hell of a lot more than I like dishonest ones."

Clifford holds his hand up in pause. "Oh, you must be Marlon. Okay, Yeah, I was eyeing up those guys down there. I- I just really like their suits."

"Yeah, that's me—Marlon," he says as he pulls out the driver's license from Clifford's wallet and starts to chuckle from the answer he gave.

"Like the suits? You're a funny guy, really. You are... Mr. uh-" looking at the ID he just retrieved from the wallet. "Mr. John McGee. Is this serious? John McGee?" He asks as he is flopping the ID in his hand. "Get the fuck out of here with this ID."

Clifford shrugs, then one of the beefcakes punches him in the face, knocking him back into the fluffy chair. Marlon continues. "This is the worst fake ID I've ever seen. And who comes up with a name like John McGee? Really?" Clifford, wiping blood from his lip says, "I dunno, I thought it looked pretty good. I paid $100 for it."

"Alright, wise-ass," Marlon continues. "How about some truth here before things start to get really physical, and not in a good way. What do you want with The Tye Brothers?"

Clifford knows there was no way to lie out of this situation.

"They're wanted men, I was hired to find them and take care of them," Clifford says with a straight face.

"Take care?" Marlon questions. "You're gonna take 'em out?"

"Yeah, that's the idea."

Marlon begins to laugh, "Taking out The Tye Brothers. Instead of Chinese takeout, it's Tye Takeout." He laughs a bit more at his own dumb joke, "Ah, I'm fuckin' hilarious! So, who put the hit on them?"

Clifford, again with a very serious face, "That's not important, but what is important is they're tracking my location as part of the agreement. My employer knows I'm here, look." He pulls out a small tracker from his back pocket. This was one of his own, but they didn't know that.

Marlon takes the paper-thin tracker from Clifford's hand. "Hmm. I see. So, I guess if anything happens to you, more people like you will show up?" Clifford nods, "Yeah, I just want The Tye Brothers, that's all."

Marlon hands him the tracker and pulls him to his feet. "What would be in it for me?" Marlon asks. Clifford, still grasping Marlon's hand says, "I'll introduce you to my client. I know you have more going on here than just lap dances. My client is very wealthy and has connections."

"I want a name first," Marlon says.

Clifford asks, "Why do you seem to be so willing to help me with The Tye Brothers?"

Marlon leans in closer and asks. "How about we share our information like civilized gentlemen? You tell me your client, I tell you about the Brothers and get you alone with them. Deal?"

Clifford sighs and says, "Eustachio Innocenzo Bandoni is my client."

Marlon takes a step back, "E. I. Bandoni? No shit. Get the fuck outta here! That's big-time shit!" Clifford nods, "Your turn now."

Marlon, still in shock that Clifford named dropped E.I. Bandoni, asks, "Who are you?"

Clifford raises his eyebrows, "We had a deal, did we not?"

Marlon says "I must know. Who are you?"

"My name is Clifford Dee."

Marlon looks him up and down with approval. "Now that is a name! John McGee?" He scoffs in a questioning manner. "Clifford Dee is a man's name," He says while clenching his fist.

Clifford gives Marlon a look telling him it was his turn to give up information.

"Okay - Okay, listen close," Marlon says.

"The Tye Brothers came in here, oh, about two years ago, to start up a hub for a gambling ring. I was broke and about to lose my business when they fronted me fifty G's. They're here to collect—plus interest, but I really don't have the cash, well, not without stiffin' my girls for the next few weeks. They told me to have it by today."

Clifford nods. "I think I've got the answer to both of our problems. All you gotta do is get me alone with them and I'll take care of it. On top of that, I'll mention you in good light to Mr. B. I'll give him your info and he'll contact you. Not the other way around. Deal?"

Marlon walks up slowly, noticeably thinking about the proposal. He shakes Clifford's hand and pats him on his shoulder. A huge smile finds its way on his face. "Clifford Dee! I think you and I are going to start a good friendship," He says with a smile, "Time to make some Tye Die."

Clifford shakes his head in disapproval of Marlon's poor humor, but finds himself smiling.

Marlon escorts Clifford out of the champagne room and toward a staircase in the back of the building. Clifford says, "I need to get a few things from my car if you don't mind."

Marlon points down the staircase and turns to one of his bouncers, "Take him out the back way and help him get what he needs. I'll cancel the card game tonight and have him set up in the poker room downstairs."

The bouncer nods at Marlon's instruction.

Clifford and the bouncer retrieve some plastic sheeting, A pistol with a silencer, and rope from his car. "What's the plan?" the bouncer asks.

"I'll lay out the plastic. Shoot 'em in the head. Take out the trash," Clifford says.

"What do I do?"

Clifford looked him in the eyes. "Just bring them to me."

Clifford hangs plastic around the poker room in the basement. He drapes it over the tables and chairs and lays it out on the floor. Standing behind a pillar, out of the main lighting in the room, Clifford has a steady view of who's coming and going.

In the distance, he hears chatter from the hall growing closer. "This way gentlemen. Don't mind the plastic. We're painting the room," Marlon's bouncer says.

Just then, Marcus Tye walks into the room and stands in the center of the plastic fortress that Clifford laid out. Clifford still did not have Darius in his sights because he's behind the bouncer.

He steps out of Clifford's line of sight, exposing both brothers. Darius looks around. "Where's the game?"

Realization hit Marcus. "Where's the paint?" he asks as the alarms trigger in his head.

"What paint?" The bouncer asks.

"You just said you were painting in here," Marcus says as he reaches for his gun.

Right before Marcus pulls the pistol from his pants, Clifford's first shot from his silenced .22 caliber, shoots Marcus dead, hitting him in just above his right temple.

Darius sees Marcus falling to the ground as if it were in slow motion. He jumps behind the bouncer, using him as a shield. He pulls his gun and starts to look around. "I will fucking shoot him!" He yells. Looking over at his once-living brother he yells, "Shit, Marcus! Shit!"

Darius peers into the darkness where Clifford is hiding, "You are going to fucking DIE, you piece of SHIT!" he screams.

Clifford takes his second shot.

The bullet whizzes between the bouncer's chin and collar bone, hitting Darius through the side of his nose and blowing out his cheekbone.

Letting out a blood-curdling scream, Darius drops his gun and falls to his knees. Clifford swiftly emerges from the shadows and points his gun square at Darius's head while kicking his gun away. He looks up at Clifford. His blurred eyes switch focus from the gun pointed in his face to Clifford as his tear-filled vision begins to clear.

"We shoulda killed you, you fucking bastard!" Darius says with confirmation just as Clifford pulls the trigger, turning off his lights for good.

"Oh my GOD, that was bad assed!" the bouncer shouts with excitement.

Clifford pulls cigar cutters out of his back pocket. He lops off their trigger fingers at the first knuckle from the tip and places them in a small jar. The bouncer, still stoked from the wild exchange, asks "I think I pissed myself a little. Wait. What is that for?"

Clifford looks him in the eyes and says, "Proof."

Clifford spends the rest of the evening cleaning Marlon's basement. Most of the blood was caught by the plastic sheeting. There are a few spatter marks on the walls outside of the sheeting but not much. He sprinkles an absorbent coagulant powder onto the bodies and rolls the two brothers in plastic like burritos so as to not spill out any bodily fluids. The bouncer and Clifford move the bodies to the back of the club while Marlon drives their car around. It's almost closing time for The Dollhouse. Marlon turns to Clifford after he and the bouncer shoved the last brother into the trunk of their car. "So, how's this going to work?"

Clifford wiping sweat from his brow, "Well, you're going to follow me and help me dump these two, and I'll drive you back."

Marlon, shaking his head in disagreement, says, "Nah, I don't like getting hands dirty and all that. Besides, I have to close up shop."

Clifford turns to him and says in a very serious tone, "I could just leave the car here for you to take care of."

Marlon sighs, "Alright, fine, but he's coming too. I ain't touching either one of those bodies."

"So this makes me the odd man here, doesn't it," Clifford says.

Marlon walks over to Clifford and puts his hand on his shoulder. "Look, you still have an obligation to me. You gotta put in a good word to Mr. B. I'm not going to mess up that business opportunity. We're gonna help you move them and their car. I just don't like getting messy. I'm wearing my white suit," Marlon says.

Clifford scoffs and says, "Okay, well let's get going. The spot's about an hour or so from here."

Marlon's eyes widen, "Jesus, an hour?!" He exclaims, "I have to close this place."

The bouncer looks over to Marlon and says, "Vinnie could close. He's done it before."

Marlon shakes his head, "Okay, fine. Tell Vincent I'm running out and he'll have to close." As the bouncer walks away, under his breath Marlon whispers to himself, "He's going to fucking lose me money again."

Marlon looks back at Clifford in disgust. "Vinnie's a fuckup when it comes to math. Last time he closed the club he was off by nearly $500, and of course, it went missing. I hope you're happy."

Clifford laughs and says, "You'll make that back in, what, twenty minutes? I saw how hopping this place was."

Marlon nods, "Yeah, she does pretty well, but Vinnie's still a piece of shit, though."

The guard returns and says, "Okay, good to go. Vinnie's going to take care of everything."

Marlon looks over to Clifford in sardonic relief.

Pulling onto the dirt road toward the church, Marlon lets out a yawn after following Clifford for about 40 minutes. "How much longer do you think?" he asks his bouncer.

"Well, he says an hour or so, right?" he asks back.

"Right, an hour. Right." Marlon says.

Clifford starts to slow down as he reaches the clearing with the church. It's charred and burnt nearly to the ground. It looks like someone recently set it on fire. Probably The Tye Brothers.

Clifford stops the car and gets out. Marlon pulls up next to him and pops the trunk just before stepping out of the car. He walks over to Clifford who's looking over the charred remains of the church.

Both stand there for a moment. Marlon nods while looking around.

"Pretty church," Marlon says sarcastically. "I might just have my wedding here," he continues. Clifford snaps out of the mini trance that he was in, "Sorry, I was going to leave them inside. I guess I have to rethink that."

Pointing, "Just tie 'em to that tree over there for the wilderness. I bet no one comes back here," Marlon suggests.

Clifford shakes his head. "No. We can't leave them out in the open. Bodies spark investigations. Not a good idea."

"Shit, that church burnt up without anyone knowin' about it," Marlon argued, "They'll be nothing but bones before anyone finds them."

Shaking his head, Clifford says "I don't think it's a good idea. We can't get caught."

Marlon looks over at Clifford. "What other options do we have right now?"

Clifford shakes his head, "I dunno. Maybe we could take them…"

Marlon cuts him off, "No, I don't wanna drive around with bodies in the trunk. I didn't even want to come out here!"

Clifford turns back to Marlon and says, "Yeah, I suppose you're right."

They both turn to the sound of the trunk slamming shut.

The bouncer looks over and says with a very sarcastic tone, "Thanks for helping."

Clifford looks over at Marlon and then back to the bouncer. "Wha- Where did you put 'em?" He asks in astonishment.

The bouncer points over to a wooded area, "Over there, in that old dried up well."

Marlon and Clifford walk over to what looks like a pile of cobblestone. It's old and broken down, at least 20 feet deep. It looks to have been dried up for years. Clifford looks down into the hole. "Well, shit!" Marlon turns to Clifford. "Good thing we brought him."

"Yeah," Clifford says, still looking at the well wondering how he missed it. Marlon returns to The Tye Brothers car and opens all the doors and pops the trunk again. The bouncer asks, "What-cha doin', boss?"

Marlon says, "We should burn it out. Get rid of any sign of us."

"Good thinking," the bouncer says.

Marlon turns to Clifford and asks, "You got any gas or anything?"

Clifford says, "I got an idea." He walks back to The Tye Brothers car and pops out a tail light. He takes off two coiled hoses from the car and shoves them into the gas tank, "Lemme have your shirt," he says, pointing to the bouncer.

"What? Why?" He asks.

Marlon looks over at him. "Just give him your shirt."

"I just got this one," He says in reluctance as he starts taking it off.

Clifford balls his shirt and uses it as a seal around the tubes. He blows into one tube and places the other into the tail light to collect the gas. He hands the gas filled tail light to the bouncer. "Pour this on the seats in the front and bring it back."

Clifford got another small amount of gasoline and poured it into the trunk where the bodies were located. "Marlon, go gather some small branches and twigs to put in the trunk," Clifford instructs.

"Why?" Marlon looked around.

"The fire needs more fuel to stay lit. The gas will burn out in minutes. We want this car on fire for at least an hour," Clifford says.

Moments later Marlon comes back with his arms full of sticks, twigs, and small branches. They place them in the car and set it on fire.

They drive off leaving the burning car and a plume of dark black smoke rising in the cover of the dark early morning sky behind them. With Clifford driving, Marlon in the passenger seat, and the bouncer sitting behind Marlon.

Marlon, sniffing the air, starts to look back.

"Yeah, my shirt smells like gasoline," The bouncer says as the other two men start to chuckle.

Clifford turns his head toward him. "That was some good thinking back there, you know, the well."

"Thanks," he says, "I get good ideas from time to time."

Clifford turned to Marlon, "You never did introduce me to him, did you?"

Marlon looked over at Clifford, "Yeah, I'm sure of it."

"I don't think you did," Clifford says. "What was your name again?" He directed to the bouncer.

"Uh, yeah, tell him your name," Marlon says with a slight stammer.

Listening to Marlon avoiding his name, the bouncer comes to a harsh realization.

"You forgot my name, didn't you?" He accuses Marlon.

Marlon, surprised, "Wha-No! No. I remember your name. I just thought you should tell him."

"You forgot my name. Unbelievable!" He says. "It's Josh….I dated your sister," He continues.

Marlon says, "Ah, Josh! Wait, you dated my sister?!" Marlon questions in false disbelief.

Clifford sits quietly, smiling.

"In college, yeah. That's how I got this job. She introduced me to you," Josh continues, not believing Marlon's jackassery.

Clifford butting in, asks Marlon, "Did you know your sister went to college?"

"Yeah," Marlon says, "I paid for it." He turns to Josh, "You were the boyfriend? Geez, I thought she dated some geeky skinny guy."

"That was me, I started working out when you said I was too small to be a bouncer," Josh says, shaking his head in disbelief.

"Oh yeah, that's right," Marlon says. "Sorry, I meet a lot of people. What happened between you and my sister?" Marlon asks.

"You made us break up," Josh says.

"Yeah, that sounds like me," Marlon scoffs, "I'm a jerk sometimes."

"Wow!" Clifford says in disbelief.

Marlon laughs, "I knew his name. I was just fucking with you guys." His laughter turned to a more serious tone as he turned to Clifford, "I did make them break up, though. My sister's not dating a bouncer at a strip club."

The early morning pushes on as the trio head back to Marlon's club. Clifford pulls his car into the front of the closed club to let Marlon and Josh out. Clifford rolls down his window as Marlon is passing the driver's side of the car.

"Hey Marlon, I'm sure that Vinnie didn't lose you too much money," Clifford says in a joking manner.

"I'll send you the bill," Marlon shoots back with a wave, "Keep in touch."

"I will," Clifford says as he starts to drive away.

Marlon heads back toward the Dollhouse where he noticed a duffel bag with a note pinned to it. The note reads: "Just in case Vinnie screwed up."

Marlon opens the bag to find it half filled with hundred dollar bills.

After Clifford sanitizes The Tye Brothers motel room, he decides to continue driving through the morning to Mr. Bandoni and collect the rest of his money.

Clifford pulls out his phone and texts "Job Complete. See you soon," to the number that E.I. called him from.

Chapter Eight

Dawn broke well before Clifford reached the Bandoni estate. He pulls up to the luxurious iron gates leading up to his property. A guard walks out from a small shack along the side of the gate and approaches the car.

"State your business."

Clifford looks up at the uniformed man, "I am here for E.I. He's expecting me. I'm Mr. Dee."

The guard clicks on his radio, "A Mr. Dee for Mr. B." Clifford could barely make out the squall that comes across the radio.

The guard leans back down to the car. "Mr. Dee, he is expecting you. Someone will escort you from the main entrance." He walks over to the gate and presses a security code on the keypad then places his hand on the butt of his gun as the gates slowly open. Clifford nods as he drives past the guard and onto the Bandoni estate.

There is a crew of gardeners already trimming, pruning, and weeding, keeping the flawless grounds looking pristine. Clifford slowly pulls up to the front steps and parks next to a white Bentley GT with gold rims. He's afraid to even ask how much it would cost to repair a ding on that thing.

Another guard with an M14 strapped across his chest greets Clifford at the top of the stairs and escorts him to an office. "Have a seat," He says as he shut the doors, leaving Clifford alone.

Moments later, Bandoni bursts into the room with gusto. "Tell me you have good news for me, Mr. Dee!" he says with huge excitement in his voice.

"Yes, Mr. B. I have a gift for you," Clifford says as he was reaching into his shirt pocket.

"Oh, I like gifts!" Mr. Bandoni says as he makes his way to his seat. Clifford pulls out the small jar with the two fingertips of The Tye Brothers and slides it across his desk.

"Wonderful!" He says looking at the jar, "What are these? Fingers? Are these their fingers?" Mr. Bandoni asks in glee.

"Trigger fingers. The rest of them are about 15 feet under the earth," Clifford confirms.

"Ah! Good, Good!" Mr. Bandoni says with contentment. "I guess this means that you need to be compensated the rest of your fee."

Clifford was always nervous talking about money with powerful people. The Bandoni family could just find a way to make Clifford disappear with no questions.

Deciding now would be a perfect time to make good on his promise to Marlon, Clifford says, "Yes. Also, I wanted to mention that I received a great deal of help from a gentleman named Marlon. He owns an adult entertainment establishment a few hours from here named The Doll House. Nice place."

Mr. Bandoni pulls an envelope from his safe and slides it across the desk in the direction of Clifford. While talking Clifford pulls out his phone to begin erasing all data he had of The Tye Brothers. "Marlon, you say? Adult entertainment?" Bandoni asks.

"Yeah, That's right," Clifford says.

"I am not one for classless smut, but I will send him a basket of fruit or something. I will not be rude," Bandoni concluded.

Clifford nods as he focuses on his phone. "Sure, That sounds reasonable enough."

Bandoni, feeling disrespected, looks toward Clifford while he's staring at his phone, "Am I keeping you from playing a game on the phone?"

Clifford looks up, "Oh, no sir, I was just deleting all the stuff about The Tye Brothers. I was tracking them yesterday and I'm trying to figure out why they left to go to an old farm."

Remembering the picture he got from Nick of Liam and The Tye Brothers with the silo and a barn in the background, Bandoni asks "Where is this farm?"

"Literally in the middle of nowhere, I have a map," Clifford says, showing his phone to Bandoni.

"Go there and look around for me," Bandoni requested.

"Yeah, sure," Clifford says. "What am I looking for?"

Bandoni, looking concerned. "A missing person. One of my men, Nicolo, hasn't checked in since yesterday."

Confused, Clifford asks, "Was he following The Tye Brothers?"

"No," Bandoni says, "Liam Stacey."

Clifford sat back in his seat. He knew that Liam met up with The Tye Brothers, but not to what extent.

"Do you think they were working together?" Clifford asks.

"I do not know. Liam is missing, too. He left yesterday and has not returned," Bandoni says.

"Okay. I'll see what I can dig up at the farm and I'll let you know," Clifford says.

"Of course, I will pay you for your efforts and I will be in touch with your friend, Marlon, was it?" Bandoni asks.

"Yes, Marlon," Clifford confirms as he gets up to leave.

Bandoni looks over toward Clifford as he reaches his door. "Please find Nicolo."

Clifford looks back and nods.

Moments after Clifford left the room, Mr. Bandoni's phone rings. He picks it up and glares at the number before he decides to answer. "Liam, I have been expecting to hear from you," He says as he answers.

"Mr. Bandoni, I know you had Nick follow me. I think The Tye Brothers got him. I can explain everything." He replies.

Chapter Nine

Clifford wants to track down his Mustang, but the request from Bandoni takes precedence. Following the map on his phone he finds the dirt road going toward the old farm. The road ends in a dirt round-about. He pulls the car over toward the grass to preserve the tire tracks left in the dirt.

Stepping out of the Jeep, he examines the tracks and determines that two separate cars were here. Luckily, the rain from a few days ago left the dirt soft enough to leave lasting impressions.

Scanning the earth, Clifford can piece together that the car that arrived first had one person, and the second car that arrived had two people, judging on the footprints in the dirt. He was even able to locate where they stood to talk.

He notices they scattered like they were spooked by something. One set of footprints ran back to the first car. The other two footprints went in the opposite direction. Clifford notices the two sets of footprints split up.

They traveled tactically as if they were flanking someone.

He follows a set of prints that suddenly stop and face the woodline. He walks toward the woods where he finds a section of vegetation was matted down from someone who looked to be using it for cover. He continues on and follows bent and broken sticks as if someone was fleeing. He approaches a tree where he sees bullet holes facing the direction where the one person would have been.

He begins to picture it in his head.

The first set of footprints were from someone trying to get someone in their sightline.

From the trajectory, he pictures the bullets whiz through the air. He steps behind the tree and presses his back against it as if he was using it for cover.

He looks around and can see a few more broken twigs and disturbed foliage as if someone was sprinting. While following the tracks left by a fleeing man, he finds dried blood on the plants and some on the ground. It was enough to deduce that someone was killed here. There are drag marks like a body was moved. As he follows the marks, he first sees a car pushed into a ditch on the side of the road and covered with brush. Stepping toward it, Clifford notices the drag marks lead toward a smaller ditch near where he's standing. He pauses for a moment then turns toward the ditch.

Inside lay Nick, lightly covered with foliage. Clifford lets out a deep sigh and picks up his phone to call Mr. Bandoni.

Chapter Ten

Clifford spends the next several weeks taking small jobs. Searching for loved ones, investigating employees' gambling problems or drug habits, the usual jobs for legit private detectives. He has enough money from The Tye Brothers job to last a while. Giving Marlon a bag full of their cash was a smart thing to do, but he can't help to think that he should have kept a little more than he did. Since work has slowed, he spends most of his time playing video games with his buddy Simon.

Upon hearing a knock at the door, Clifford pauses his game and walks over to answer it. "No cheating," He quips to Simon as he goes to answer the door.

"Would I do that?" Simon questions.

"Yeah! You would!" Clifford shouts across the room. On the other side of the doorway was Jaime.

"Hi!" She says as she pushes into Clifford's office to see Simon looking wide-eyed at her with a controller in his hand.

"So, this is your idea of training?" She asks the guys.

Clifford stammers a bit, "Simon came over, but we, I mean—I was,"

"Yeah that's what I thought," Jaime continues, "Get your butts off the game and into the gym."

"Yes, Dear," Simon says as he secedes from the couch and turns off the TV. Both men sulk downstairs.

Jaime continues to lay into them, "You guys promised me ninety minutes today and I am holding you to it. Call Of Duty does not count as a workout."

She really kept Simon and Clifford on point with their physical training. The ninety minutes came and went, and Clifford is physically exhausted. He limps upstairs after doing weighted squats and leg lifts to round out the last few minutes of the workout. He saunters into his office and over to his room. He kicks off his shoes and plops down onto his bed.

Just then, he hears a ring at the door. Aching, Clifford stands back up and walks over to answer the door. He swings open the door and finds a sad-looking middle-aged man standing as if he were in dire need of some good news.

"Can I help you?" Clifford asks.

"I hope so, I'm looking for a detective," The man says.

Clifford looks him up and down. "I'm a private investigator, but my office is kinda closed right now, can you come back?"

"Yeah, that's what I meant. Sure, I can come back. What time?" The man wondered.

Tugging on his sweat-soaked shirt, Clifford says, "Uh, give me an hour, and we can sit down here and chat. I just need to freshen up a bit."

"Okay, an hour? Sure. I'll just grab something to eat and come back," The man says.

"Alright. See you then," Clifford says as he shut the door.

After finishing his shower and getting dressed, Clifford fixes himself something to eat. Sitting at his kitchen island and just about to sink his teeth into the best-looking lean chicken breast sandwich anyone has ever seen, the doorbell rings again.

Dropping the sandwich onto the plate and letting out a sigh, Clifford gets up and goes to the door. It was the same sad-sack as before.

"Hello sir, me again. I know it wasn't quite an hour, but so, uh," the man stammers, trying to make a sentence.

Clifford waves him in as the man continues trying to make a coherent thought. "someone - a friend recommended you. I would like to hire you for your services."

Clifford shuts the door behind him.

"Sure, let's have a chat," he says pointing toward his office. "Have a seat in there and I will be right with you."

Clifford walks back into the kitchen and grabs the plate with his sandwich and takes it into his office.

"I hope you don't mind, I'm eating lunch," Clifford says as he shuffles into his office. "No-no, not at all, please. It is your office," the man says.

"Thanks," Clifford says. "Well, let's start with the basics. What's your name?"

"Oh right. I'm Luther, Luther Buckley," The man quickly says. "Well, Mr. Buckley, what can I do for you?" Clifford asks.

"Do? Uh, my wife..." Luther pauses...a bit too long.

"You want me to DO your WIFE?" Clifford says, half trying to clarify and half trying to make a bad joke.

"No. Well. Someone else already is - at least I think," Luther stammers out. "I think my wife is having an affair."

Clifford, happy that he did not mean he wants him to kill her, or have sex with her, for that matter, taps his fingers on his lunch plate. "I'm sorry to hear that you think that," Clifford says with a more serious tone. "So, what makes you think she's having an affair?"

"Well," Luther takes a deep breath, "She stopped coming home right after work. I won't see her 'till after dinner. I'm finding that she's hiding fancy underwear in her purse.

Like, ya know, the lacey panties." Clifford, listening intently, continues to nod as Luther talks.

"She takes secret phone calls. There's so many things, I can't even think of 'em all."

Luther seems to have a few valid points regarding suspicious activity surrounding his wife.

"Okay, sounds pretty serious. When did this all start?" Clifford asks.

"I dunno, really. It seemed like she was always sneaking out here and there, but more recently over the last several weeks," Luther started rubbing his brow, trying to remember.

"Okay, it doesn't really matter," Clifford says. "I'm gonna need some work from you first. Are you okay with that?" Clifford asks.

"Work, what do you mean?" Luther asks.

Clifford pulls open a drawer and rifles through some papers to eventually pull out a contract. "Okay, this is a contract. You fill out your information and sign below agreeing that you'll provide me a deposit of $1000 into a retainer to start," Clifford says pointing out some lines on the paper, "Down here, please write a brief description of what you need me to do. It doesn't have to be super descriptive. Just a basic reason for hiring me."

Luther nods.

"I'm gonna step away and let you read that. I'll be right back," Clifford says, retreating to the kitchen with his sandwich. Clifford left Luther with his thoughts. He didn't need his money and he almost felt like turning him down.

But first, his chicken sandwich.

Clifford takes a few big bites of his sandwich to finish it off before leering in the refrigerator for a drink. He grabs a vitamin-infused water, opens it, and takes a huge swig. He grabs a second bottle of water and closes the fridge. Walking back to his office, he sets his drink down by his chair and hands Luther the other water bottle.

Luther was finished filling out the paperwork and was ripping a check out of his checkbook.

"So, I guess this means you're ready to proceed?" Clifford questions.

"Yeah," Luther says, handing him the contract. "If you're as good as my friends say you are, I want to get started as soon as possible."

Clifford looks over the contract and confirms that it all looks legit.

Luther hands Clifford a check, "Here, it's $2,500. It's a bit more than the deposit you asked for, but I want you to get started sooner rather than later."

Clifford takes the check. "Okay, I'll get started. Let's see here." He starts mentally checking off the list of information he needs to get started as he reads the informational sheet attached to the contract.

"Everything looks alright, but I have a few questions that were not on the sheet."

"Okay," Luther says.

"Number one," Clifford starts off, "What will you do if I find nothing?"

"Uh, well—" Luther pauses. "I guess I will owe her an apology and maybe ask her what's going on."

"Ask her what's going on. That's good," Clifford says, "Why haven't you done that yet?"

"Well. I've tried talking to her, but she just—" Luther pauses and looks as if he's going to burst into tears. "She's just so distant and never wants to talk."

"Hmm. Okay. Do you still want me to continue with this?" Clifford asks.

"Yes," Luther says with a serious tone, "I need to know for sure."

"Fine, and number two," Clifford raises two fingers in the air with a huge pause, "What will you do if I find exactly or worse than you fear?"

Clifford carefully watched Luther, trying to judge his reaction. Luther pauses for a moment and the realization of what Clifford is asking just hits him like a truck.

"I would never hurt her if that's what you're implying!" Luther says with passion. "I'm still in love with her and I would not-" Just then Luther bursts out in the tears he was fighting ever since he walked into Clifford's office.

Clifford hands him a tissue. "Hey, I'm not implying anything. I just needed to hear it."

Luther dries his face with the tissue. "Hear what?" He questions. "Your love," Clifford says. "I know for sure that you have good intentions. You just need to know."

"Yeah. It's hard," Luther says with a slight sob.

"Okay, do me a favor," Clifford demands. "What's that?" Luther ponders.

"Get yourself a stiff drink. Just one! But a nice one, and relax. I'll let you know what turns up." This is Clifford's 'go-to' line when he has emotional clients.

"Yeah, sounds like a good idea. I have some good bourbon that I've been waiting to bust out," Luther says turning his sobbing face into a grin.

Clifford jokes, "So invite me over for that Bourbon," He says with a grin.

"Sure. When you're done with your investigation," Luther says, starting to find his smile.

Clifford takes the rest of the afternoon to prepare for the new case. He has plenty of time to look into it since this is currently his only contract. He starts with a few online searches, looks for traffic violations, and the only thing that he finds is a ticket for running a red light camera. The strange thing about the ticket is it's from across the city from where she works and lives. There's no logical reason for her to be in that area at that time.

It's a lead.

Clifford decides to take a drive. It's pretty nice outside, and he loves riding with the top off of his Jeep. The area of the city where she got the citation leads directly into the center of the city;

Full of businesses, a town hall, and many important people with very important jobs.

Since this lead could have many different angles or outcomes, it would be like looking for a needle in a stack of needles. Clifford decides to retreat and try a different strategy.

Chapter Eleven

Grabbing her keys and leather satchel, which she uses for a laptop bag and purse, Mrs. Buckley hurries out of her office, shutting and checking the door to be sure it's locked. She heads down the hall toward the elevator and passes Ben in the hallway.

"Oh, hey Ben?" She exclaims.

"Hey Cindy, what do you need?" questions Ben as he whips around.

"I need to review the Templeton portfolio. They just hired a few new employees and we need to get the HR packages over to them tomorrow," Cindy says.

"No problem, I'm here for another hour and I got all that information in our Sharepoint already. I can get that over to you for your brief with them tomorrow," Smiled Ben.

"You, sir, are a lifesaver!" Cindy says turning and walking away.

Cindy is a brunette with very slight signs of aging. You can tell she's a bit more mature than what her face suggests she is. She looks forty, but is closer to fifty. She's curvy, but not overweight. She's full of cheer and always smiling. Everyone loves working for her, and the men of the office love watching her walk by.

As she reaches the parking lot, the sunlight hits her face and accentuates some of the few grey hairs poking out from behind the curtain of dark brunette locks. She hits the unlock button of her car remote and the grey Benz parked in the spot, "Reserved for the Deputy Director of Human Resources," chirps. She opens the passenger side door and tosses her brown leather satchel on the white leather seat. She shuts the door and walks over to the driver's side and gets in.

After checking her makeup in the mirror, she fluffs her hair and straightens her collared shirt. She pulls out of the parking lot and drives down to the first light. From across the street, Clifford's Jeep pulls out behind her at the light. Clifford follows Cindy into the area where she received her citation. She's driving as if she knows exactly where she is going, and like she's been there several times.

Clifford's having a bit of trouble keeping up with her aggressive driving. Not only is she speeding, but she's also weaving in and out of traffic. After several minutes of city driving, she pulls into a garage. Clifford decides to find street parking.

He walks to the corner and hits the button to cross the street. He looks back toward the garage and sees her pull out and drive in the opposite direction. Wondering if she made him, Clifford rolls his eyes and lets out a sigh.

He slowly walks back toward his car when he decides that he would just walk a bit down the street and get some food since he already fed the meter.

As he reaches the street that Cindy turned down, he turns his head to see that she has parked a block over, next to the side of a corporate legal firm office. Across the street is the District Attorney's office, next to a few more legal firms. There were many business offices in the immediate area, the district court, as well as the police station, a block over. She could be visiting any of these places.

Curious, he walks down to the firm she parked in front of and goes inside.

The building has a huge empty lobby on the first floor with a big waiting room. There is an information board that shows several different firm offices with their corresponding floors. He walks over to the seating area, sits, and grabs a magazine from the table across from him.

Clifford has a nice view of the hall leading toward the elevators. He also sees Cindy's car to his left. She is not getting by him without him noticing.

His ears perk up as he hears an elevator ding. He peers over the top of his magazine trying to get a glimpse of who's coming out.

A bunch of lawyers with suitcases and portfolios in their hands come pouring out of the elevator doors while talking about their respective cases. Clifford shoves his nose back into his magazine and continues to pretend he is reading.

Some motion catches his attention toward where Cindy is parked. He notices that her car is driving away. He looks but cannot tell if there was anyone in the passenger seat. Clifford gets up and walks over to the window.

"Dammit." He says to himself.

He steps outside, knowing that he bet on the wrong building, looks around at the surrounding buildings. She could have been in any of them. He at least has the area down. Clifford walks back to his car, never getting anything to eat. He just isn't in the mood anymore.

He jumps into his Jeep and heads out of the city towards home. Clifford spent several hours looking up the businesses and other offices in that corridor where Cindy parked. He finds several business owners, more legal firms than he could count, and that he was really wasting his time.

The next morning Clifford sets up shop, bright and early across from Cindy's office. He watches as she pulls into her designated parking spot and walks into her office building with a newspaper and a cup of coffee in her hands. Picking up his cellphone, he calls Luther.

"Hello?" Luther answers.

"Hey, Luther, it's Mr. Dee, what time did your Mrs. get home last night?" He asks.

"Ten-ish. Maybe later. She said she had to work late to get some files done for a big client or something, but I could tell she was lying. Why?" Luther responds.

Clifford let out a small sigh. "Well, I tracked her into the middle of the city yesterday," He says while holding up one of his digital trackers.

"She parked around a bunch of professional buildings. You know, a bunch of law firms, businesses, and such. Do you know of any reason she would be there?"

"Law firms?" Luther asks, "Like, divorce lawyers?"

"Well, they were mostly business law. The DA's office is over there too, so I guess there could have been family law as well. But why go all the way into the city when there are family lawyers all over? I don't think she was seeing someone for business if you know what I mean," Clifford says.

Luther stammered a bit. "I—I don't know. She may be thinking about divorce and got referred to someone or something. Are you sure she wasn't there for work?" Luther says worriedly.

"Ninety percent," Clifford says, pausing. "Well, more like ninety-eight percent sure. There's always that chance, but she was driving and parking like she didn't want to be spotted. She pulled into a garage, stayed for a minute, and left to only drive a few blocks over and park on the street. It was almost like she was talking to someone and they told her that street parking was open, or to meet them somewhere else. Something like that."

Clifford pauses to think. There has got to be a reason why she would first drive into the garage if she did not know she was being followed.

"Is she a paranoid person, Mr. Buckley?"

"No, not at all. I mean, she basically flaunts her infidelity at home. She knows I suspect something, but does nothing to hide it. I mean, she is secretive - sure, but not paranoid at all," Luther replies.

"Hmm," Clifford says, rubbing the stubble on his cheek with his knuckles. "Okay. I'll let you know what I find out tonight. Take care." Clifford didn't wait for Luther to say goodbye. He was all full of questions that Clifford could not answer now and he has work to do.

It's almost lunchtime when Clifford gets a notification that his tracker is moving. He's having lunch at a deli nearby, so he is able to get to his car and follow Cindy from a few miles behind. She drives to the same area of the city and Clifford is able to spot her car from about fifty yards away.

No one was inside.—Clifford waits.

His phone begins to vibrate. "Mr. Bandoni, how are you?" Clifford asks in a surprised tone.

"Mr. Dee, I hope I did not catch you at a bad time," Bandoni replied.

"No, not at all, I am just waiting for someone."

Bandoni stopped him, "About that, Mr. Dee. I would like you to stop your current investigation on Mrs. Buckley."

Confused Clifford asks why.

"I will not repeat myself. Just leave her alone."

"Uh, okay. I'll stop looking into her," Clifford says.

"Good," Bandoni says just before hanging up the phone.

Clifford starts to process what just happened when a black Escalade pulls up next to Cindy's car. Clifford, quick with his camera, was able to snag a few shots. The passenger door opens, Cindy steps out and walks to her car. The SUV speeds away, around the corner. Clifford is parked the wrong way to follow, but he did get a pic of the rear plate after it drove past him.

When Clifford turns back around, Cindy is driving away. He had an idea that she was probably going back to her office. Even though Bandoni told him to stop, he really wanted to know who was in the SUV. After Cindy clears the intersection, Clifford drives the opposite way, around the block. He opens his laptop and uses his phone as a hotspot for internet connectivity. He begins researching the SUV and plate.

The name Kristen Neil was staring him in the face.

The image of several campaign signs begin to flash in his mind. He could see her face on billboards and road signs all over the city. Kristen Neil is the newest firecracker District Attorney for the Commonwealth. She has become quite popular in getting crime off the streets. In the last four years, she had a ninety-seven percent conviction rate with several hundred convictions. As well as, successfully convicting seven major career criminals, and put away a cartel kingpin for twenty years. She is up for re-election this year and it has been a vicious election. Her opponent is claiming she is corrupt, but has no ground to stand on. Everyone loves Neil, apparently, including Mr. Bandoni.

Clifford picks up his phone and calls Luther.

"Hey, Mr. Dee!" He says cheerfully.

"Hey buddy, I'm truly sorry to do this. I am going to refund all of your money. I have to stop the investigation."

"What? Why?" Luther asks.

"It's, uh, complicated," Clifford says, "Just come by my office tomorrow morning and we can chat."

Chapter Twelve

It's just after midnight and the app on Clifford's phone linked to the tracker starts chirping. Clifford sighs and rubs his eyes. He opens his phone and can see that the tracker was still alive, and Cindy has driven outside of the city, almost an hour away. Clifford notices that she was at an upscale hotel. He only laid in bed staring at the ceiling for a few minutes before the curiosity got the best of him.

Clifford walks inside the hotel holding a suit bag in one hand and waves at the check-in clerk while walking by. She smiles back at him, assuming he is already a guest. He has no idea where Cindy could be, but he wants to get a good layout of the hotel. He drops the suit bag onto a cart in the hallway. The lobby is curvy and spacious. It has plenty of seating for guests and a small bar over to the left where there were a few people sitting, having idle chit-chat.

Clifford walks over to the bar and orders a drink. A man approaches Clifford and tosses a twenty onto the bar. "It's on me!" he exclaims.

Clifford looks over. "Thank you, but I can pay for my own drink."

The man looks at him with a bit of a squint. About a second or two later, he snatches the twenty off the bar. "Fair enough, but I have a question for you," He says sternly.

"What's that?" Clifford asks. The man looks at him and asks, "What are you snooping for?"

"Snooping?" Clifford half asks, and half refusing to admit. "Who's snooping?"

The man smiles. "Do we really need to do this? C'mon, I know," He says.

"Oh!" Clifford says with mild surprise. "What do you know?"

"I know you were told to drop the case you're on," The man says.

Clifford's mood changes and he takes another swig of his drink. "What do you know about the case I'm on?" Clifford asks.

"Hmm, pesky jealous spouses," The man says with a smile. "You should just do what the boss says and let this one go. No more warnings."

With that, the man pushes away from the bar and walks back out into the lobby and out of sight.

"Last Call!" the barkeep yells.

Clifford sits for a few more minutes and finishes his drink. He stands up to leave when he notices Cindy Buckley walking in from outside. He sits back down. She turns to the door when District Attorney Kristen Neil walks in behind her. They both walk toward the elevator and press the button. Clifford walks over to get a better look. As the elevator doors are closing his eyes grow wider as he witnesses them kissing. In shock, Clifford slows his stroll and walks over toward the small newsstand. His head is filled with more questions than ever. He checks his watch and then looks back at the elevator to see that it stops on the fifth floor.

Clifford nonchalantly walks back to his Jeep and climbs in. He drives to the rear of the hotel and looks at the windows on the fifth floor. There are only three rooms with lights on. One of them has to be their room.

He holds his cell phone to his ear and pretends to make a call. "This is Luther Buckley, where is my wife?" Clifford shakes the idea from his head. "Hello, this is Cindy Buckley." He says in his best feminine voice. "No, that could never work. How the hell am I going to do this?" He says under his breath.

"Sara!" he exclaims.

Two cute lovers are warmly nestled in bed at 2:30 am when the phone begins to ring. Sara opens one eye and looks over at Tracy who doesn't even flinch from the sound of the phone. Letting out a disgruntled sigh she reaches over and looks at the caller ID with one bloodshot eye.

"Clifford DEE" the ID displayed.

"Jesus!" She says very unhappily. She answers the phone and puts it to her ear. "What do you want? It's 2 a.m., Dee."

Clifford quickly states, "Well it's 2:30 actually."

"What? Why?" Sara asks, still partially asleep.

"I need a huge favor. Please please please please." Clifford continues saying please while Sara swoops her legs off the side of the bed and sits up.

"Okay okay okay! Shut up. Jesus, you're a brat. What do you need?" She whispers as she walks out of the room, leaving Tracy sleeping soundly.

The phone in the hotel lobby rings twice before it's answered.

"Thank you for calling Hotel GranDelux, this is Janet, how may I help you?" The receptionist belts out.

"Yes, hi," Sara starts. "I'm in Room 526, and I'm looking at my calendar, and wanted to confirm checkout. The name is Cindy Buckley," Sara says with confirmation.

"I'm sorry Ms. Buckley, I have you in 524, not 526 and you have reservations until Sunday morning," The receptionist confirmes.

"Oh, 524! Right, that's it, I'm sorry. Yes. I see it now, Sunday. Thank you so much for your help! Bye!" Sara says with a cheery tone in her voice.

Clifford sits in his car anxiously awaiting a return call, when his cell phone rings. "Hello, Did you confirm?" He asks.

"It's Room 524 and it's reserved until Sunday. You owe me a bottle, Mr. Dee. Tonight!" Sara demands.

"Yes, of course. Tonight. I will wrap it in ribbons," He says.

"Rainbow ribbons. Rainbow is my favorite color," She says.

"You are such a lesbo," Clifford says in a joking tone.

"You like it!" Sara laughs.

Clifford smiles, "You have no idea. Thank you, get some sleep."

"Way ahead of you," Sara says just before hanging up the phone.

Clifford drives out of the hotel parking lot and down two blocks. About a half-mile away, there is an abandoned professional building that sits about 4 stories high. He cuts the chain which is locking the fence and drives his car onto the compound. He reconnects the chain link with a small amount of solder wire, so it looks undisturbed. He drives up to the rear entrance away from the road and enters through a broken window. With a pack full of gear, he climbs four stories and finds a birds-eye view of the hotel.

Clifford digs into his pack full of equipment and sets up a long-range digital camera. It has infrared settings to locate body heat and a laser sound recording microphone that can translate the vibrations on the hotel window glass into audible sound. It cost a pretty penny, but was well worth it.

He tests the camera on a darkened room on the sixth floor where he noticed a bit of movement. He was able to capture the sound, and an infrared silhouette, of a man, really going to town on a woman in the doggy style position. The slaps of skin and moans were coming through in crystal clear HD quality.

"Justporn.com eat your heart out," He says just before he refocuses the camera back to his target room. They must have left the room again, as he was not picking up any movement or sound.

So he waits,

and waits.

The sun starts to make an appearance and a bright light beam shines directly onto the sleepy face of Clifford Dee. He shakes awake and checks his monitors. He can see the heat signatures of the women sleeping in the bed. He must have fallen asleep and missed them coming back to the room.

Clifford decides to leave his gear set up but takes a copy of the video back to his office. He plugs a thumb drive into his laptop and proceeds to copy the video onto it. Halfway on the journey home, he gets a notification that Cindy's car is moving. He just assumes that she is headed back to work.

Since he is in the neighborhood, he makes a slight detour and decides to stop at the small café near her office building. Cindy parks in her assigned place as Clifford is looking on, enjoying a fresh cup of coffee. She hurries into her office and Clifford sits complacently knowing where she is and that he can take it easy for a few hours before going back to the to check the camera. He takes his last sip and places the cup back on the coaster and heads to his car.

Just as Clifford approaches his Jeep, two shots make an impact on both driver's side tires. The sound was like two giant balloons popping. Clifford dives in behind a trash can. After a few screams, the pedestrians on the sidewalk cower and look on in fear. Clifford looks in the distance to see if he can identify where the shots originated, but he can't.

It's almost lunchtime before Clifford makes it back home. Sara meets him on the stairs of their building. "Get my bottle yet?" She asks.

"Damn girl! No I haven't got your bottle yet!" Clifford returns. "My tires were shot out. It's in the shop getting new ones."

"Wait, shot out?" Sara asks. "As in shot by a gun? With bullets?" She continues.

"No, as in a flu-shot, yes with bullets." Clifford's sarcastic response causes Sara to tilt her head in disapproval.

"It was just a warning. I'm not sure who fired it, but I am sure it was about this case." Clifford says. Sara looks at Clifford with concern. "The case where you had me pretend to be this Cindy Buckley?"

"Yeah," Clifford responds.

"Oh my God, Dee. Seriously?" Sara asks in a concerned tone.

"Yeah, but they only know about me," Clifford says.

Sara shakes her head. "It's not about that! You need to be safe. I don't like people shooting at you."

"It's part of the job. Sometimes you get shot at," Clifford shrugs it off like it's not a big deal.

"You just make sure you shoot them first," Sara says.

"That's usually the plan," Clifford fires back as he starts up the stairs.

"Oh, Dee! Before you go in," Sara pauses.

Clifford slowly turns his head toward her. "Yeah?"

"Go get my bottle!" She demands.

"Jesus woman, you'll get it," he says as he heads back toward the door.

In his office, Clifford plops down with a sandwich and pulls the thumb drive out of his pocket. He sticks it into his computer and starts watching the video in fast forward while eating his turkey and swiss on rye. He slows the video to normal speed when he notices activity in the room. The light flips on and the two women are in mid-conversation. The heat signature silhouettes are walking around the room having a conversation. It's difficult to make out who each person was, but the voices were unmistakable.

Kristen Neil: .... *"and the Templeton portfolio should be delivered tomorrow afternoon to my office. Once we get it, we will process the release. The money for the clients will be ready, available, and clean for them to use. We just need that portfolio before the release is processed so there are zero hiccups."*

Cindy: "I got it! They'll be ready. I have everything under control, Kristen. You don't have to worry."

Kristen Neil: "I...You know I worry. I will always worry. These are not easy people to please. I.... Just don't want anything to happen to you. I love you."

Cindy: "I know you do. I love you, too, Kristen."

....

Kristen Neil: "I need you to understand what this means."

Cindy: "I have it under control. It'll be delivered on time."

Kristen Neil: "Okay, I believe you. I trust you."

The heat signatures get closer together and there are audible sounds of kissing. Clifford shuts the video off when he hears a knock at his front door.

"One Second!" He blurts out as he is checking the video footage of the front. He likes to check to see who is there before going to the door. It's Luther.

Shaking his head, he walks over to the door. "Come on in, Luther," he says as he walks to the foyer.

"How'd you know it was me?" Luther says as he opens the door.

With a smile, Clifford says, "I make it a habit of knowing who's at my door."

Luther steps in and follows Clifford to his office. Clifford points to a chair and he sits. Clifford plops on the corner of his desk. "So, I have decided to drop the case. I will refund your money, All of it."

Luther asks, "Why? Did something happen?"

Clifford starts rubbing his jeans with both hands nervously. "Let's just say that Cindy is involved with someone rather important and continuing my investigation could lead to me not having a job in the very near future." This was as truthful as Clifford could get without telling him everything.

Luther looks shaken, but like he expected this news. "Who is he? Just tell me."

Clifford pauses for a moment before saying, "She."

"What?" Luther asks.

Clifford continues, "It's a she. Cindy is with a woman. That is all I can tell you."

Luther has a look of disbelief on his face. "A woman?" He asks, still shocked.

"A woman," Clifford confirms again.

Luther stammers, "I had no idea- I mean- She knew- She told me she was a Christian woman!"

Clifford took this time to start writing out a check to reimburse Luther as he is going through every human emotion imaginable while he processes this new information.

Clifford rips the check from his book and Luther snaps to. "Here and do me a huge favor," Clifford says, handing him the check.

Luther looks at Clifford, still in disbelief, as he continues. "Just go home and tell Cindy you want a divorce. Tell her that you want to make it as easy for her as possible. You know your relationship is over, you told me so yourself. I just wanted to confirm that this is exactly what you thought and because I can't help you any further, I am giving you a full refund. Do not make it difficult or harass her. Believe me, you will regret it."

Luther looks at Clifford, takes the check, and slowly stands. "What do you mean, regret it?"

Clifford sighs, "Well, I am backing out of this investigation. What's that tell you?"

Luther nods, "Oh. Okay." he says as he gets up to leave the office.

Clifford walks him to the door as his phone starts to ring. "Have a good day, Luther," he says as he reaches for his phone.

"Yeah?" Clifford says, pulling the phone to his ear.

"Hey Mr. Dee, this is Scotty, BK Auto. Got some good and bad for you."

"Jesus. Uh, bad first," Clifford says.

"Okay, so whoever shot your tire out, got the rim on both tires, so you need new rims too," Scotty continued. "You're pretty lucky that's all the bullet did. Damage could've been a lot worse."

Clifford yawns and says, "Okay, so the good news?"

"We have some great rim options in the shop here. If you come down now we can cut you a deal. Oh, and if you haven't yet, you should talk to the cops. One of the slugs was recovered from your left rim and we can save it for ya."

"Yeah, actually I did talk to them this morning. I'll head over there now. Save that slug for me, please," Clifford says.

"Okay, see ya in a few?" Scotty asks.

"I gotta walk, so in about twenty minutes," Clifford says.

"We can send a car out to get you right now, we got your address here," Scotty offers.

Glancing at his watch, Clifford says, "Yeah, that'd be great."

"Okay, we'll see you in a minute," Scotty says.

Clifford walks back to his room to take a leak and grab some extra cash from his safe. He opens the safe and counts out a few bills when the security system trips, triggering the red lights in his room. It seems someone was in his office.

He slides open the false wall and closes it behind him. "Luther, did you forget something?" He blurts out, thinking that he returned to the office. He turns the corner and looks in, but no one's there.

He sees something in the center of the floor. It's casting a long shadow from the sun peering in through the blinds from the other wall. He slowly walks towards it and eventually notices that it's a knife stuck to a note, plunged into his wood floor.

"No more watching Buckley," is scribbled on it. This must have been from the same person responsible for his two new wheels. Pulling the knife from the floor leaves a huge gash in the wood, which made Clifford wince in disappointment.

Although he can't quite place it, something about the pearl-handled knife strikes Clifford as familiar. Even the handwriting on the note feels familiar.

"Mr. Dee?" A young voice questions from the hallway, along with a knock on the door.

"Yeah, It's me. I'm here," Clifford says as he folds the knife and shoves it into his pocket.

"Uh, I'm from BK Auto here to pick you up." Clifford turns around to find a pimply kid in his late teens standing in his doorway. "Sorry sir, uh, your door was open. I didn't mean to intrude like this," says the driver.

Clifford looks him up and down. "Well, let's go," Clifford says, motioning to the door.

Clifford spends close to an hour going over rim and tire options with Scotty. Clifford is not really a car guy so all the details of each product seemed to meld into nothing and everything at the same time. Clifford eventually points "That one. How much is that one?"

Scotty turns and looks at the rim. "Oh, they call that an 'Assault Tire.' Pretty cool, huh? It's pretty pricey, but it could stand up to all the wear and tear your Jeep can take. Not sure about direct hits by bullets though."

"Okay, I'll take it," Clifford says. "So, you do want all four replaced, right?" Scotty asks.

"Yeah, all four. And four of those assault rims next to it," Clifford says pointing at the display. "Oh," Clifford continued, "and will I get a discount for the two that are not shot up?"

"Yeah, uh. Let me give you a quick breakdown," Scotty says mashing on a calculator.

"Mm-kay, four rims," Scotty says mumbling to himself. "Tires. Now discounted rate for the labor. Okay, okay, okay," Scotty continues.

After another minute of mashing on the calculator, Scotty looks up and smiles a bit, seemingly proud of this deal he put together. "I know it's a lot of money, but it's a really good deal," Scotty says just before Clifford lays out a bunch of hundreds on the table.

"Do you still have that slug?" Clifford asks. Scotty, staring at the bills nervously says, "Yeah, I have it here for you."

He reaches on top of a filing cabinet and pulls off an envelope. He cashes out change and hands both to Clifford.

"Thanks, I want to take it to my buddy at the precinct. Maybe I can find out who it belongs to," Clifford says.

"Okay, sure. Uh, two hours at the most. We close at six p.m.," Scotty says to Clifford as he's turning to walk out.

"Just call my cell when it's ready," Clifford says as he leaves the office.

Chapter Thirteen

Clifford always feels slightly uncomfortable in police stations. He feels that the police do more of the biddings of the state and corrupt bureaucrats than they help people in need. He knows they are mostly good people trying to make a living, but when push came to shove, they would protect the state and their laws over the people. He spots his buddy Martin down the hall from his office. "Hey, Detective DiPietro!" Clifford blurts out.

"Dee, you're back, What's up buddy?"

Clifford hands Martin the slug. "What's this?" Martin asks.

"I just came from the shop. It was lodged in my rim," Clifford says with an uneasy smile.

"Nice, We can have our tech run it. Maybe we can find something useful," Martin says.

Clifford reaches into his pocket. "Yeah, there was also this in my floor," Clifford produces the ivory-handled knife from his pocket, handing it over to Martin.

"Whoa, buddy! That was *in* your floor? Hold up."

Martin grabs a tissue from the desk next to him and takes the knife using the tissue.

"Yeah, like stabbed into my floor. I think it was another warning," Clifford says.

"Two warnings in one day? What have you gotten your-self into?" Martin says as he bags up the knife. "I'm going to run this for prints. I'll let you know," Martin continues.

"Yeah, I think it might have something to do with my last client. Not sure," Clifford says.

"Wasn't that an adultery case?" Martin asks. "This is a pretty serious warning for just a cheater," He continues, "If you're into something deeper than you know. Give us the details of the case and let us help you."

Clifford shakes his head. "Nah, it's nothing that serious. Besides, I dropped the case."

"You dropped a case?" Martin asks. "You never drop cases."

"I caught her cheating red-handed, but the husband was a real prick about it. So I told him I was out. That's it."

Clifford forgot Martin knew about the case he was on and decided to play it down as if it was no big deal.

Martin looks unimpressed. "You hiding somethin'?" He asks.

"Oh come on, my client hired me to do some tailing and dirt-digging. That's all I did. You can investigate the bullets in my car," Clifford says in a serious tone.

"Yeah, yeah. Okay, fine," Martin says, "Just be careful."

"I'm always careful," Clifford says as he turns to leave. "Oh, and let me know if you get anything from that knife."

"Yeah, I'll get on that right away, sir!" Martin says with a smile.

Clifford flashes a middle finger as he exits the office door.

Halfway back to the garage, Clifford gets a call from them telling him his car is ready. Tired, he reaches the garage and Scotty is there with a big smile on his face. "Hey man, you're good to go."

"Great!" Clifford says, "My feet are tired of walking everywhere." Scotty tosses the keys over to Clifford and says, "Well, take a load off and enjoy your new wheels."

Clifford catches the keys, midair, and waves as he walks out of the office.

He jumps into the Jeep and heads to the liquor store to get a bottle for Sara.

Clifford was emotionally worn after a rough day. He feels as if he is slinking up the stairs to his apartment. Sara snakes around the corner, trying her best to walk like a thug, "Yo Dee!" She says in a tough girl voice. "You got my stuff?"

Clifford sighs, "Yeah, I got it," As he raised a brown paper bag. A very girly "Ooh!" escapes out of her mouth in excitement.

"That didn't sound very tough at all," Clifford says.

"Shut up, Dee, and give me my bottle," Sara says using her tough voice again.

"Yeah, that's more like it, you alcoholic," Clifford says as he hands it over.

Sara reaches into the bag and pulls out the bottle inside.

"Wha? This is like a $400 bottle! Seriously?" She says in disbelief.

"Yeah, it's all yours," Clifford says.

"Wait, you ain't dying are you?" She asks.

"What? No. I'm not dying. I just appreciated your help and figured I would make it worth your while," Clifford explained. Sara jumps on Clifford and gives him a huge kiss.

"Oh, God, you're stubbly. Gross!" Sara says.

"Yeah, well, I think you made it move, So I guess I enjoyed it," Clifford says sarcastically.

"Oh, you men are so nasty," Sara says. "Oh, Lover!" She says turning to her apartment. "Look what the nice man across the hall got us!" She continues as she walks into her place. Clifford just shakes his head and walks inside his apartment.

The next morning Clifford wakes, refreshed. He decides to go out for a jog and wants to see if Simon will join him. He walks down to his place and knocks on the door.

Jaime answers, "Hey Dee, what's up?"

"I just wanted to see if Simon was up for a jog in the park," Clifford says.

"Well, he is pretty tired from jogging around my bush, if you know what I mean," Jaime says with a wink.

"Ha, I bet it was a short jog," Clifford says with a smile.

"Oooh, good comeback," She says with a smile, "I'll go get him." About a minute later Simon comes to the door.

"Hey, I just woke up. Haven't had any coffee yet," Simon says, trying to avoid the jog.

"Tell you what, I will buy you a cup across the way at that coffee place you like," Clifford says, trying to convince him. Simon sighs, "Yeah, okay, I guess. Gimme five."

Clifford waits outside on the steps of the building and sees the same black guy in a wheelchair rolling through the park. He stops and looks over toward Clifford sitting on the stairs. Clifford waves, as he always does, but after about a minute, the young man turns and starts rolling down another path, away from Clifford and the building.

"Weird," Clifford says under his breath.

"What's weird?" Simon asks, sneaking up on Clifford.

"Uh, The guy over there looked at me and just sat there for a minute and then rolled away," Clifford says.

"Oh, that guy?" Simon says "Yeah, I saw him sitting on the corner over there a day or two ago. I think he's new to the neighborhood."

Clifford shakes his head. "I see him all the time now in that park. I think the first time was a few weeks ago."

After a thirty-second pause, Simon asks, "So you promised coffee?"

"Yeah, let's get some Java," Clifford agrees.

After the jog, Clifford heads back up to his apartment for a shower when he gets a call on his phone. "Hey, What's up, Detective?" Clifford answered.

"Dee, can you get down to my office?" Martin asks.

Clifford looks at his watch. "I can be there in an hour, is that cool?" He asks.

Martin says, "Sure, I'll be here."

Clifford walks into Martin's office but he isn't there. Clifford sits down and starts fiddling with the desk name-plate sign. Martin walks in and says, "Hey, Dee, we got a problem."

"What is it?"

"The knife you brought in," Martin says. "We found blood."

"Wait, blood?" Clifford asks "Whose blood?"

"Well, that's the thing," Martin says. "It's Kelly Kinton's blood."

"Who?" Clifford asks.

"Kelly Kinton is the last of the 'Tree Girls,' we found murdered in the woods over two months ago," Martin says.

"Oh my god!"

"Yeah, but that's not the worst of it. The knife has two sets of prints," Martin continues. "Yours, obviously, because you touched it, but the others belong to a wanted criminal. Darius Tye."

Chapter Fourteen

The Police station always had a stale smell of coffee and justice. Martin's desk is cluttered with papers and notes he has on cases. One of the piles is about The Tye Brothers. He looks across his desk at Clifford who has a strange look on his face. Clifford shakes his head, "Did you say Tarrius?"

"Darius Tye" Martin corrects, "He's part of a crime duo with his brother, Marcus. They're bad news."

"Oh, I see," Clifford says, playing dumb.

Martin sets the report down onto his desk. "We 've been looking for a lead in this case and you just handed it to us on a silver platter. Now, we know, for a fact, that The Tye Brothers are the killers we've been looking for."

"That's good to know," Clifford says.

"But why stab this in the middle of your floor? What do you know about The Tye Brothers?" Martin asks.

Clifford couldn't grasp any logical excuse at the time.

"Not sure, I'm just learning about 'em now. It's not like I got a lot of time on my hands to watch the news. Maybe the girl I was investigating?" Clifford starts rambling. "Nah, couldn't be. That doesn't make sense. No, I don't know."

"Okay, well, look, we need to know everything you've been doing in the last 48 hours to prompt a reaction out of The Tye Brothers. We need to know about your last case, and anything that may have prompted this," Martin demands.

"Martin, C'mon now. You know I can't give my clients info like that," Clifford says.

"Hey, this is a huge investigation and this is our only lead. We need your cooperation. Otherwise, we 'll hold you until we get a warrant to take your case files."

Clifford leans forward in his chair. "You wouldn't!" He says, offended.

Martin looks dead in Clifford's eyes, "Yes, yes I would," Martin says. "Friendship aside, we have a community to protect. If you get in the way of that, I will take evasive measures."

"Fine, I'll give you my files and make a statement," Clifford says, sitting back in his chair.

Clifford knows that the case will not lead the police toward The Tye Brothers. It will lead them to a dirty DA and get him in trouble with Bandoni. With any luck, the police can continue where he left off and he can avoid dealing with Bandoni. This may turn out to be the best situation.

"Luther Buckley was my client. He hired me to tail his wife, Cindy. He assumed an affair. He was right. With whom, I'm not sure, but all the tell-tale signs are there," Clifford says.

"And who shot out your tires?" Martin asks.

"I have no idea, The Tye Brothers? Maybe?" Clifford sits back in his chair and throws his hands up.

"So is that when you called me?" Martin asks.

"Yeah, and towed the car to the shop, went home, found the knife in the floor. You know the rest." Clifford says.

"Huh!?" Martin says with a confused look on his face. "Why would they bother you over an affair?"

"I just started this case. You tell me" Clifford says.

"Okay, okay. Can you get me the case files and all the info you got on the Buckleys? There has to be more to this story. We're missing something," Martin says.

"Yeah, Not sure what," Clifford says back.

"Just get me the files."

"Yes sir," Clifford snaps.

"Shut up," Martin says, "I'm trying to help you."

"That isn't what you said before. You're 'helping the Community'," Clifford says with air quotes.

"Just get me the files," Martin repeats.

"You'll have them by tomorrow morning," Clifford says as he gets out of the chair.

Martin rubs his thick black hair. "Dee!" He calls out as Clifford is heading out of the door.

Clifford stops and turns his head back toward Martin.

"Thanks." Martin continues.

Without a word, Clifford walks out of the office and proceeds to leave the station.

Chapter Fifteen

The club lights at the Dollhouse flicker and flash as Marlon looks on at two of his girls doing a strip battle routine on the stage.

It is the main attraction of the night. Most of the club is out of their seats and tossing bills everywhere. Marlon has seen this so many times, it's just routine and mundane.

He gets up and walks back to his office. He can still see the stage through the mirrored glass, but he never pays attention because he's usually there to conduct business.

The sound of the music becomes muffled as he shuts the door. He sits down in his chair and lets out a huge sigh. He opens a cabinet and pulls out a bottle of a top-shelf rum and pours a little in a glass. Something about being a rum guy in bourbon country makes him wonder why he moved out of the south. The Jamaican blood pumping through his veins just enjoys the rum better. He leisurely inhales, takes a sip, and then sets the glass on top of several unpaid bills and sits behind his desk. Marlon leans back in his office chair and tilts his head back. He takes off his stylish fedora and rubs his slick brown head.

He feels a slight vibration in his jacket pocket. He reaches into his inside breast pocket and pulls out his phone to find a text message.

DEE: "We need to talk. I'll come to you."

Marlon hadn't heard from Clifford since he dropped him and Josh off in front of the club a few weeks ago. He was starting to wonder if he would ever hear from him again.

Clifford pulls up in front of the recently closed club. Some of the customers are still scrambling to their cars. A few of them are way too drunk to drive. Clifford walks up to the front of the club and spots Josh standing by the door.

"Hey Dee, that you?" Josh asks.

"Yeah, I need to talk to your boss. You might want to listen, too."

Josh had an unsure look on his face. "I can't right now, I have to make sure the parking lot clears out. Girl's safety and all," Josh says.

"Yeah, I get that. Can I go in?" Clifford asks.

"Yeah, yeah. Go ahead," Josh says, stepping aside from the door.

Clifford enters the club and all the lights are on at their brightest. It gives a completely different appeal. The smut is so much more attractive when you see it in dim light. A few of the girls are still in costume having a drink at the bar, talking.

Clifford walks over, "Ladies," He greets them.

"Honey, the club is closed. You're supposed to be outta here," One of the girls says.

"I'm here for other business. Can one of you direct me to Marlon's office?" Clifford asks. The girl points over her shoulder toward the wall on the side of the room. Clifford sees the mirrored wall with a door next to it and figures that would be the best place for an office in this establishment.

Just before he knocks, Clifford hears "Motherfucker, get in here!" from the other side of the door. He opens the door and Marlon is sitting behind his desk. Clifford enters and shuts the door behind him.

"So, what?" Marlon asks.

"What, what?" Clifford asks back.

"You wanted to talk to me? I got the text over two hours ago."

"Yeah," Clifford says. "We might want Josh in here too. It involves both of you."

Marlon stands up from behind his desk and slowly walks over toward Clifford. With an angry face, he looks him up and down, then wraps his arms around him.

"You're an asshole, you know that?" Marlon says as he gives Clifford a hug.

Clifford pulls away, "Wait, what did I do?"

"I got a rotten fruit basket from your Boy E.I.," Marlon says. "So much for a good word."

"Hey, I mentioned your name and said you were a huge help," Clifford shoots back.

"Yeah, well, the good that did."

"I can't make the guy like you, Marlon," Clifford says.

"Still, you could have tried harder."

"Well," Clifford says pausing. "I'm not on the best terms with the family."

Clifford sits in the chair next to Marlon's desk. Marlon grabs a glass out of his cabinet and his bottle of Appleton Estate and drops about two ounces into the glass. "Here," He says as he hands the glass to Clifford.

Clifford knocks it back with one swoop and sets the glass down.

"Easy pal! That's $50 a pour at the bar!" Marlon says.

Clifford reaches into his pocket and pulls out a crisp $100 and sets it on the table.

"Hit me again. I need it."

"Only if you promise to respect it this time. This is sippin' rum," Marlon says, already pouring it into the glass.

"Oh! this is rum?" Clifford asks, smiling.

"Bitch, I will put that right back into the bottle!" Marlon threatens Clifford, but laughs as he takes a small swig.

"Oh, this is good!" Clifford says.

"Yeah, you can taste it this time, huh," Marlon says. "Now, why don't you start telling me what is so important that you needed to come out here in the middle of the night."

"I want to wait for Josh. It involves The Tye Brothers," Clifford says.

Marlon grabs his glass and motions to the door. "Let's go sit at the bar and wait for him."

The two men continue idle chat as they walk up to the bar. A gorgeous topless brunette walks past Clifford. He glances at her perfect breasts as they bounce when she walks. He turns his head and gets a nice glimpse of her firm ass. "Rebecca. But she goes as Babs," Marlon says, "She's new here," He continues.

"Oh. Good addition," Clifford says.

"Yeah, really comfortable in her skin. She used to be a nude model for artists. She's still learning to dance, so it'll be a bit before she can be a lead girl," Marlon says.

The men sit at the bar and continue their chat about the girls. Marlon complains about how slow the business has been when eventually Josh makes his way over to the bar.

"Boss, the girls are safe to leave, the lot's clear," Josh says.

"Alright, hit the light and let the girls know, but we have to talk so get your ass back here when you're done."

"Safe to leave?" Clifford asks.

"Some pricks get emotionally attached and think it's okay to meet the girls outside when they're going to go home. So we put this procedure in place. Josh and his boys make sure everyone's gone, then they give the girls the proverbial green light," Marlon explained.

Suddenly a green light detailing the frames of the ceiling comes on, giving the club a greenish glow. Marlon motions Josh toward his office and slides out of his chair.

"Let's go back to the office," Marlon says.

The two gentlemen meet Josh by the office door. All three enter, closing the door behind them. Marlon plops into his chair and says, "Okay, spill it. How much trouble are we in?"

"Well," Clifford says. "I have more than trouble. That's for sure."

"What?! What happened?" Josh asks.

"It's been a long couple of days. I think someone is trying to point the cops in my direction regarding The Tye Brothers. The cops took some case files from me and they're digging for info," Clifford says.

"Are the cops on to us 'bout The Tye Brothers?" Marlon asks.

Clifford stares at him then slowly looks away.

"No. At least, I don't think so. I had no records of The Tye Brothers. But, I don't know what all the cops know. That's the least of my worries right now," Clifford says.

"What do you mean? That seems pretty serious!" Marlon says.

Clifford continued, "Well, someone shot my Jeep up the other day and stuck a dagger in my office floor. I thought I was being clever turning it in to the cops and it turned out to belong to The Tye Brothers. Now the cops are wondering how I'm involved in this. Someone is trying to get the cops looking my way. I just don't know who."

"Bandoni?" Marlon asks.

"Nah, he wouldn't. It would be too dangerous for him as it could lead his way," Clifford says, "It has to be someone else."

Marlon rubs his face, "This better not come back on me," he says.

Clifford shook his head, "No way. But I may need you to have my back."

Against his better judgment, Clifford decides that he should do his own side investigation on why Darius Tye's knife was stuck into his floor. He jumps into his Jeep and heads back to the abandoned warehouse to collect the recording of the hotel room where Cindy and Kristen stayed. He got to the site and was relieved the camera was undisturbed after being there over the weekend. Before he packs up everything to take it back to his office, he removes and pockets the full memory card and replaces it with a new one.

"I don't want to lose this," He says to himself.

Clifford pulls up along the front of his building where the 15-minute parking is. He gets out of the car and notices the black man sitting in the park facing the building. He locks eyes with him and the man starts shaking his head 'no', warning Clifford not to go inside.

Clifford pauses and starts walking over toward the man. The man turns his chair and rolls away from him. Thinking that chasing down a crippled man in the park in broad daylight would give people the wrong impression, he walks back toward his Jeep.

Approaching his Jeep he notices a man sitting in his driver's seat. He stops in his tracks and starts to walk in a different direction when another man comes out of nowhere.

"Get in the car Dee." He says. Clifford looks over and the man in his Jeep has a gun pointed at him.

"Passenger's seat," he says. Clifford climbs in and the other man gets in the back.

As the men approach the grounds of E.I. Bandoni, things became very clear to Clifford.

"What does Mr. B. want with me?" Clifford asks.

The men were silent.

Approaching the gate, the guard looks out the window and lets them in at just the sight of the driver. They continue through the well-groomed grounds of the estate up to the main entrance. "Let's go!" the driver says as he throws the Jeep into park.

They walk up the steps and into Mr. Bandoni's office. Bandoni, sitting behind the desk, is waiting for Clifford.

"Mr. B. How are you? You know you could have called," Clifford says.

"This required a face-to-face conversation," He says as Clifford plops into one of his chairs.

"You disrespect me in my own home?" Bandoni questions.

"Oh!" Clifford says and begins to stand up.

"You can remain seated. But a gentleman asks to sit. Remember that!"

"Sorry, sir," Clifford says with a more respectful tone.

Bandoni leans forward in his chair. With a very stern tone in his voice, he says, "That is more like it. I want your ears right now, not your lips. You open them, I cut them off."

Clifford nods.

He continues, "Good. You are meddling in something that could cost me money. You had a client, Luther Buckley, right?"

Clifford nods again.

"Good, he's going to find himself dead. His wife, Cindy, is working for me. Understand?"

Clifford nods.

"Good, now we are getting somewhere. Did you stop your investigation like I asked you?"

Clifford nods.

"Okay, so, let me hear your voice now. How is your mom doing in Florida?"

A concerned look falls onto Clifford's face. "Good. Well, I assume. I haven't talked to her in a while," he responds.

"Oh, no?" Bandoni asks "Shame, she has a lovely home in Tampa."

"Okay, I get it," Clifford says.

"Oh, you do?" He asks. "Well, hopefully, your Mom or your little sister in Augusta won't have to get it. Or your

Buddy Simon and his pretty girlfriend Jaime, or your lesbian neighbors," E.I. continues.

Clifford realizes that Bandoni had someone gather intel on him. He sits there nodding to show his understanding.

Just then the two goons that drove Clifford interject.

"Hey boss, check this out," One of them says while carrying Clifford's recording equipment.

E.I. looks over. "What is this, Clifford?" He motions to the equipment.

"I was surveilling, uh, I set up surveillance," Clifford stammers.

"Surveilling?" E.I. asks.

"Yeah, on Cindy. As part of my investigation," Clifford says.

"What else do you have?" Bandoni asks.

"This is pretty much it. I have some paperwork signed by her husband at home, but I just started looking into the case, so this is all I have. I had this set up for a while. Before you asked me to stop. I was just collecting it," Clifford confirms.

"Well, good. If you are lying to me. So help me God, I will take it out on your friends."

"I'm not, you have everything," Clifford says.

"Good. I am glad you are starting to understand," Bandoni continues. "I might have some more work for you in the near future. I will be in touch." Mr. Bandoni motions to the door to excuse Clifford. Clifford gets out of the chair and heads to the door.

"Wait!" He says "I do have something for you now."

Clifford turns toward Bandoni and starts to walk back to his desk.

Bandoni scribbles an address onto a notepaper from the desk.

"You have a week. Take care of everyone at this address," He says handing Clifford the paper.

"Why? What did they do?" Clifford asks.

"Does it matter? You are a hitman!" He heatedly fires back.

"Right. No, it doesn't matter. The Price?" Clifford asks.

"Price?! No Price! You are doing this to show your loyalty. I should not have to drag your ass in here and screw up my day. This is your payment to me."

"Yes, Mr. B., I completely understand," Clifford says.

With that Clifford pockets the address and leaves the compound. He is extremely uncomfortable with Mr. Bandoni's tone.

He knows he's slipping out of favors and didn't want to stick around to see his temper. Not many people survive the wrath of Eustachio Innocenzo Bandoni's Temper.

Chapter Sixteen

It's **midafternoon** before Clifford makes his way back to town. In desperate need of a drink, he pulls into the garage and jumps out of the Jeep. He walks into the building and continues up to his floor. Cruising inside his kitchen, he opens his fridge. The beer is gone. He isn't much of a liquor drinker so he doesn't have much of anything in the cabinet.

Across the park is a small bar where he could find something to sip on, so he walks down to ask Simon if he wants to join him, but he isn't home.

Clifford shrugs and heads through the park toward the bar.

While walking, he sees the same wheelchair-bound man feeding the birds. Spotting Clifford, he begins to roll away. Clifford shakes his head over how skittish this guy has been and plans on leaving him alone, but after a moment, he changes his mind.

"Hey!" Clifford says, picking up his pace and walking toward the man.

The man begins rolling faster.

"Wait, I want to talk," Clifford says, now starting a light jog.

The man shouts, "Leave me alone."

Clifford, now at full sprint, runs up in front of the man and grabs his chair.

"Bitch, why you grabbin' at me like that? Motherfucka, I said leave me alone!" The man says as he tries to pull away from Clifford.

"You saw something earlier today. I just wanna talk. You drink?" Clifford asks.

The man scoffs, "Do I drink?" He asks, "Hell yeah, I drink. You buyin'?"

"If you talk to me, I am. Cool?"

"Shit, yeah, man. I'm game," He says.

"You gotta name?" Clifford asks.

"Uh, yeah. It's James Bailey. But people just call me Bailey."

"Bailey, huh?" Clifford asks "Alright. Drinks on me. I'm Clifford Dee."

"I know who you are," Bailey says.

"How do you know me?"

"Drinks first, Dee," Bailey says.

The bar is dimly lit. The neon lights cast a strange glow on the walls making it difficult to see the patrons inside. Clifford and Bailey sit in a dark corner sipping on some drinks having a conversation. Clifford takes a swig of his stout and sets the mug down.

"You're obviously new in the area, Where ya from?" Clifford's first question was not the first one he wanted to ask.

"Indy," Bailey says with a nod. "Well, I grew up in Alabama. Then Indy, and now, here."

Clifford takes another sip of his beer, "That's a pretty big move, 'Bama to Indy," He says.

"Yeah, I moved after my brother died. He was shot on a job and I just had to get the hell outta there. My cousin lived in Gary, so I decided to crash with her for about two years before moving here."

Bailey's tone makes it clear he's reluctant to tell this information to Clifford and he notices.

"Okay, let me ask you this, Why did you tell me that?" Clifford asks.

"Thanks for the drink," Bailey says as he starts to push away from the table.

"What are you scared of?" Clifford asks. "I'm not a bad guy."

Bailey stops and looks over at Clifford. "I ain't scared of you."

"Then, what? You can trust me," Clifford says.

Bailey rolls back up to the table. "I do have trust issues," He says.

Because of his skittish behavior, Clifford knows that he needs to take it easy with him and slowly move the conversation along.

"Okay, look I'll start. What do you want to know about me?" Clifford asks.

Bailey looks at him. "Well, let me tell you what I think first and you can just correct me."

"Okay," Clifford says with a smirk.

"You're a PI. But not just any PI. You take 'other jobs' on the side."

Clifford's smirk disappears from his face and a sense of worry replaces it.

Bailey continues. "You ain't from here. I want to say somewhere closer to me, like Georgia or Florida or some shit. You were military, Imma guess you were in the Army, special forces or a Marine or some shit. Right?"

Clifford nods.

Bailey grabs his beer and takes a swig while holding his finger in the air, pausing the conversation for a moment. Setting his beer down swiftly and letting out a huge satisfactory 'aahh.'

He looks across the table seeing the slight worry on Clifford's face, he asks, "How'd I do?"

"Not bad," Clifford says, "How did you—" Clifford pauses.

"How did I deduce such correct information?" Bailey asks.

"Yeah."

"Well, Mr. Dee, I read people well. You're confident. Despite your limp, you gotta certain walk, like you were taught to march like they do in the force or military. You have the eyes of a killer, but they're soft. This made me think that you were special forces rather than a pig. Your accent is different, but familiar. That's why I am thinking, Georgia or Florida. Oh, and I saw your PI flier."

"You think I'm a hitman?" Clifford asks.

"The mob was looking for you," Bailey says. "I put the two together and made me think that you do... jobs."

Clifford nodded in approval. "Very good."

"Yeah," Bailey says, "Now you can understand why I was worried about meetin' you. You seemed to be bad news."

"And what do you think now?" Clifford asks.

"You seem okay to me," He says with a smile while raising his beer.

"Okay, so your story?" Clifford asks.

Bailey looks at him, "You tell me, you're the PI."

"Dude, c'mon" Clifford says. "I'll investigate. Do you want me to start looking into you?"

"Nah, I'll tell you. Since we're sharing and all," Bailey starts. He takes another big swig of his beer, finishing it. "So like I said, I grew up in 'Bama. Birmingham, to be exact. My brother and I used to get bus fare after school and take it down to Bessemer. Lot's of petty theft down that way and not many cops to stop it. We would just boost cars and drive them back to the shop in B-ham."

Clifford, still sitting and sipping on his beer, is listening intently and stops him for a moment. "Wait, you stole cars?"

"Yeah, I haven't been in this chair forever, ya know. We would boost two and race back. We'd get around about five

G's a piece. Easy money for a kid in school and then go back and do it the next day. Cars, bikes, whatever we could get our hands on," Bailey says.

"So what happened?" Clifford asks. "Is that how you got in the chair? Car accident?"

"I'll get there man, don't worry," Bailey laughs. "So, a few years ago, my brother snatched up this truck. He was starting to drive away and he was shot by a shotgun totin' redneck. I mean defending property an all, but still, he killed someone. No amount of property is worth my brother's life, you know what I mean?" Bailey says.

Clifford looks over and signals the bartender that they were ready for more beer.

She nods and starts pouring their drinks. "Hold that thought," Clifford says, leaving to get the beer. Returning, Bailey gives Clifford a nod and a slight smile.

"You miss your brother?" Clifford asks.

"Yeah, of course," Bailey says, "That dude was funny as shit. Anytime I was feeling down he could make me laugh."

"So," Clifford says, taking a swig of his fresh beer. "What happened next, I assume you made it out of there," He says.

"Yeah, after my brother died, I moved in with my cousin, JJ. I was ready to get out of Bama. The whole area made me think of my brother."

"Yeah, that's understandable," Clifford says.

"Yeah, but my cousin's a bit relentless. I was 18 when I left town. Shit, that was over ten years ago," Bailey says, starting to rub his brow. He takes another sip of his beer and sets it down, thinking about the time that passed.

"Anyway, so my cousin ran a small crew in Indy. She got a gig in Chicago and needed me to drive. She had me and this other guy drive out to scope a location for a meeting. It went south fast. They spotted us and thought we were tryin' to drop someone or somethin'. They put a few shots in the driver's side of the car and one got my spine. That's how I got in the chair. I recovered, but she moved out of Indy and took over a larger crew in Chi-town. I couldn't run jobs for her anymore, so I left."

Clifford shakes his head in disbelief. "Wow, That's an amazing story. I got one for you that I don't tell everyone."

Bailey leans in closer to the table. "Aight, let's hear it."

"So you mentioned me being a soldier, right?" Clifford asks.

"Yeah," Bailey returns.

"Well, I was out visiting 'stan' in the sand, if you know what I mean. We were hunting for splinter cells off of a major terrorist group."

Bailey nods as Clifford continues.

"We were cruising in the desert when our truck hit a mine. It blew the rear axle off of the vehicle and threw the entire truck end over end."

"Oh shit!" Bailey exclaims.

"Shh," Clifford says, trying to calm Bailey's excitement from attracting listeners.

"Okay, yeah, so it gets worse. Six were dead. I was thrown from the truck with a concussion and a bad head injury. My sergeant was screaming my name because both of his legs were crushed and his arm was blown off."

Bailey winces.

Clifford continues, "It looked like hamburger meat on a stick. Pretty messed up."

Bailey still wincing, "The fuck dude?"

"Well, while my sergeant was calling for me, he suddenly started telling me to run. He was in front of the wreckage and could see about fifteen towel-heads running toward us. I was so confused, I had no idea what the hell was going on. I was captured."

Bailey, looking astonished, "Shit, you're a POW?"

"Yeah, if you look at it that way, yes," Clifford says. "So fast forward a bit. A cage was my home for about a week before I was found and rescued."

"Damn dude," Bailey says, "Now that's a story."

Minutes turn to hours and the two men sit drinking more beer and exchanging stories.

Bailey and Clifford begin to try outdoing each other with their tales until Clifford mentions The Tye Brothers.

"Tye Brothers?" Bailey asks.

"Oh, forget I said that," Clifford says.

"You talking about Darius and Marcus Tye? From the news?" Bailey continues to ask.

Worried, Clifford says, "Just forget I said anything."

"They boys of yours?"

"No, no. Not friends. At all," Clifford firmly says, "Let's talk about something else."

"Damn, okay," Bailey says, realizing he touched a nerve. "So why'd those guys come to see you?"

"Well, that was a warning, I guess. Told me to stay away from some lady named Cindy I was following. Husband thought she was cheating. She is, with the District Attorney, of all people," Clifford rambles.

"Cindy Buckley?" Bailey questions while looking past Clifford toward the TV.

"Yeah, how the hell did you know her name?" Clifford asks.

"Wait, that's the name of the lady you were watching? With the DA?" Bailey asks with a confused look while pointing toward the TV in the corner. Clifford turns around slowly to look and sees that the news is claiming that Cindy is the latest victim of The Tye Brothers Killings.

"You sure you don't want to talk about those boys?" Bailey asks.

"I just- I can't right now," Clifford says.

Chapter Seventeen

Kristen walks out of her office with a thick envelope with the word, "Cleveland," written on the front. She walks down the stairs and around to the back of the building and enters the parking garage. From the dark corners, two shadowy figures emerge and one asks, "You have the file."

She hands over the packet, turns heel, and walks back inside.

The shadowy figures slip back into the darkness.

Hours later a file comes across her secretary's desk stamped, 'Urgent.'

The secretary opens the file and her eyes widen.

She bursts into the office, "Ms. Neil, Ms. NEIL!" She nervously exclaims.

Kristen looks up from her files. "What is it, Sherry?"

Sherry sticks her hand out with the paperwork. "It's about Cleveland Kendall."

"Just set it on my desk. I'll get to it."

"It's Urgent. I think it's release papers," Sherry says with a hint of fear in her voice.

"That's impossible!" Kristen says, snatching the papers from her hand. Reading over the papers Kristen is muttering over the verbiage in the document.

"Thank you, Sherry." She says barely glancing from the file. Upon leaving the office Sherry can see a slight smirk on Kristen Neil's face.

Clifford wakes up around 10 am with a slight hangover from drinking with his new friend.

He sits up out of bed and sluggishly shuffles toward the bathroom and gets himself some water.

His cellphone begins to ring in the other room. He slowly walks back to answer it, but just missed the call. He looks at the Caller ID.

MARTIN.

He tosses the phone onto his bed and rubs his face. He walks to the bathroom and turns on the shower. The voice mail tone dings and a notification light flashes on the phone. Exiting the shower, Clifford throws his towel down on the bed and reaches for his phone.

The alarm system trips.

Clifford lets out a huge sigh. "Again?" he mutters under his breath while walking in the dim light over to his camera. Looking in his office, he sees nothing alarming until suddenly a sliver of paper the size of a legal envelope slides under the door of his office.

He steps into sweatpants and walks out into his office and grabs the envelope. Inside it is pictures of a large home and an address. It's on the other side of town and was a beautiful home.

On the back of the picture, it says. 'Everyone in the house. EVERYONE.' Clifford slams it down in anger. He knows that he has to do this or everyone he cares about could be in danger. He walks back to his room and throws the envelope onto his nightstand. He picks up his phone and dials his voicemail to hear Martin's message.

'Dee, we need to have a chat. Come into my office as soon as you can.'

Clifford tosses the phone back onto his bed and continues to get dressed.

He steps out of his apartment, into the garage, and heads toward his car.

Echoing across the concrete pillars he hears "Dee."

Clifford stops and looks around. Outside of the garage, he can see Bailey wheeling toward him quickly.

"Get in the car," he says in a slight panic.

Clifford jumps in the car and pulls out of his spot, throws it into park, and gets out to help Bailey into the Jeep. He grabs his chair and tosses it into the back. Clifford jumps back into the Jeep and takes off.

"Where am I going?" Clifford asks.

Bailey looks at him and says, "Your place is being watched. The guy that delivered that message is bad news."

"Are you watching my place?" Clifford asks.

"Bruh, I pretty much live in that park across the street."

Clifford shakes his head and sees in the rear-view a car mirroring his every move.

"Did you see the kind of car that messenger was driving?" Clifford asks

"Yeah it was an impala, Green, I think," Bailey says.

"Huh, okay," Clifford returns.

"Why?"

"Well," Clifford says, "He's behind us. Don't look," He says when Bailey turns his head to see.

"What are you going to do?"

Clifford peers into the rearview mirror, "I'll shake him, no worries."

Clifford continues to drive and he presses the call star button in his Jeep.

The voice from his speakers chimed "Hello Dee, Call Star ready!"

Clifford enunciates, "Call Martin!"

"Call Martin, is this correct?"

"YES," he enunciates again.

Clifford is keeping his eye on his company as Martin picks up the call.

"Dee, Did you get my message?"

"Yeah, I did. But I can't come in right now."

"Why not?" Martin says.

"I can't say, but I need a favor," Clifford says.

"What?" Martin says unenthused.

"I need you to come pull me over."

"What? Why?"

"Well, I'm being tailed by someone that I really don't want knowing that I am visiting the cops. You want me? Come get me," Clifford says.

"Where are you? I'll send a black and white," Martin says.

Clifford gives Martin his location. A few minutes later, a cop pulls out from behind an alley and starts following the impala behind Clifford. The blue lights turn on and the Impala slows down and starts to pull over.

The cop darts past the Impala and pulls over Clifford and Bailey.

The Impala continues past and onto a side street.

The squad car chirps its siren and flashes its light and then pulls away. Clifford pulls a u-turn and then makes his way to the police station.

Pulling up to the station, Bailey looks over to Clifford and says, "Kidding, right?"

"Nah, man. My buddy Martin works homicide," Clifford says with a smile.

"Of course," Bailey says, "I'll wait."

"Suit yourself," Clifford says, jumping out of the Jeep. Clifford runs into the station and Bailey is sitting looking around. Suddenly a car pulls up next to Clifford's Jeep and a man looks over toward Bailey.

Bailey looks over and notices that the man is staring at him.

"Shit!" He says under his breath.

The man gets out of the car and begins to walk toward Bailey. Bailey presses the call star button.

"Hello, Dee, Call star ready."

Luckily Dee was still in range of the car.

"Call Martin!" Bailey screams.

"Bluetooth signal low, calling", the voice announces.

The phone rings twice before Martin picks up, "Dee, what's up?" Martin says.

"This is Dee's friend, I'm outside in his car, I need help!"

The phone disconnects and Martin stands up from behind his desk. He starts walking down the hall and toward the stairs. In the hall, he spots Clifford. "You have someone in your car?"

"Yeah, Why?"

Martin takes off in a full sprint. "Come on!" he shouts. Clifford turns and runs along with Martin. Outside, they run up to Clifford's car. Bailey is gone, but his wheelchair is still in the back. In the driver's seat there was a note: "Do your job!"

Clifford spots the note before Martin, snagging it and shoving it into his pocket.

Martin is looking around and asks, "Dee, what's going on?"

"I don't know," He answers. Clifford stammers for just a moment before asking, "I can trust you, right?"

Martin looks at Clifford and says, "Of course you can, with anything."

Clifford rubs his brow, knowing that he needs to get Martin involved. "It's about that case, I stumbled onto something."

"Let's go talk," Martin says.

Chapter Eighteen

That night, Clifford drives out to the address on the note left in his apartment. He parks outside the gates of the huge home. The lights in the foyer and living room are still aglow.

He waits patiently for the lights to turn off. When they do, he waits some more. After about two hours, he safely assumes that the residents in the home are fast asleep. Clifford leaves his car and inspects the house. He can tell that there's an alarm system, but doesn't spot any cameras. He walks around to the back of the house and scales the iron fence surrounding the property. He makes his way around the back and tests the patio door.

Locked.

He pulls out a lock pick set and quickly unlocks the door. Like a swift wind, Clifford swoops into the living room. By the front door, he sees an alarm system that states, 'Silent Alarm triggered.' He pulls an electronic device out of his pocket and places it over the box. The box flashes, beeps, and goes back to 'Armed-Home.'

He quietly climbs the stairs and passes a room in the hall on his way toward the master suite. Clifford can see a soft glow of light from under a door. From that room, he hears a toilet flush.

Clifford presses his body as close to the wall as he can. He sinks into a door jam of a closed room as the bathroom light peers out of the open bathroom door. He looks on as a little girl, no older than nine years of age, walks out of the bathroom and into her bedroom at the opposite end of the hall.

'Take care of everyone in the house. EVERYONE.'

Clifford shakes the memory of the note from his mind. There is no way he can ever bring it upon himself to kill a child or leave one orphaned. He continues into the master suite and looks over the sleeping parents.

He knows that this is an impossible task that Bandoni bestowed upon him. He can't leave them alive or they will kill Bailey and then his friends and family shortly after, but he already decided that he can't kill them either.

Clifford takes a step toward the bed and a loud creek squeezes out of the wood floor.

The wife opens her eyes and scoots toward her husband beside her at the site of Clifford. The sudden movement jolts her husband awake. He looks over and screams, "Hey!" at the sight of the intruder.

Clifford pulls out a gun and says, "Shut up! I'm here to talk."

The wife's heart is pounding and her eyes become wide at the sight of the gun.

She is frozen in fear.

The husband moves closer to his wife and angles his body in front of her in the act of a shield. "What do you want?"

"Listen!" Clifford says, now beginning to whisper, "Your little girl is in the other room awake. I was sent here to kill her and you, but I am not a killer. I don't know why, but some very bad people want you all dead."

The wife elbows the husband, "Dammit Raymond, I told you not to take that money."

"Shut up!" Clifford exclaimed in a whisper. "I don't care what you did. I am not going to kill you, but I have to make it look like I did, and you need to leave town. For good!"

The couple nods as Clifford continues.

"If you don't leave town, or if you tell people that you're alive, they will send someone else that WILL kill you. Understand?"

The couple nods again.

"Your car, is it in the garage?" Clifford asks.

The woman nods.

"Okay, good, I don't think anyone is watching the house right now, so I want you to pack a bag for you and your family, load up the car and go."

Clifford begins to pace, rubbing his forehead in thought.

Raymond asks, "What's wrong?"

Clifford looks over and says, "I just need to figure out how to deliver proof."

The wife slowly raises her hand, "I have an idea."

After a discussion, the wife leaves and returns a few moments later with their daughter.

Clifford can hear her talking from the hall. "Listen, honey, there is a man here, don't be scared, he is going to help us with the Halloween prank."

The tired little girl says in confusion, "But, Mommy, Halloween is so far away."

"I know, Sweetie, this is for a prank. I'll explain later, okay?"

"Okay."

After using makeup to paint blood and contusions on the face, Clifford tells them to lay down.

He takes a few photos with his cell phone and says, "Okay, that should do it."

The wife turns to the father and says, "Raymond, why don't you take her to pick out some clothes for our trip."

Confused, he says, "Okay, sure," and turns to his daughter, "Alright, Sweetpea, let's get some clothes for a trip."

"Where are we going, Daddy?" She asks as he escorts her out of the room.

The wife turns toward Clifford, "Come with me," she demands.

Clifford's eyes follow her as she leaves the room. "What are you doing?" He asks.

"Let's go!" She demands again.

With that, Clifford picks up his feet and follows her down to the kitchen. She turns to him and says, "If I sent you to kill someone, I wouldn't likely believe some pictures of people in Halloween makeup. You need more proof."

Clifford's eyes narrow, "What do you mean?"

She reaches for the knife block on the counter and draws out the butcher knife. She wraps a large lock of her hair onto the blade and cuts off some of her hair. She then palms the blade and runs it through her hand, letting out a grimace as the blade slices through the meaty flesh of her palm.

"What are you doing?" Clifford exclaims.

She tosses the bloody knife into the sink and drips blood onto her severed hair and all over the counter. She grabs a towel and wraps her hand.

"Take the blood and hair to use as more proof. They will be able to tell it's real," She says as she walks away. She opens a cupboard and grabs a plastic bag and hands it to Clifford.

"You're hardcore, you know that!" He tells her.

She grabs a cigarette from a hidden spot in the cupboard and lights it with a grill lighter.

"I knew my husband was going to get into trouble sooner or later over his activities. He always seemed to have a lot of extra money we couldn't account for," She says letting out a puff of smoke. "He thought I didn't notice. But I knew."

Clifford smiles and says, "He's lucky to have you."

With their daughter wrapped in his arms, Raymond walks into the kitchen and says, "I thought you quit smoking?"

She raised her hand with a blood-soaked rag wrapped around it to grab the cigarette from her mouth, "Sorry, honey, It just seemed like a good time to start back up," she says.

With his mouth agape, Raymond says, "What happened to your hand?"

Clifford raises the baggy filled with hair and blood, "She told me I should have better proof."

Clifford pushes the button to shut the garage door after the family drives off. He reaches into his pocket and pulls out his phone to call Martin.

"Hey, buddy. Remember, only people you trust or else I'm dead. Here's the address..."

Clifford walks upstairs toward the bedroom of the home-owners and pulls out his gun. He fires his gun three times. He walks down to the kitchen and fires it again. He grabs some paper towels and takes the bloody knife out of the sink. He walks to the front door, opens it, and bolts from the house as fast as he can. He drops the knife in the front yard as he runs across the street and up the hill. As he's running, he notices the neighbor's lights coming on and some of them looking out of their blinds. In the distance, he can hear the sounds of the police sirens.

He turns the corner at the top of the hill away from prying eyes and jumps into his Jeep. He pulls out his phone and calls Bandoni's assistant.

"It's done, but I ran into a snag."

"What snag?"

Clifford, out of breath from running says, "I can send a picture, but I had to shoot them and the cops were coming so I had to get out fast. I was only able to get a little bit of the woman's hair."

"Okay, whatever you got is fine. We can verify other ways," he says.

A plain-clothes cop strolls up to the house and approaches Martin. "Hey Detective, What's going on?" He says as he tries to walk past him.

Martin walks out in front of him to stop him from going into the house. "What are you doing here?" He asks.

The cop responds, "I heard it on the scanner and thought I could help out."

Martin shakes his head, "Nah, we got this under control."

The cop tilts his head in confusion, "So, why are you here?"

Martin let out a slight smile, "The Captain called me from home and asked me to handle this. Shots were reported so he wanted someone from homicide here."

"Ah, okay. I guess I'll see you in the morning then?" The cop says to Martin as he's backing away down the driveway.

"Yep," Martin quips back.

Another uniformed officer interrupts them and says, "Detective, We found this in the yard. It has blood and hair on it," as he presents the knife in an evidence bag.

"Put that with the other stuff," Martin says as the plain-clothes cop smiles and strolls away from the scene.

Chapter Nineteen

A cheap hospital wheelchair is pushed up against the wall in a dimly lit room. Bailey is sitting in a folding chair with a shock collar around his neck. His nose is bloodied and there is dark bruising under his eyes. There is no doubt that his visit with the Bandoni family has not been very warm and welcoming.

Hearing the door creak open, Bailey looks over to see one of the goons approaching him.

"Haven't had enough, huh?" Bailey says.

"Shut your yap! Boss wants to see you!" He fires back.

"Ooh, lucky me," Bailey says mockingly.

With that, the goon hit the remote for the shock collar sending Bailey into a brief electric convulsion.

"Not feeling so lucky now, huh?"

Bailey regains his composure and says, "You're so funny."

He smiles and says, "Yeah, everyone tells me that," as he's helping Bailey to his wheelchair. Bailey is wheeled from his room and taken through a hall leading into a garden. He can see a man sitting at a table with breakfast set up for two.

As he gets closer to the table, he can smell the bacon and eggs, as well as cinnamon toast. There is a glass of orange juice in a nice crystal glass sitting next to a steaming hot cup of coffee.

Bandoni lowers his newspaper, folds it, and sets it next to his plate as Bailey is being wheeled up to the table next to him.

"What is this?" Bailey asks Bandoni.

"Breakfast. Please eat."

"I didn't think my stay here included the continental breakfast," says Bailey.

"You are a very clever man," Bandoni says. "I feel that we got off on the wrong foot."

Bailey scoffed, "Yeah, torture is a very wrong foot to get off on."

"Torture? You thought you were being tortured? Please. You have all fingers. You have no broken bones. A little 'scratch' on your head, and just a few bruises. We were being..." Bandoni twirled his fork in the air while trying to grasp the right word, "... Assertive in our communication."

"Assertive?"

"We want to be sure you understand that what we talk to you about is to be taken seriously," Bandoni says, passing a plate of eggs over to Bailey.

"You see, Clifford Dee is an employee of mine who is very good at his job, but has been slipping in his duties."

Bailey begins scooping some eggs onto his plate. "So what do you want from me? I just met the guy," He says, taking a huge bite of eggs.

"He needs someone looking out for him, and you seem perfect for that job."

Bandoni's attention was grabbed as a man walked into the garden and confronted one of the guards. Bandoni wipes his mouth with his napkin and excuses himself.

Bailey grabs a piece of buttered cinnamon toast as he looks on to what is a seemingly tense situation.

Bandoni became loud and blurted out "He was stopped by COPS?! He IS a cop?" Just then Bandoni pulls a gun out of his inside jacket holster and shoots one of the men. He casually walks back to the table as the guard is cleaning up the mess.

Bandoni puts both hands on the table and says "Change of plans. I need information. I will pay you a thousand a day to get info from Clifford and bring it back to me."

Bailey looks over at the man struggling with a fresh corpse. "And if you don't like the information I bring you? 'Cause, you clearly have no problems shooting the messenger."

"Bringing me information will be your job. His job was to bring me confirmation. I shot him because he did not do his JOB!" Bandoni says furiously.

Bailey tries to squeeze a sentence in, but Bandoni cuts him off.

"If I have no need for you, I have no use for you."

Bailey could see a pulsating vein in Bandoni's neck and knew that he was fighting off killing him right then and there.

"Understood, Mr. B," Bailey says knowing that he is on very thin ice.

Chapter Twenty

Kristen Neil's secretary, Sherry, rushes back to a ringing phone. "Kristen Neil's office, how may I help you?"

She pauses for a moment and answers the voice on the other end of the line. "Yes sir, Mr. Russo. I will let Ms. Neil know."

She scribbles a note on a sticky pad and places it on top of a folder. Kristen was clearly a very busy woman. Sherry walks down the hall and into a conference room where Kristen is reviewing a case file. She takes a look at the sticky note and asks, "How long ago did Mr. Russo call?"

"Just a moment ago. Maybe three or four minutes." Kristen pushes away from the desk, picks up her cell phone and walks into the hall. The only bit of the conversation Sherry heard was "Hey, Tony, it's Kristen."

She spends the majority of the call listening to Mr. Russo talk. Kristen can barely even get a few "Uh-huh's" or "Ums," into the conversation before the call is over.

As soon as she hangs up the phone, Sherry asks, "Everything okay?"

Kristen looks over, "I have to go sign some papers for Cleveland's release. They're doing it right now and they need me to sign an affidavit of wrongful prosecution."

"But you weren't the DA when he was sentenced, You didn't prosecute him."

Kristen runs her hands through her hair and says, "Yeah, well, I'm it now, so I have to do it." As she storms off to meet with the opposing counsel. Kristen breathes a huge sigh of relief as soon as she turns the corner. It's clear that she's stressed about this entire ordeal. She catches her breath and continues heading toward the office of Mr. Russo when she is met by Detective DiPietro. "Ms. Neil, can you come with me for a second?"

"What's going on?" She asks as two other officers walk toward her, surrounding her.

"Am I in trouble?" She continues to ask.

"Ms. Kristen Neil, you're being detained for questioning regarding the death of Cindy Buckley. Please come with me," Martian demands.

"I'm sorry, I can come down to the station after work and give you a statement," She says, trying to brush Martin off.

"I could bump that up to an arrest with an official arrest record if you like. Or, you could just come with me and answer my questions now," Martin says, grabbing her arm.

"Fine!" Kristen says annoyed.

She pulls out her phone and sends a text message "Sorry, I have to cancel an appointment real quick."

Martin nods, "Alright, when you're ready."

On the other end of the text message, Bandoni reads: *"Being detained re CB. Must answer ??s"*

He texts back: *"It will be taken care of."*

It's mid-morning when Clifford walks up to his building and sees a familiar face shrouded by a purple hoodie and some sunglasses. "Bailey!" Clifford says running toward his new friend.

"Hey Dee," He says, looking up at Clifford

"HOL-LEE-SHIT!" Clifford says looking at his face. "What did they do to you?"

"Visiting Bandoni was a unique experience," Bailey says.

"How long have you been here and where did you get that dinky wheelchair?" Clifford asks.

"Not long, forty-five minutes maybe. It's a cheap chair. Courtesy of Bandoni."

"Did they drop you off? How did you get here?"

"They let me go, conditionally," Bailey says looking around.

"What does that mean, 'Conditionally'?"

"Yeah, you gonna love this one. They want me to snitch on you."

"Snitch? About what?" Clifford asks.

"About a job you were supposed to do. How about we go inside?" Bailey suggests.

Clifford and Bailey head toward the elevator and go up to his floor, not saying much to each other. Once inside, Clifford closes the door and says. "Okay, so?"

"They said something about no body, no proof. Were you supposed to kill someone?"

"Yeah, I was."

"And?" Bailey asks. Clifford looked at Bailey with a slight untrusting glare.

"Man, I ain't no snitch. You should know that."

Clifford looks away and says, "Yeah, I know that. No, I didn't kill them. There was a kid, too. I don't kill kids."

"I get that," Bailey says, removing his sunglasses.

Clifford looks closer at Bailey. "What is it, Dee?"

"Your eyes, the dilation is off. I think you're concussed," Clifford says.

"I'm good, man."

"Let's get you to the hospital," Clifford says.

"Man, I can't afford that."

"I got it. We're going," Clifford insisted, "You're also going to need some stitches for that cut."

Clifford smiles and asks, "You know who gets stitches, right?"

Bailey chuckles back, "Man, shut up, I ain't no snitch."

"I know. Hey, your chair's in my Jeep."

"Sweet!"

On the way to the hospital, Bailey looks over at Clifford and says, "Hey man, I just wanted to tell you, Bandoni's got cops on his payroll."

Clifford looks back at Bailey briefly as he's driving, "I know, but why are you telling me that?"

Bailey says, "He was bitching about one of the cops not being able to confirm your kill."

Clifford smiles at Bailey, "I knew he was going to try that shit. I had a feeling."

Bailey says, "Yeah, but I'm just wondering..."

"Wondering what?" Clifford asks when Bailey didn't finish his thought.

"Your boy at the precinct. Can you trust him?"

Clifford scoffs, "Martin? Hell yeah, I can trust that guy. He's the one that blocked Bandoni's guys from the crime scene. Martin's cool. He's legit."

Bailey nods, "Okay, but as you know, I have a genuine distrust for the po-pos. The fact that some of them are working for guys that want to harm me outside the law doesn't make it any better."

"Yeah, I get that," Clifford says, as he pulls into the hospital parking lot.

Bailey puts his hand up to his eyes and begins rubbing his brow. "Man, I think I'm okay. Just take me home so I can rest a bit and I'll be fine."

Clifford looks in concern, "Not a chance, for two reasons. One, you are clearly concussed and need to see a doctor. If you go to sleep, you might not wake up. Two, if they got to you and know who you are, they're watching your place. I am sure it's all full of bugs right now."

Bailey looks up with a bit of worry. "You think they bugged my place?"

"I wouldn't put it past them. Especially if you're supposed to be an informant," Clifford says.

Bailey shakes the throbbing pain from his head and continues to rub his brow. "Yeah, okay. I'll go see your witch doctor and get my voodoo medicine," he says in his best mocking tone.

Clifford gets out of the car, grabs the chair from the back, and helps Bailey into it.

"Oh man, it's like fitting into an old glove. Those hospital chairs are so cramped and uncomfortable."

Clifford tosses the old chair into the back and walks behind to begin pushing him. "You can tell a difference?"

"Oh yeah, huge difference," Bailey says letting out a sigh. Clifford parks Bailey over near the waiting area and heads over to the check-in desk to start filling out paperwork. He fills out the majority of it and then takes the paperwork over to Bailey.

"Hey man, I filled most of this out, but I can't answer these questions for you."

"Okay," Bailey continues to mutter to himself as he's reading the paperwork.

"Hey, I gotta piss, I'll be right back," Clifford says as he gets up and walks away.

Clifford finds his way up to the maternity ward after a stop at the gift shop to buy some flowers. He walks up toward a nurse with the flowers behind his back. "Excuse me, Ms. Davis. I believe these are for you," Clifford says as he reveals the flowers.

Ashlea turns around and her eyes widen. "You!" She exclaims. "I should call the cops right now."

"I know, I came back to apologize to you."

"Do you have any idea how much trouble you caused me?" She asks.

"Yeah, I know. I'm sorry. See, flowers!" Clifford says shaking the bouquet.

Ashlea threw a quick smile. "You really think you can buy me off with some flowers?" She says as she takes the flowers from him.

Looking it over she noticed the tag. "Get Well? Really? You got these from the gift shop downstairs?"

Clifford shrugs. "Well yeah. I didn't have many options."

"I see, so, you didn't come here for me. Why are you here?" Ashlea says setting the flowers on the nurse's station counter.

"A buddy of mine needed some care. He got roughed up real bad, and since I was here, I figured..."

Ashlea interrupts, "You wanted to kill two birds with one stone?"

"No, Well, Yeah, but no. I wanted to thank you properly for saving me. I really did. But in my line of work..." Clifford pauses for a moment.

"Your line of work? What are you a spy or something?" She asks. "You know, I'm pretty sure that Kyle isn't your real name."

"It's Clifford."

"Clifford? Clifford what?" She asks.

"Clifford Dee."

"D? Is that your last initial?"

"No, it's my name D-E-E, Dee," Clifford explains.

"Huh, okay. Clifford D-E-E." She says, mockingly.

"It's really my name. I'm a Private Investigator," Clifford says, handing her a business card.

"Seriously?"

"Yeah, seriously," Clifford says. "I was on a case and there were bad people out to get me. I couldn't have any run-in with the police because some of the police are on their payroll."

"And this is a real story that I should believe?" Ashlea says with doubt.

"Hey, you don't believe me, walk down to admissions and look for a black guy in a wheelchair. His name is Bailey. He looks like he went a few rounds with the champ and then got hit by a truck, got up and then walked into a door, possibly even fell down a flight of stairs."

"What? A wheelchair? Did they cripple him?"

"No, that was pre-existing, but he was roughed up by some really bad people," Clifford says. "I'm just trying to get him fixed up. He's my friend."

Ashlea says, "I see. I'll make sure he's taken care of."

"Thank you. It was pretty much my fault because he wouldn't be in this situation if it weren't for me. Actually, I have to get back to him." Clifford starts to back away from Ashlea and waves goodbye.

"Nope," She says, "You can't walk out of here without promising me dinner," She continues.

"Dinner, promise!" Clifford says.

"When?" She asks.

"Tomorrow, six?" Clifford asks.

"Pick me up, here, at five." She says.

He turns, with a smile on his face, and heads back down the hall toward the elevator. Clifford walks out of the elevator and heads toward the waiting room. He noticed a nurse pushing Bailey's wheelchair down the hall. "Uh, where is the man that belongs to that?" Clifford asks.

"Oh, you brought him in?" The nurse asks.

"Yeah, he's my friend."

141

"He was admitted. You should probably wait in the waiting area. You can't see him right now," She says.

"Wait, what happened?" Clifford asks.

Chapter Twenty one

Martin DiPietro walks into the interrogation room with two cups of coffee and hands one to Kristen Neil. "It's warm, been sitting a while."

"No thank you," she says refusing the cup.

"Well, I guess we can get down to the brass tacks," Martin says. "How do you know the victim?"

Kristen sits tight-lipped with arms crossed. Martin takes a huge swig of the warm coffee and swallows hard.

"This is how we're gonna do this?" Martin asks.

"You know how this works, Detective," Kristen says, "I wait until I have my attorney present before we talk."

"Aren't you the D.A.? You are an attorney."

She scoffs, "I'm saying nothing."

"Okay, be right back," Martin says excusing himself from the table.

He walks into the room behind the mirrored glass and the Captain turns to face him. "Not talking, huh?"

Martin looks over to his Captain, "Nah, but I figure we can wait for her attorney before dropping any truth on her. Give her a false sense of security."

The Captain rubs his brow, "Your buddy, Clifford, really got mixed up into something bad here."

Martin chuckled, "Yeah, he's really good at stirring up some shit."

"Do you trust him?" The Captain asks.

Martin nods, "I really do. He's a good guy and an even better detective."

The Captain stands quiet for a moment and looks over at Martin. "Okay, detain her for forty-eight before making an arrest. I'll notify the Chief. She wants to know how we're going to proceed," he says as he starts walking past Martin to leave the room.

"Hey, Brian," Martin says. "Are you going to have her come in?"

He nodded, "Yeah, Probably. She's not happy with this one. She's gonna want to see this for herself."

The Captain walks out of the door and down the hall while Martin stares through the mirrored glass at Kristen. He shakes his thoughts from his head when he can hear that shady attorney, Tony Russo, in the hall demanding she is let go.

Martin grabs a file from a small table and heads out to the hallway.

"Mr. Russo, I'm the arresting officer, please, your client is this way."

"Thank you!" He hastily blurts out as he brushes past Martin.

"Which room?!" He demands, "Which room!?

"Uh, Number three, She's in number three," Martin says quickly to his abrupt rudeness.

They both enter the room and Tony blurts out, "K, I am so sorry. Grab your things, we're going."

"Woah, not so fast, Mr. Russo. We need to have a little chat first?" Martin says setting the file onto the table.

Tony looks down at the file and back up at Detective DiPietro. "What's that?" He asks.

"Something that I have questions about," Martin replies.

"Fine, get it over with so we can go," He says in exasperation as he pulls a chair out to take a seat. Martin pulls the file aside and opens it so only he can see the contents. He closes the file and sets it back down. He looks up at Tony who has his arms folded and clearly is not in a mood for the Detective's games.

"Well? Questions?" Tony asks.

"Yeah," Martin says, "How do you know Cindy Buckley?"

Tony rolls his eyes and looks at his client, "You don't have to answer that."

"No, she does," Martin says.

"Why? What's in the folder?"

Martin pulls out a photo of Kristen and Cindy talking on a street corner and slides it across the table. "So?" Tony says dismissing the photo.

"So?" Martin scoffs "So.... Cindy was murdered and we need to follow all leads."

The two men begin to banter when Kristen blurts, "She was helping me with a case. We met a few times. It was confidential."

Tony sighs and under his breath says, "Fine, do what you want. Why am I even here?"

Martin looks over to Kristen, "Thank you for answering the question. What was the extent of your meetings?"

"What does that mean?" Kristen says.

"I just want to know what the extent of your meetings were," Martin says,

"They were purely professional," confirmed Kristen.

"Oh, purely professional? No outside contact other than for this confidential case of yours?"

"Nope," Kristen says, annoyed.

Martin reaches into the folder and pulls out a heat map image of her and Cindy in the bedroom of the hotel in a very compromising position and slid that across the table. "I guess this is considered part of your professionalism?"

Tony grabs the photo and yells, "There is no way you can tell that my client is even in this photo. This is evidence of nothing!" The photo flops in his hand as he shakes it with rage.

Martin looks at him and says, "Mr. Russo, That's not a photo. It's actually a screen capture of a video with audio. If you have a moment, I can bring the AV cart in here an…"

Tony interrupts him. "No, we don't have time, we are leaving." Tony begins to stand up when Martin raises his voice a decibel.

"Mr. Russo, I don't think you understand what's happening. Your client is not leaving this station."

Kristen lowers her head because she knows what he is going to say next.

"She is going to be detained for the next 48 hours for further questioning."

Tony puts his hand up to silence Martin, "Give me a moment with Kristen."

Martin nods and walks out of the room and back behind the glass. He watches their conversation in silence and he can tell by the body language Kristen is not happy at all.

Chapter Twenty two

Clifford swings his feet from the bed and as they meet the floor, his phone rings.

Clifford glances at the caller ID and sees it's Simon. "Hey buddy, what's up?" He asks, answering the phone.

"Breakfast? Yeah, breakfast sounds wonderful. I'll be right down. But I -uh - can't stay long. I gotta meet someone in a little bit," Clifford continues.

Clifford walks into the little diner on the corner where he would meet Simon and Jaime on occasion. He looks over and spots them in the corner and walks over.

"Hey, look who the cat dragged in," Simon says jokingly.

"I feel like I was dragged in," Clifford says as he plops down next to Jaime.

"You look like you were dragged in," Jaime quips. "What have you gotten yourself into?"

"Work," Clifford says, being short.

"No Shit?" Jaime says. "Doing what?"

"You okay, man?" Simon asks.

"Yeah, It's just that the last few days have been putting me through the wringer."

"It looks like it," Simon says.

With a concerned look on her face, Jaime asks. "Are you sure you're okay? If you need to get away, we can look after your place. My aunt has a house up in Jersey that..."

"No, I'm good," Clifford interrupts, "I've just been puttin' in a lot of hours and the case I'm on is pretty stressful. It'll all blow over soon."

"Okay, but the offer still stands. Just let us know how we can help," Jaime offered again.

Clifford smiles. "Thanks. Let's order some brekkis."

Simon chuckles. "We ordered already. Just waitin' on you."

"Thanks," Clifford says.

Simon takes a sip of his coffee, "Hey, you said you were meeting someone. Someone, I know?" Clifford stammers, "Ah, no. I don't think so. It's a guy I met."

"A guy? I thought you had a date. So is it a business thing? Are you allowed to talk about it?" Simon asks.

"Yeah, it's just that I'm a bit concerned about him. He was jumped the other day and I just want to check up on him."

Simon sets his coffee down. "Jumped? That's terrible. Well. I hope he's okay, too."

With a concerned look on her face, Jaime says, "Please send him our best wishes."

"I will, thanks," Clifford says, "But funny that you mentioned a date because I am taking someone to dinner," he continues.

Jamie's eyes widen, "Let's talk more about that!" She says with a smile.

In a dank office, Marlon is going over bills and crunching numbers. Even though The Tye Brothers are out of the picture, he is still treading water. It seems that whatever he does, he still breaks even. He shuts his laptop and lets out a sigh of disgust knowing that he is slowly going broke. He just needs one or two good weekends to get back on top.

He gets his phone from his desk drawer and shoves it into his pocket.

He grabs his coat and walks out into the club. The girls left several hours ago and all of his staff was gone, too. It was just him and his thoughts.

He leans against the railing looking down at the floor below.

Marlon tosses his jacket on, grabs his bag, and heads down the stairs. He makes his way to the back of the club and out to his car.

He fiddles with the radio trying to find a song he likes. He stops on the song, "Sex and Candy," scoffs and says to himself. "You smell sex and candy? Try owning a strip club."

Marlon pulls into a diner to get some hot food in his belly before heading home.

He sits in a booth and a waitress pours him a hot cup of coffee. She hands him a menu and walks away.

His phone vibrates in his pocket just before his ringtone goes off, startling him.

He reaches for his phone and sees that it's Clifford. "Yo Dee, what's up?"

"Hey, I need your help."

Chapter Twenty three

The distinct smell of a hospital is unmistakable. Bailey wakes to the sounds of the monitors and machines and no recollection of why he was hooked up to them.

He presses the call button he finds next to his bed.

Moments later a nurse walks into the room. "Look who's awake!" She says, cheerily.

"Why was I asleep?" Bailey asks.

"Sir, you went into Hypovolemic Shock and passed out."

"Hyper-what?"

"It's when you aren't getting enough blood to your organs. Your injuries were a little worse than you thought."

"How long was I out?"

The Nurse looks at her watch, "Little more than a day. I'd say about twenty-seven to twenty-eight hours."

"Twenty-eight hours," Bailey says under his breath. "Am I okay?" He continues.

"Oh yeah, you'll be fine. Your blood pressure dropped and you blacked out. We stitched you up, gave you an IV with glucose and some pain reliever. Now all you need is some good old-fashioned rest."

The nurse turns and walks out. Bailey puts his head back on the inclined hospital bed and gently closes his eyes.

What seemed like a moment was a little over an hour. Bailey opens his eyes to find Clifford sitting next to his bed. "Dee, What's up, brotha?"

"Hey buddy, how're you feeling? The Doc filled me in. Says you had a dizzy spell from the blood loss."

"Yeah, I guess I went into shock. They told me that I just needed to rest up. What time is it?"

Clifford looked at his watch "Ten A.M. Sunday."

Bailey jolted up "SUNDAY?!? Aw, shit man, I'm supposed to be at Bandoni's by noon. He wants updates on you, man. I can't fuck this up."

"It's going to be okay. Don't worry," Clifford assures.

"These are bad dudes, man. He shot a guy right in front of me for giving him bad news. They have zero chill," Bailey says, getting worked up.

Clifford pats his arm. "I have a place for you to rest up. We're going to get you out of here soon. I just have to sign some papers and you are free from this place."

Bailey looks concerned. "But.."

"Trust me. I got you," Clifford says, leaving.

A very irritated E.I. Bandoni waits in his garden for a crippled informant who is never going to show. His patience is already thinner than silk. He motions for his assistant and whispers in his ear. The assistant walks into the house and down the hall.

He makes his way past several offices and down the stairs toward the main foyer of the home. He continues on through the foyer and down another hall to a rear door. The assistant opens the door and walks in. "You're being reactivated," He says.

"It's about time," Liam Stacey says, sitting up in his chair.

"Boss has decided to clean house. He wants you to run the contingency plan - Rifare"

"Rifare, oh? Things must be bad. That's good for me!" His grin peered through the darkness. "I finally get to kill Clifford Dee!"

Chapter Twenty four

A little over six years ago, fresh out of his criminal justice training, Clifford thought that being a PI was going to be easy. He didn't realize that some of the jobs included acting and pretending to be someone you're not. Other times it's doing something stupid and desperate. Clifford knocks on the door holding two pizzas up to the peephole to hide his face.

A guy looks out, but can only see the boxes. "It's pizza!" He says to the other man in the room.

"Did you order anything?" He asks. "Nah," The other says back.

Through the door, the guy says, "We didn't order pizza."

Clifford says, "It's paid for. If you won't open the door, I'll just leave it."

"Fine, leave it!" The guy says.

Clifford set the boxes down and walked away from the door.

about a minute went by and the man slid the chain lock from the door and unlocked it.

The door started to swing open as Clifford, full sprint ran up and threw his shoulder into the door. The door smashed the guy in his face and sent him flying backward into his partner.

Clifford paused for a moment looking around. He spotted a journal on a desk and he ran over to grab it. The men, dazed, stumbled to get back to their feet as Clifford dashed out the door.

"Get him!" Exclaimed the brains of the duo, as Clifford ran away.

The thug got to his feet and darted out toward him. He shields his eyes from the bright sunny day as he aimlessly leaves the room. A shot rang out of nowhere hitting the brawn right in his temple, killing him instantly. His handler runs out of the room, "Did you kill him?" He asks, as he too, was shielding his eyes from the sun. He sees a body on the ground and slowly walks to it. He gasps when he realizes it's his partner. Upon his realization, a second shot rang out.

Clifford stood with his hands in the air as a man shot and killed the thugs who were chasing him.

"Clifford Dee?" The man asks. "Yeah?" Clifford says, squinting in the sunlight.

"My name is Liam Stacey," He says, "I have something for you. A gift."

Coming to the realization that he cannot flee, and that he wanted to give him something, Clifford puts his hands down.

"A gift?" Clifford asks.

Liam steps out from behind a car. He was in all black, with a black fedora. He had a white pearl six-shooter on his hip, like some sort of old western cowboy.

"Howdy Partner," Clifford says. "That's some pistol."

"There's a story behind this gun. I'll tell you later. First, here!" He says as he tossed something in Clifford's direction. It was a medallion.

"What's this?" Clifford asks.

"These guys had that in their car. I think that is what you were hired to find," Liam says.

"Oh, but did you have to shoot those guys?" Clifford asks.

"They were going to kill you, and my employer wants to hire you. He can't if you're dead."

Clifford smiles, "Who's your employer?"

"His name is Bandoni."

Chapter Twenty five

Clifford and Bailey are on the way back from the hospital when Bailey notices a smile on Clifford's face.

"What did you do when I was in the hospital?" Bailey asks.

"Me? Nothing, Why?" Clifford says with a grin.

"Dee?" Bailey continues to question "Why you smilin'? Did you get some ass?"

Clifford laughes. "What?" He asks.

"Oh my God!" Bailey exclaims in realization.

"What?" Clifford asks with a smile.

Bailey continues, "You were getting ass when I was passed out in the hospital."

"It was a good day, okay. I found my Mustang in the impound. It was lost for like six weeks and.." He pauses.

"And what? Bailey asks.

"And I went on a date with a nurse."

Bailey laughs, "And you got some ass!"

Bailey can't help to think that he always needed a friend like Clifford. The bill for his hospital stay was not cheap, but he paid it in full, cash, no less. Bailey, still smiling, turns to Clifford and says, "Hey, Dee."

"What's up, buddy?"

"Thanks man," Bailey says.

"Yeah, no problem."

Bailey starts to get serious for a moment. "Nah, I mean it. No one's ever done anything like that for me before. I appreciate it."

Clifford smiles and looks over. "Dude, I got you. I told you that I had your back. I meant it."

Bailey joking says, "That hitman money must be good to be able to pay off bills like that."

Clifford looks over and says. "The health benefits suck, but yeah, the pay is good."

A serious look fell onto his face as he turned to Bailey. "Hey, you know the only client I do hit jobs for does not like us very much, right?"

"Well yeah," Bailey returns.

Clifford says, "I wanna get square with Bandoni, then get out. I'm out and going straight, No hits."

"Uh Dee," Bailey says.

Clifford looks over, "Yeah, I know that it's going to be difficult," Clifford returns.

"No, Dee!" Bailey says sternly.

"What?" Clifford says.

"Look!" Bailey exclaims, pointing toward the rear.

A dark black car speeding up behind him suddenly rams the Jeep.

Clifford slams on the accelerator to create some space. He hands Bailey a sidearm he pulls from a concealed compartment in the dash. "Use it!" Clifford yells.

Bailey points over his left shoulder and squeezes off three rounds, one hitting the windshield.

"This is difficult for me, Dee!" Bailey says. "I can't turn completely around."

Clifford motions to Bailey to take the wheel. "Okay, switch."

Clifford takes the gun and Bailey takes the wheel.

Just then the car rams the Jeep again and accelerates, causing the gun to jolt from Clifford's hands and into the back. Clifford hits the cruise control. "Keep it steady, Bailey!"

"Okay!" he shouts back.

Clifford dives in the back as he sees the driver pull out a shotgun. A shot rang out from the back and Clifford could hear the pellets bouncing off the metal Jeep frame. Another shot rings out. He starts to look for the gun in the back as the driver of the other car pulls alongside. Clifford peeks over the side of the Jeep as the car slowly pulls aside them and watches as a shotgun emerges from the passenger side window. Clifford ducks down and braces himself as the driver unloads a shotgun round into the Jeep's back driver's side rim. Clifford looks over the edge of the Jeep, to his surprise, finds the tire completely unscathed.

"Assault Rims!" He exclaims as he remembers Scotty from the shop, mentioning how durable they were.

The dark car backs off and then rams the Jeep again, this time causing the gun to slide right in front of Clifford.

He grabs the gun, jumps up from his cover, and pops several rounds into the dark car. The driver jolts the car away and spins out of control. The car, spinning sideways, hits the curb and then slides into a telephone pole.

Clifford watches as the driver, wearing all black steps out of the car and looks at them as he is unscathed.

"Dee!" Bailey says. "Runnin' out of road here!"

Clifford jumps back into the front and takes control of the car and drives off, leaving the devastation behind him.

"What the fuck, Dee? Who was that?" Bailey asks in a panic.

"That was Stacey," Clifford says. "Liam Stacey. He used to be a hitman, but now he's a cleaner. He hates me, always wanted my jobs, but he was too sloppy and reckless for Bandoni's liking so he only uses him to clean. If he's after us, Bandoni doesn't care anymore." They continue away from the crash at a quick pace as they can hear sirens in the distance.

"We need to get some stuff from my place and lay low," Clifford says.

"No doubt, man. but I ain't likin' this Stacey guy. He's got bad intentions," Bailey quips back.

"You don't know the half of it," Clifford says.

———

Two years ago, Clifford Dee sits with a camera waiting for a target to come out of a building when his phone starts to ring. "Hey Mr. Bandoni, I'm on that job you gave me. I should have the photos shortly."

Bandoni says, "Forget that, I need you in my office now. My home office."

Clifford swallows hard because he has never been invited to his home before. "I don't know wh-"

Bandoni cuts him off, "Shut up and listen. Be here in an hour. Here is my address."

Clifford drives straight there. He approaches the gates of the Bandoni estate with shot nerves and sweaty palms.

A guard approaches his car.

"What?" He asked.

"Mr. Bandoni asked me to come by," Clifford says with confidence, even though he's scared as hell.

"Name?" The guard asks.

Clifford let out a little nervous smirk. "Clifford Dee."

The guard backs away from the car and calls into his radio. "Mr. Clifford Dee for Boss."

A few seconds go by and Clifford could barely hear the squawk over the radio.

The guard walks back to the booth and opens the gate. He waves Clifford through and goes back inside. Clifford glances in the rearview mirror and watches the gate slowly close behind him as he continues up the groomed car path to the house.

Upon reaching the house, Clifford sees two guys out front waiting for him. He parks and gets out of the car and walks up to them.

"He's waiting, let's go," one of them says.

They escort him to an office and open the door. Clifford walks in alone and the men shut the doors behind him. He can see Liam standing in front of the desk.

Bandoni swivels around in his chair. "Ah, Mr. Dee. Please have a seat!" He says pointing to the chair next to Liam.

Clifford looks over to Liam and turns back toward Bandoni "Why is he standing?" Clifford asks.

"Only gentlemen sit," Bandoni says with a scowl emerging on his face.

Clifford reaches for the chair, pulls it out, and sits. He looks up at Liam and notices that he has a bloodied lip and he's quivering a bit.

Bandoni adjusts his glasses and looks over to Clifford. "I am promoting you. You are no longer my ears and eyes, you are now my hands."

Not understanding Clifford says, "What do you mean by that?"

Liam sighs and says, "You're his hitman you twit."

"SHUT UP!" Bandoni exclaims. "You only talk when you are spoken to!" He continues.

"Yes sir," Liam says.

Bandoni turns his focus back to Clifford. "You will be doing all my top jobs now. I need someone that has patience, such as yourself. I can no longer afford to deal with reckless abandon and clean up messes all the time," He says as he looks back over toward Liam.

"Mr. Stacey" Bandoni continued. "You will be working my cleanup detail since it is your fault I lost that employee. Mr. Dee is careful, I am sure you will have very little to do. Am I right, Mr. Dee?" He asked again, returning his focus back to Clifford.

"Yes sir, I am always careful," Clifford says back.

"Good. I will call you with the details of your next job. You can go. As for you," Bandoni says pointing at Liam, "You are lucky I found a use for you, otherwise someone else would be cleaning YOU up."

Liam nods, "Understand, Sir," he says looking over with disdain as Clifford carefully stands and starts to walk out of the office.

Clifford pulls into the garage near his house. He jumps out of the Jeep and grabs Bailey's chair from the back. As he pulls it out he notices that it is sprayed with buckshot, leaving holes through the back of it, rendering it unusable.

"Damn, dude. Sorry," Clifford says.

Bailey looks at his chair, "Shit man! What the fuck! I'm going to kick that motherfucker's ass. This shit is ruined."

Clifford says, " I still got that hospital chair inside, but I can get you a better one man, don't worry."

"Yeah, okay. Shit's your fault anyway," Bailey says with a chuckle. "Get what you need, I'm going to wait here."

"Okay, It'll only be a minute."

Bailey looks behind him as Clifford runs off. "Hurry up, motherfucker!" He shouts over his shoulder.

Clifford quickly rifles through his paperwork to grab anything incriminating against himself or Bandoni. He wants to make sure that the cops will have absolutely nothing on him and more than enough to go after the mob. He wants to make good on the promise to Martin that he would get him enough to incriminate them.

Clifford's cell phone rings.

It's Bandoni.

Clifford answers angrily and says, "You put Stacey on me, you asshole?"

"I needed your full attention."

Clifford scoffs, "Well you got it and my Jeep is riddled with holes now. You need to get him some target practice."

Bandoni, audibly eating and smacking his food with his lips, begins to speak. "I need your work notes Mr. Dee. If I do not get your notes, it will be a very bad thing for you and your friends."

Clifford sighs loudly. "Do you have to eat while on the phone?"

"Mhm, Mr. Dee," Bandoni repeats as he shuffles food around his mouth to speak. "I need those notes. I still consider you a usable asset. But your negro friend outside your apartment, I do not. He is no longer of use to me. Disposable."

Clifford walks to a window and peers out.

"I am always watching you, Mr. Dee. You have two hours to get me those notes or you and the rest of your friends are dead."

Clifford stammers, "The rest?" he questions.

"When was the last time you talked to your friends Jaime and Simon?"

Clifford looks at his phone in disbelief as it goes dead.

He shoves it into his pocket and races down to the apartment below.

A knife dripping with blood is stuck in the door of Simon's apartment. Clifford pushes open the door to find Jaime on the floor in a puddle of her own blood with her throat slit.

"Oh God, NO!" Clifford says as he drops down to check on her.

It was too late.

Gasping for breath Simon calls out, "Dee," in a whimpering weak voice.

"Simon!" Clifford says as he quickly makes his way across the room to him.

"He made me watch," he says in a whisper.

Clifford holds his head up and realizes that he is mortally stabbed in the neck. He places his hand on top of the wound to stop the bleeding, but it's too late.

"Don't talk. I'm here, buddy." Clifford says as he was dialing 9-1-1 on his cell.

Simon's face is pale and faded. His eyes begin to gloss over as he hears Clifford calling for an ambulance. "I'm sorry, Dee," he mutters as his consciousness subsides.

Dee walks out of the apartment covered in his friend's blood. He notices thick black smoke pouring from the garage and he begins calling out for Bailey.

There's no response.

He hurries over to the garage and notices his Mustang fully engulfed in flames. He covers his face but still gags and coughs as he makes his way over to the Jeep.

But, It's empty.

Chapter Twenty six

Clifford, covered in dried blood, is sitting in a cell at the station. Martin bolts into the room, "Jesus Dee, I'm going to get you outta here. I know this wasn't you."

"They said I was fleeing the scene. Actually, I was returning to it."

"What?" Martin asks.

"I was with my friend Bailey, he was in my Jeep when it happened. After I found them, I went to Bailey to see if he was okay, but my Mustang was burning and Bailey was gone." Clifford was still in a bit of a daze.

"Who did this, Dee?"

"It was one of Bandoni's guys. Stacey," Clifford says putting his hands to his face. "Stacey just doesn't want me dead, he wants me to suffer. That's why he torched my Baby!"

"Your Baby?" Martin asks.

Looking off into space Clifford says, "My Mustang is my baby. He wants to torture me. He killed two of my friends and took another. He torched the car because he knew I loved it. It was a message."

Martin shakes his head in pity.

"Jesus, Dee. What kind of mess are you in with Bandoni? This is some serious shit," Martin started in a panic.

"You know that guy walks among powerful people," Martin's voice begins to lower to a whisper. "I think that he owns half of the department, if not more."

Clifford nods in agreement, "The DA's working for him, for sure. I'm surprised he doesn't own you."

Martin scowls at Clifford, "He could never. My price tag is way too high," He shoots Clifford a smile to show him he isn't mad. "Dee, if you want my help, I need to know everything."

Clifford runs his clammy hands over his face and looks up at Martin, "Put a pot on, It's a story."

The car breaks hard, jolting Bailey awake from inside the trunk. He shakes the pain from his throbbing head as he hears Stacey get out of the car. The voices are muffled, but he can make out most of the conversation.

"You need to take out Neil."

"How am I supposed to do that?"

"Make it look like a suicide. Like she hung herself."

"Okay. I can cut the feed to the holding cells and do it right before shift change. There is about a fifteen-minute window where no one will be watching."

"Get it done. I have some bait I need to set a trap with," Stacey says as he pats the trunk of his car.

"Anything I can assist with?"

With a hint of determination in his voice, Stacey says "Nope, this one's all mine."

Bailey was awake for what seemed to be a long ride to the destination. He could hear the classic rock bellowing from the radio and Stacey's attempts to sing along with it. The car comes to a sudden stop on what sounds like a gravel or dirt road. Bailey closes his eyes and acts like he's still asleep.

Stacey steps out and pops the trunk again and says, "I know you're awake."

Bailey opens his eyes, looks at him, and says "And I know you're a terrible singer."

Stacey scoffs at Bailey, hitting him again and knocking him out.

Clifford and Martin are walking back from booking in conversation when they hear a lot of commotion coming from the offices.

"Stay here," Martin says to Clifford as he runs to find out what was going on. Clifford can only make out a few words but 'Kristen Neil' were two of them.

Martin comes back out to Clifford. "Dee, you gotta go. The DA just hung herself downstairs." "Yeah right!" Dee fires back. "You know she didn't!"

Martin points toward the door. "Just go!" The Captain grabs Martin, "You are on this one. Find out what happened."

"Yes sir," Martin says.

Martin walks into the surveillance room to pull tapes of the holding cells. He notices a guard with a huge scratch on his face that looks very fresh. "Nice scratch," Martin says.

"Cut myself shaving," the guard says.

Martin gave him a bit of side-eye as he left the room. He begins looking for the digital files on the computer for the videos of Neil's cell. When he finds the footage, he clicks play. The video cut from Kristen Neil sitting alone to Kristen Neil hanging from the bars of her cell. Martin rewound the video and watched the timestamp jump 9 minutes as if someone erased part of the file.

Clifford, waiting for the uber he just called, gets a call. It's Stacey.

"Lose someone, Dee?"

"Where is he?"

"Remember where we first met? You can find him there."

The phone goes dead.

A car pulls up and the driver leans out the window, "Clifford Dee?"

"Yeah," Clifford affirmed. "I'm your Uber… Wait, is that blood?" The driver asks.

"No, it's… Uh," Clifford stammers, looking at his stained clothing. "Yeah, it's blood. I witnessed a murder."

"Uh, bye!" the driver says, and immediately drives off, leaving Clifford in a cloud.

"It's dry!" Clifford shouts to the car fading in the distance.

Clifford begins walking home, knowing that he would probably not find another Uber to pick him up. A few hours later, Clifford finally gets to his condo. Upon reaching his door, Sara jolts into the hall. "Dee, Oh my God. I thought they got you, too."

Sara and Tracy both wrapped around him like a blanket.

Sara slowly looks down in shock, "Oh my god, is that from Jamie and Simon?"

Clifford pulls away from them and says, "The guy that did this has a friend of mine. I need to find him."

Tracy runs into the apartment and returns shortly. "Dee, this guy came up and stuck this in your door about two hours ago." She hands him a business card. The address on the card was a lot in an industrial park across from the motel where he first met Liam. "9pm" is scribbled on the back in Blue ink.

Clifford looks up at the girls, "I need your help."

Martin pulls the sheet back from Kristen Neil's body. The medical examiner, Mina, looks over the body. She looks up at Martin as he walks in, "What are you looking for? Suspect something?"

Martin looks over, "I suspect everything, Mina, but what makes you think I suspect something?" She smiles at Martin and says, "I'm glad you said that. Look here. This bruise on her neck wraps around to the back. See?"

"Yeah, so?" Martin says as he looks on.

"The noose was made from bed sheeting. First of all, It's difficult to die from a broken neck from a bedsheet. The bruising, the way it wraps around, was from forced trauma, not a hanging," Martin nods in agreement as she continues.

"If you look further, you can see bruising on her elbows, as if she fell to the ground. A couple of broken fingernails. There are also bruises on the fingertips, and what I find most interesting...." She pauses as she points to her wrist.

"Bruising on her wrist?" Martin asks.

"Yep. Fractured, like she braced a fall," Mina confirmed.

"That is interesting," Martin says.

"Either she was extremely clumsy and fell a couple of times, and then broke her own neck, or the hanging was a coverup."

"I could kiss you, Mina!" Martin exclaims.

"I know, but that would be unprofessional," She retorted with a smile.

Martin pulls a ringing phone from his jacket pocket.

"Hold that thought", He says as he answers the phone. "Dee, what's up? You okay?"

"I need your help. Please, it's important."

Martin covers the phone. "Mina, Can you sit on this information, just for a day?" She cocks her head to one side. Martin mouths please again with prayer hands.

"You have until tomorrow when my report is due, that's all I can do. You owe me a drink," She says with a smile.

"Thank you. I'll buy you two. Oh, and when you test her nails, see if anyone's DNA from the department matches what you find." Martin says as he walks out of the room.

"Dee, What do you need me to do?"

Chapter Twenty seven

Stacey splashes Bailey with a bucket of water. He's sitting in a chair, his arms bound with leather straps connected to a chain from the ceiling. Bailey starts to talk through his gag. Stacey walks over and pulls the gag from his mouth. "What?"

"Come on man, What's with the chains? You know I can't just get up and run on outta here," Bailey says, in a joking manner.

Stacey shoves the gag back in Bailey's mouth. "Listen, I don't need your smart-ass comments. Clifford is a dead man. The DA should already be dead by now and you're my ticket out of this fucking mess."

Stacey pauses for just a moment. "Bandoni's a fucking idiot! That bastard fucking told me to kill you!" he shouts as he begins pacing the room. "He didn't realize you're connected, but I figured it out. I know who you really are!" His rants were almost therapeutic for him as he had a lot of pent-up animosity toward Bandoni and Clifford.

"Dee's a piece of shit. He and Bandoni fucking deserve each other. I'm gonna kill him and send his puny head to Bandoni. Then you and I are going to take a little trip up north to see some friends. They've been looking for you."

Stacey continues in his rant. "They thought you were dead until I said your name. Ooh, they perked up and they are really fucking interested."

171

Bailey seems like he is trying to chew through his gag, but Liam continues.

"You cost those people lots of money up there, didn't you. That's why you ran like a little piece of shit and hid down here. What else did you cost them? Respect? Cred? When I deliver you, I'll be the one everyone wants! I'll take over this town and kick Bandoni out on his fat Italian ass!"

Liam starts shaking in his own raging fantasy. He pulls out a small coke vile from his pants pocket, opens it, and snorts some through his left nostril.

"This is fucking what Bandoni gets! Really, it is! You know why? Wanna know why?"

Bailey shakes his head as he listens intently.

"Because he trusted that little brown-nosed shit face Dee! That's why! He was a SNAKE! He never had the best interest of the family in mind!"

Stacey starts shaking his head.

"Why did he fucking give The Tye job to him? That was the last straw. THAT was MY JOB!"

Stacey was so enraged that spit rocketed from his mouth as he spoke.

"Bandoni KNEW that The Tye Brothers were supposed to be my target. It was MY Blood they spilled, NOT DEE'S! What do I get for my effort? My loyalty to the family?"

He asks Bailey with no expectation of an answer.

"A FUCKING Back SEAT! That's what I get!"

Stacey begins to calm down a bit and grabs Bailey by the face with both hands.

"This is my chance to get what I have worked for. This is my chance to get everything I deserve."

Stacey begins to wrap a small rope around his fist. Bailey's eyes widen because he knows what's coming next.

Day turns to night and Bailey, bloodied and bruised from a fresh beating, remains tied up while Stacey, now calm, waits. He hears a commotion growing louder outside, looks over at a barely conscious Bailey, and decides to go investigate. He steps outside of the warehouse and rounds the corner, slowly, so he isn't seen. As he makes his way around, seeing several cars across the lot and a few young adults having a good time drinking beer and playing music around a trashcan fire.

Stacey looks on for a moment before deciding to walk over. "Hey, what's going on here?" He asks as he approaches the group.

Tracy turns around and says, "Oh, hey man, we're just listening to music." She reaches into an ice bucket and pulls out a beer and hands it to Liam. "Beer?" She asks.

"No, get the fuck out of here. It's private property," He says.

Tracy, trying to be diplomatic says, "Chill with us we got some good music."

Liam is completely out of chill. He walks over to the radio, picks it up, and tosses it into the trashcan fire. A guy jumps up and says, "Hey, that was my radio!" and tries to push Liam.

He grabs the boy's hand, twists him around, and kicks the back of his knee, forcing him to the ground. He pulls his gun out and puts it to the back of the kid's head. "You have two minutes to leave," Liam says.

A few people jump up out of their seats and start running.

Tracy looks over at Liam and says, "Woah! There is no need for that! We'll go! We'll go!"

Liam holsters his gun and pulls the young man up. "Pack your shit. Two minutes," He says as he stares at the remaining group.

A few guys start packing up and heading to their cars. Tracy glares in anger at Liam watching as they pack up.

Liam looks over at Tracy and says, "I'll be more than happy to remove that look from your face, Sweetheart!"

She purses her lips in attitude and looks away with disgust.

After a minute, they finish gathering gear and walk back to their cars.

Stacey walks back to the warehouse.

As he reaches the door to the warehouse, he sees Clifford standing there, pistol in hand.

"Care to step inside?" Clifford says with a smile. "Dee, how nice to see you," Stacey says, "You did this? Slick!"

"I may have called a few friends who called a few friends who called a few friends and rumored about a party here tonight. I needed something to distract you."

Stacey half-smiled. "Well done, but you almost got those kids killed."

Clifford uses his pistol to motion toward the door. Stacey walks in and slowly raises his hands.

"Okay, turn around there, Stace," Clifford says. Stacey turns around with his hands still in the air, and Clifford begins to lightly frisk him. He pulls his pearl-handled gun from his holster and says, "I see you still have this piece of shit," then tosses it on the ground and continues to pat him down. Stacey looks at Clifford with an irritated look on his face and says, "Dee, you know I am going to kill you, right?"

"You can try," Clifford says with a smirk, "Now go untie him," and motions over to his now unconscious friend. As Stacey starts to untie Bailey, he jolts awake.

"Wha-" Bailey stammers and begins to look around. Clifford came into focus. "Dee, oh thank God."

Clifford looks at Bailey and says, "Nope, it's just me."

Stacey couldn't help but grimace, "You always did have a God complex, Dee."

Clifford shakes his head, "Nah, you just thought highly of me."

Stacey finishes untying Bailey and turns to Dee. "So, how do you plan on carrying Mr. Bailey out of here while keeping your gun on me?"

Clifford pulls a walkie-talkie from his pocket. "Okay, ready!" He speaks into it. Clifford smiles "Didn't I say I called a friend who called a friend?"

Outside a car pulls up and the tires slide across the gravel. Moments later Sara walks into the warehouse pushing a wheelchair. She helps Bailey into the chair and pushes him away. Bailey uses the last bit of energy he has to raise his middle finger in the air as he is being wheeled out of the door.

"Bandoni is going to kill you and all of your friends. You know this right?"

Clifford childishly shrugs it off.

Stacey smiles at the immature gesture, "You and I are businessmen, and we can't just walk away from the business. I tried. He won't let you, and I won't let you."

Clifford starts to back away and says, "We'll see about that."

As Clifford turns to walk away, Stacey yells "This is NOT over. You know this!"

Clifford drives around the corner and continues down the street with Sara and Bailey in the car. He pulls into a small parking garage where he previously asked Martin to meet him.

Clifford and Sara hop out of the car.

"Okay, take her home and I will call you later. We have to lay low for now and Bailey needs rest. He's hurt."

Martin looks over at Bailey resting in the passenger seat of the Jeep. "What the fuck is going on?" He asks.

"It was Liam Stacey," Clifford says.

Martin, furious, says "God Dammit Dee! Why didn't you just have me go in there and arrest that piece of shit?"

Clifford shook his head, "I didn't want to chance it. If he even smelled a cop, he would've started shooting. People could've been hurt, but I can have him come to you."

"How?"

"One second," Clifford says as he disappears to the back of the Jeep.

Sara chimes in, "I can help. Can I come with you Dee?"

Clifford shakes his head, "No, I really don't want you involved. You've already done too much. This is dangerous shit." He rustles around in the storage compartment and pulls out a black wand-looking thing.

"Is that?" Martin begins to ask.

"Yep," says Clifford, "a tracker finder. He would never leave my Jeep alone without leaving something to track me with." He waves it around and over his car. It starts to beep faster and faster until he comes to the rear wheel well.

"Ah, here ya go," Clifford says as he hands the tracker over to Martin.

"Now, get her home and find a place to wait. Stacey will come to you."

Martin shakes his head. "I don't like this plan at all. If you want me to lead Stacey away from you, I am not taking Sara with me."

Clifford nods. "Good point. Sara, You're coming with me and Bailey," he says as Sara jumps in excitement and lets out a slight squeal.

"Thank you! Thank you! Thank you! I promise I will keep a low profile," She says.

"Let's get going," Clifford says as he looks over at an unconscious Bailey. Martin jumps in his car and motions to Clifford. He walks over to his window as Martin rolls it down. "You would have made a lousy cop, you know that right?" Martin says.

"What?" Clifford cocks his head to one side, squinting in confusion.

Martin continued, "You want to do the right thing way too much. Most cops only go far enough to do the legal thing. Just know, when the shit hits the fan. I'll have to side with the law." With Clifford speechless, Martin speeds off without letting him get a word in.

Sara walks over to Clifford as Martin's speeding car gets smaller in the distance. "What did he mean by that?"

Clifford shook his head, "That is just his way of telling me not to go too far off the reservation."

Sara says, "Maybe that was his way of telling you not to trust him one hundred percent."

"Maybe," Clifford replies.

Clifford turns around to find Bailey passed out in the back of the Jeep and the chair already in the back.

He looks over to Sara in disbelief that she muscled him in there.

"What?" She asks. "I'm much stronger than you think."

Clifford gives her a smile. "You are," he says back to her as he puts his arm around her.

Marlon looks at his ringing phone as the name "Dee-hole" is displayed. He picks it up and places it to his ear. "Dee, what's going on? You call me and say you need help and then I don't hear from you for four days?"

Clifford replies, "I had to drop some heat first. Things are getting out of hand."

Marlon scoffs. "Why should I help you?"

"Dude!" Clifford says in a mildly irritated tone.

Marlon replies. "We aren't even that close, bro."

"Are you fucking serious right now?" Clifford says angrily.

Marlon lets out a huge laugh, "Nah, I'm just fucking with you."

"Not a good time to fuck around, Marlon. I'm coming in and I need you to play host."

"Host?" Marlon asks.

Clifford replies, "Yeah, a buddy of mine is banged up and needs to rest a few days, and they'll be scouting hospitals for him."

"Jesus, Dee. I ain't a hospice," Marlon says.

"I know, I know, but he's got nowhere else to lay low," Clifford says.

Marlon says, "He can't rest in a club, man," then is silent for a few seconds. "Actually, I have an idea."

Clifford's Jeep pulls up in front of the Dollhouse where Marlon and one of his girls are sitting out front. Clifford and Sara step out. Clifford looks at Marlon and points to the obvious off-duty stripper.

"Who's this?"

Marlon pats her on the back. "Sugar."

Sara's eyes widen, "Hey, Sugar!" She says as she looks her up and down.

Clifford does a double-take toward Sara. "For fuck's sake."

Sara breaks her trance and looks at Clifford. "What?" she asks. "I'm hot-blooded."

Sugar extends her hand to Clifford, "It's Maggie, actually."

Marlon chimes in, "Maggie? Yeah, I like calling you Sugar better."

"Yeah, I know," Maggie says, "Because you're an asshole."

Marlon laughs, "Yeah, I am."

Clifford shakes her hand, "Okay, obvious question, why's Maggie here?"

Marlon steps forward. "Sugar," he says condescendingly, "Is studying as a medical professional and is using my club to help pay for her student loans. I told her that if she helps your friend, you would float her some bills."

"How many bills?" Clifford asks.

Maggie holds up five fingers and says, "Five to watch him during the day. I'll work a half shift at night and stay with him for a few hours before going into work."

"Okay, he might need a few days to rest up," Clifford says.

Maggie nods, "Pay two days now and you can pay me the rest later."

Clifford retreats to his Jeep and pulls an envelope from a secret compartment under the dash. He walks back and pulls some bills out of it and counts out ten one hundred dollar bills.

"Here's a grand," He says as he hands the cash over to Maggie.

Marlon chimes in. "Do I get like a moderator fee? Ya know, for organizing this."

Clifford looks at Marlon and cocks his head in disbelief.

Marlon smiled "No? Cheapskate. Alright, let's get going."

"Going?" Clifford asks.

"Well, he's not staying in the club," Marlon says.

Maggie chimes in. "The club isn't a suitable atmosphere for someone who needs rest and healing. It's loud, busy, and it'd probably prolong his progress."

"Okay, so where?" Clifford asks.

Maggie says, "We were thinking you would put him up in a hotel or something."

Clifford says, "I know a place."

Clifford figured the same motel The Tye Brothers stayed in would be fitting. It's a bit off the grid, quiet, and wheelchair accessible. It was also cheap.

Clifford and Sara gingerly push Bailey into the room and over toward the bed. After Bailey is settled, Maggie says,

"Okay, I'll be here until midnight then I'll go into work. I should be back by six a.m."

Marlon smiles and says, "I have all your routines pushed back a few hours. You won't lose any tips, okay?"

Maggie smiles and nods. "I'll be here if you need me."

Clifford hands her a burner phone. "This is clean, I should be the only one calling this number."

Clifford and Sara follow Marlon back to his club and walk inside. "Wow!" Sara says as she walks inside. "From the looks of it on the outside, I thought this place would have been a dump, but it's pretty nice in here. I should bring Tracy here on a date."

Clifford and Marlon both slowly turn to look at her.

"What?" Sara asked. "We go on dates."

Clifford shakes his head and continues inside and sits next to Marlon at the bar.

Marlon looks over at Clifford, "We open in an hour. I know you don't want to be here when the clientele starts showing up. Sug—Maggie's a good girl. She isn't the typical stripper around here that does anything for a buck if ya know what I mean. She'll take care of your boy. She's got morals."

Clifford nods, "Thanks."

"So, what's your deal with him? If you don't mind me asking, I mean, you ponied up a pretty penny for a retired street thug," Marlon questions.

Clifford sighs. "Truthfully? It's when I was in the war, the sandbox. He reminds me of my section Sargent, Williamson. We were hit by an RPG. Ambushed. His leg was blown off and I was concussed and had no idea what was going on. All of my buddies were dead. There were body parts and blood covering the sand. My buddy, Somers was screaming at me to run away, but in my state, all I could think about was collecting all the body parts to put my buddies back together. I thought I could save them, or something."

Marlon's jaw drops. "HOLY SHIT!" He says. "Don't ever tell anyone that story again. DUDE!"

Clifford chuckled at Marlon's reaction, but then bit his lip. "This is a true story, man,"

Marlon replied. "Okay, but damn!"

"It was hell. I was captured and tortured for like a week before a team rescued me. I was about two hours away from being the next star on the Al-Qaeda reality tv show."

"Woah, that's—That's terrible," Marlon says in shock.

Clifford continues. "So yeah, I couldn't save my team. Bailey's now my team and I'm going to do what I can to save him."

Marlon nods. "I get it, man. Dude, I get it."

Clifford looks over at Sara. "Let's get going."

Sara's still looking around the club. "Yeah okay, but I'm coming back later."

Marlon laughs. "I'll buy your first lap dance."

"Really? Awesome!" Sara happily exclaims.

"Okay, let's go, or I'll tell Tracy you were flirting with every girl in here," Clifford says.

Sara laughs. "She would totally believe you, too."

Chapter Twenty eight

Martin parks his car downtown and walks over to a curbside stand. He grabs a paper and a drink and tosses two bucks on the stand. "Keep the change," he says as he walks across the street and sits on a bench. He has a straight-line view of his car on the corner.

Just when he thinks that Stacey wouldn't show, a car drives slowly past his car. Martin stands up from the bench and starts walking toward him.

Liam spots Martin and speeds away.

Martin races to his car and speeds off to follow Liam. He jumps on the radio and calls in his tag as he closes in.

A few sharp turns, then Liam jolts down a side alley and Martin overshoots it. He turns down an alleyway and continues on. He jumps on a different side street and pops out just behind Liam.

Liam sees Martin, floors the gas pedal, and bolts down the street, dodging cars and pedestrians as he swerves dangerously around them. Martin continues on the radio, giving updates as he begins losing ground on Liam.

Two, then three, black and white police cruisers join the chase and force Liam to swerve around a blind corner. His car hits a newsstand spilling newspapers into the street. Martin is now back on his tail and gaining, and continues to gain on him to the point where he can almost attempt a PIT maneuver.

Liam approaches a turn to the entrance of a freeway, cuts the wheel, and skids sideways just before Martin could attempt the PIT and connects the ramp to the freeway. The car jolts and skids, bouncing off the jersey wall. Liam speeds off and leaves Martin in his dust.

The other black and white squad cars approach just as Martin calls in that he lost him in the pursuit.

Chapter Twenty nine

C lifford is closing in on his neighborhood when he gets a call from Martin. He hits the Bluetooth icon on his dash. "What's up, Detective?"

"Your buddy, Liam, took the bait and tracked me to the inner city, but he spotted me and got away."

Clifford winced. "Damnit! How did Stacey get past you?"

Martin shook his head. "He can drive through a crowd like it's nothing. I couldn't keep up."

"Yeah," Clifford says, "He told me once that he was a get-away driver for hire in Detroit. I didn't believe him."

"Well, Dee," Martin says, "He wasn't joking, and that information could have been useful to know upfront."

"Like I said, I thought he was joking! Sorry, man."

Sternly, Martin says, "Well, now he knows the cops are onto him, and he's probably pissed. God knows what he will do to get back at you for this one."

Clifford says, "Yeah, I know. I am taking Sara home and I have to get out of town. I need to visit someone."

Martin pauses for a moment. "Can you tell me where you're going?"

"No," Clifford says. "I have to do this alone, and bringing a cop with me would be suicide. You have to trust me on this one."

"Okay, but be careful. This Bandoni case is gaining traction in the office. I've been trying to push the case, but the whole thing falls apart when I do. Honestly, I think you're the key to making this thing stick," Martin says.

"Yeah, keep pushing it," Clifford says. "I'll need the department's help on this one."

Clifford pulls up to the front of his condo to drop Sara off. Sara jumps out of the car and walks over to the driver's side door.

Clifford smiles and says "Hey, Chickie, keep your head down. I'll be back in a few days."

Sara lets out a nervous grin. "Please be careful."

"You know me," Clifford shoots back as he begins to pull away.

"That's why I'm nervous!" Sara shouts at the back of his Jeep as it drives away.

She slowly walks up the stairs and heads up toward her apartment to find her door open.

"Tracy? Are you home?"

She slowly pushes the door wider to find a pool of blood surrounding a body on the floor in the hallway.

Chapter Thirty

A few hours ago, Clifford thought that he was taking a trip out of town, but here he stands holding his sobbing friend as the coroner's techs are wheeling Tracy's body from their apartment. Martin looks over in sorrow while listening to statements from passers-by. As they finish up Martin thanks them and walks over to Clifford and Sara.

"It was Stacey. The witness was in the park and saw him walk into the building and thought they heard a scream, but wasn't sure."

As her head is still nestled in Clifford's soggy, tear-filled shirt, Sara's bloodshot blue eyes look up in anger. "I'm going to kill that son of a bitch."

Martin put his hand on her shoulder. "We'll get him. He's our number one priority right now. We will be paying Bandoni a visit as well. He and Stacey have connections, so I hope that he'll cooperate with his apprehension."

Clifford scoffs, "Don't count on it. Bandoni has several employees that can do the work Stacey does, but..."

"But what?" Martin asks, waiting for him to continue. Clifford just stares, knowing that he shouldn't finish his thought out loud.

Martin continues, "You two need to lay low for a while and let us do our jobs. You can't go all vigilante here. I won't let you."

As Martin turns and walks away Clifford pulls Sara back into his chest as she begins to sob again. Hours pass and Sara is calm but still processing. She's staring at a cold plate of eggs and soggy buttered toast.

"Honey, are you going to eat that, or stare at it?" The waitress says as she approaches the table. Clifford looks over, "Hey, let her be. She lost someone today." Sara glares at the waitress and pushes the plate away. "Take it."

"Oh, honey, I'm so sorry. I'll get you some more coffee. And pie. I will get you pie. On me." The waitress hurries away, embarrassed.

"I am going to kill that man. You know that, right, Dee?"

Clifford looks up from his coffee. "Yeah, I know that, but I need your help first. I want you to come with me."

"Where?"

"I'm going up to Chicago. You need to get away from here right now and I need help if we're going to take on Bandoni."

Sara looks confused. "We're taking on Bandoni? I thought we were laying low. What's in Chicago?" Her questions flutter out like butterflies as they form in her head.

The waitress plops down a huge piece of pie with a scoop of vanilla next to it.

"This Caramel Apple is the best you will ever taste," she says as she starts to pour some more coffee into her mug and reaches into her apron, and pulls out a fist full of little cream containers.

"Eat, please. This is good for the soul," she says.

Clifford smiles at the waitress as she walks away then turns his eyes to Sara.

"Eat. You need your strength. I'll tell you what's in Chicago."

The pie was probably the best piece that Sara had ever eaten. With every bite, a little bit of her smile returns to her face. After a few minutes, Sara is scraping the ice cream and pie filling goop up with her fork and licking it off.

"Let's get going," Clifford says with a slight smile. As the two head out of the diner, Clifford walks up to the waitress. "Thank you."

He says as he palms her a $50 bill and walks away.

She looks down at the money and smiles.

Clifford opens the passenger door of the Jeep for Sara and says, "We can get about an hour or two north, but we should stay somewhere and finish the trip in the morning. It's getting late."

Sara nodded, "Sounds good. Let's get the hell outta here."

Chapter Thirty one

Martin pulls up to the gates of the Bandoni plantation. A guard leans out of the tower and Martin flashes his badge.

"Yeah, so?" The guard says.

"Your boss here? I need to talk to him," Martin says.

The guard peers at Martin for a moment before saying "Hold on." He can barely make out what the guard was saying in his shack, but he did make out the word "Fuzz." Martin could only wonder who refers to the cops as, "Fuzz," anymore. He hadn't heard the term in a long time.

The gate guard pops out of the shack again and points toward the house.

"Go up the driveway and keep left, and park near the front entrance. Someone will escort you to Mr. B."

With that, Martin gives a confirming nod and the guard presses the button to open the gates. Following his direction, he pulls up to find another one of the hired goons waiting by the top of the steps. He parks and proceeds to exit the car and walk up the stairs.

"Beautiful day, isn't it?" Martin says.

"I suppose. This way," The guard responds as he motions behind him and starts back into the house.

The guard escorts Martin to the back of the home and out onto a patio that overlooks a pristine golf green. He proceeds down a cobblestone staircase that leads down toward the green and motions to Martin to get into a golf cart.

They drive up to a driving range where Mr. Bandoni is practicing his swing.

"Mr. Bandoni, I presume?" Martin says. Bandoni looks over and gives a smug smile. "Of course, and you are?"

"Detective Martin DiPietro. I wanted to ask you about one of your employees."

Bandoni hands his driver over to his caddy. "Which employee?"

Martin pulls out a picture and hands it over to Bandoni. "Ah!" Bandoni says, "Mr. Stacey. He hasn't been in my employment for quite some time."

"When did he move on?" Martin asks.

Bandoni took a moment to think. "Two, maybe three years back. I suppose."

"Why did he leave your employment?" Martin asks.

"Oh, it was…. disciplinary. He was, how can I say this nicely? An addict. Because of his little problem, he was no longer a valuable asset," Bandoni says.

"A drinker, huh?" Martin asks. Bandoni shook his head. "It was a bit more than mere alcohol." Martin nodded. "Ah, okay. What was he doing for you?"

"Liam was a handyman, but because of his problem, he was constantly doing sloppy work. I had to hire others to fix his mistakes. It was counterproductive."

"I see," Martin says.

"Is there anything else I can help you with?" Bandoni asks.

"No, not at this time," Martin pauses. "Well, actually, you wouldn't happen to know his whereabouts?"

"I do not," Bandoni says, "Do you mind if I ask why the interest in my former employee?"

Martin smiled, "I need to ask him some questions regarding a wrongful death."

"Wrongful death?" Bandoni asks with an inquiring tone. "Murder?"

"It looks like it is turning out that way. So, any information you have on Mr. Stacey would be greatly appreciated," Martin says.

"Indeed," Bandoni says, keeping it short.

"Well, if there is nothing else, I will have my associate drive you back to your car," Bandoni says motioning toward the golf cart. Martin glances at the cart and back to Bandoni.

"Thank you. I'll be in touch."

Martin climbed back into the cart and was whisked away.

Bandoni looks over to his caddy. "I assume he isn't on my payroll?"

"No, sir."

"Can we get him a message?" Bandoni asks.

"I'm already on it," the caddy says, picking up his phone.

In a dark storage room, Liam Stacey is connecting wires to a chipboard when his phone rings. He jolts in surprise and lets out a huge sigh. "Fuck!" he says in frustration, followed with "Hello?" as he answers the phone.

A voice from the phone calmly states, "You have been benched. Do not come in. We are being watched, but we are working on it."

"Okay. Got it," Stacey says.

"We will be in contact when the situation changes."

The call ends and Stacey puts the phone down and continues his work.

Chapter Thirty two

C lifford and Sara pull into a roadside motel. Sara looks over to Clifford, "Motel? Isn't there something nicer nearby?"

Clifford pulls out his phone and opens up a map, "Nope, this is the closest place," He says with a smile.

"Ugh," Sara says irritated, "You know what I meant. This place looks beat."

Clifford looks around. "It's not too bad."

He pops out of the car. "Stay here," He says as he heads over to the office.

Sara shouts back "I want my own room!" Clifford gives a thumbs-up as he walks away.

The clerk was behind a desk watching a fuzzy tv. "Yeah?" He says without even looking in the direction of Clifford.

"I need a room with two beds."

"Nope, ain't got none. Only doubles left," The Clerk says.

"Nothing?" Clifford asks in surprise. "Maybe a room with a couch or something?"

The clerk's emotionless face tells Clifford that there are no rooms with a couch.

"We only got single rooms for $99 a night," the clerk says.

"Only single rooms?" Clifford asks.

Somehow the clerk's face shows even less emotion than before. "$99," He says, being brief.

Clifford thinks for a moment again. "Do you have adjoining single rooms?"

The clerk, annoyed, picks up a ledger and proceeds to thumb through it. "Yeah, last two in the back are next to each other. Looks like they're connected."

Clifford smiles, "So, $200 for both rooms for the night, right?"

The clerk looks up at Clifford. "Yeah, cash or credit?"

Clifford sets two bills on the counter one at a time and smiles.

Returning to the car with the keys Clifford notices that Sara isn't in the car.

"Sara?!" Clifford yells while looking around.

"Over here," She yells back.

Clifford runs toward her voice and sees her on her knees looking over a younger man.

"What's going on?" Clifford asks.

Sara, helping him to a seated position says, "He was attacked."

The young man began touching his head and pulling away bloody fingertips. "Aw, jeez!" He says in surprise.

"Hold on, I got something in the car," Clifford says as he jogs away. Sara looks into his eyes for evidence of a concussion. "Why did they hit you?"

"I owe their boss money," He says.

Sara moving her attention to his head asks, "So, what's your name, cowboy?"

"Daniel. Why did you call me cowboy?" Daniel asks.

"The boots," Sara says with a little laugh. Clifford returns with gauze from his make-shift first aid kit and helps Daniel to his feet. Sara looks over to Clifford and begins introductions. "The Cowboy here is Daniel. I'm Sara, and this is Dee."

"Dee?" Daniel asks. Clifford places the gauze on his head, "Clifford Dee, but friends call me Dee. Let's get you off of the street and go get you some ice."

Clifford and Sara help Daniel into the room and Clifford motions him to sit on the bed. Sara pats him on the back and walks over to her room.

"So, what are you, nineteen?" Clifford asks, trying to start some conversation.

"Twenty-one. Almost twenty-two," He quips back like he practiced saying it a million times trying to convince others of his maturity.

Clifford looks at him in disbelief.

"Yeah, okay. I just turned twenty," Daniel says.

"So," Clifford says. "How does a twenty-year-old get a nice thump on the head like that?"

Daniel sighs, "It's complicated. I borrowed some money and I'm having trouble paying it back."

"That doesn't sound complicated at all. Money for what?" Clifford asks.

"Huh?" Daniel asks back confused.

"Why did you need the money?"

Daniel put the ice down. "My mom. She took my dad's death pretty hard. He died two years ago and she started drinking and taking drugs. She lost her job and then got into a car accident. I left college and have been taking care of her. She passed away about three months ago. The hospital bills have been killing me. I started dealing to pay off the bills, but couldn't get the cash fast enough. I borrowed the last grand from a rival supplier and..."

Clifford nods, "Yeah, I get it. It's rough."

Daniel looks up at Clifford, "My supplier didn't like who I borrowed money from, so I don't even have product to sell anymore. I'm kinda stuck."

Daniel paused for a moment, debating on how much information he wanted to share.

"Wait, you're not a cop or anything are you?"

Clifford laughs, "No. Not a cop."

Daniel let out a nervous laugh. "Okay. I just don't know what to do."

Clifford nods and sits down next to Daniel. "You sound like a good guy that was dealt a terrible hand."

"Yeah, I guess. Thanks," Daniel says, clearing his eyes.

Sara walks in toward the end of the story, "You're in good hands here. We can help you," She adds more ice to the gauze on his head.

"Oh, you're good," Daniel quips, "and, thank you. I appreciate it," he says toward Sara flashing her a smile.

Clifford let out a little laugh at his subtle flirtations, "You aren't her type."

Daniel looked over to Clifford, "oh, I'm so sorry. Is she your..."

Clifford cuts him off, "Friend, she's my friend, but she's a woman's woman if you know what I mean."

"Huh?" Daniel questions.

"I'm into the ladies," Sara says.

"Oh!" Daniel says in realization. " I'm sorry, I didn't mean to be forward."

"Forward?" Sara laughs, "It's okay. I thought it was cute."

Daniel asks, "So do you have a, uh, a girlfriend?"

He saw the change on Sara's face. "Had," She says in a serious tone. Swallowing hard, she continues, "She was murdered yesterday."

Daniel's eyes open wide as he begins to stammer. "I... I'm so sorry. I don't know..."

Sara stops him. "It's okay, you didn't know."

Clifford chimes in, "You know what, it's getting late, Daniel, why don't you stay here with me? You can have the bed, so you can keep your head propped up. I'll sleep on the floor."

Daniel looks at Clifford, "I don't want to impose on you guys."

Clifford asks, "Is there somewhere I can drop you off tomorrow?"

"I've got no one…." Daniel says in a sobering tone.

"Hmm, we're going to leave first thing, I guess the room is yours until ten or so," Clifford says.

"Uh, okay. Sure," Daniel says in an unsure tone.

"Get some sleep," Clifford says, turning toward Sara. "We leave early."

Sara motions to Clifford, "Let's talk in my room real quick."

The two leave the room and close the door adjoining the rooms. Sara turns to Clifford. "Listen. You need to hire this kid."

Clifford says, "Hire? For what?"

"Think about it, dummy! Bandoni wants you dead. They killed Tracy, so they know me. They put Bailey in the hospi- well, hotel-hospital. Your detective friend, Martin, can only do so much."

Sara continues, "We are going to need some muscle, you know, someone who doesn't have PTSD and a bad knee."

Clifford shocked, "That was low….that hurt, Sara."

"I'm not saying that you aren't able. I'm saying that we could use the help, " Sara says in a very compassionate way.

Clifford nods, "Let me think about it. Get some sleep," He says as he turns to walk out of the room.

Chapter Thirty three

Martin is sitting alone in his apartment with a Bourbon soda in his hand watching late-night tv. He still hasn't gotten over his wife leaving him two years ago. Especially since she took his daughter back to Chicago.

He is startled by a knock on the door.

He slowly gets up, and sets his drink on the end table next to him, and grabs his revolver from the kitchen counter.

Martin makes his way to the door and asks, "Who is it?"

"Martin DiPietro?" the voice asks from the other side of the door.

Martin carefully unlocks and opens the door, "What do you want?"

The man hands him a padded envelope and says, "I live in the building across the street. This is for you. It came to my apartment, but it's addressed to you."

Martin notices the lack of postage. "How did you get this? There's no postage."

The man, looking annoyed, says "Look, it was in my box. Do you want it, or should I throw it away?"

Martin reaches out and takes the envelope. "Sorry, thanks."

He slinks into his apartment and opens the envelope as he walks back toward his kitchen. He dumps the contents onto the counter and out tumbles a stack of hundreds wrapped in a sheet of paper. He opens the paper and inside is written, "Leave Stacey alone."

Martin tosses the money into the envelope and crumbles the note in frustration.

Night turns to day and Martin stumbles into the shower, slightly hungover from his late-night bourbon. After some breakfast, he pours coffee into a travel mug and heads to the station, but not before he grabs the envelope full of cash.

At the station, Martin plops the envelope onto the desk of Internal Affairs.

"What's this?" the IA officer asks as he's digging into the envelope.

Martin looks across the desk, "A man handed it to me at my door last night."

Pulling the cash out of the envelope, he says, "This is like ten thousand dollars!"

Martin nods. "Look at the note."

"Who's Stacey?" asks the IA officer.

Martin says, "He's the main suspect in my case. I'm sure you heard about the big car chase? That's Stacey."

Still looking in the envelope, "This is a lot of money to look the other way."

Martin grits his teeth. "I am not someone who can be bought. So, I'm filing a report and turning in the cash."

The IA officer scoffs, "Better man than me."

Martin looks up from the paperwork, "You wouldn't turn it in?"

He stammers a bit before saying, "Of course. It's the right thing to do. I was just joking around."

"Oh, okay," Martin says annoyed, as he continues to fill out the forms. A few minutes later, he aggressively rips his copy of the paperwork off the pad and leaves the IA office, giving the IA officer a stern glance.

E.I. Bandoni sits in his nook overlooking the back of his estate scooping out his grapefruit with his silver spoon while reading a newspaper.

His man-servant walks up with a phone. "Sir, the telephone is for you."

Bandoni reaches for the phone and places it to his ear. "Yes?"

The voice on the other end can be heard saying, "Bad news, DiPietro turned in the cash, to me of all people."

Bandoni clears his throat. "That is bad news for Detective Martin DiPietro."

Maggie returns to the motel room where Bailey is resting and takes his pulse. She then circles around and begins checking his breathing and takes his temperature.

"All normal," she says in a breath of relief. She grabs some clothing from a gym bag, kicks off her sneakers, and walks into the bathroom to start the shower.

She takes off her flowy tank top and slips off her sweats. She tests the temp of the shower with her hand when she realizes that she forgot her toiletry bag.

She grabs the body towel to cover herself and slips out of the bathroom. Maggie jogs across the room to her bag and grabs her toiletry tote when Bailey starts to awake from his sleep.

"Oh, damn, and I thought my dreams were good," Bailey says as a towel-draped Maggie came into focus.

"Oh, shit!" She says as she hurries back toward the bathroom. "Stay there, I will explain after my shower," She yells as she shut the door.

"I ain't going nowhere," Bailey says. "Unless you want me to slide in there and wash your back. I'm a good back washer," he continues.

"Good morning to me!" Bailey says under his breath while giving his arms a light stretch.

Clifford and Sara watch over Daniel as he sleeps. Sara leans over and whispers, "So what did you decide?"

Clifford looks over at Sara, "I'm taking your advice."

Sara smiles at Clifford.

Clifford notices the smile and says, "Shut up."

Daniel startled awake at the sound of Sara laughing. "What's going on?" He asks.

Clifford sat down on the bed. "I talked with my associate here, and we decided to make you an offer."

Daniel rubbing the sleep from his eyes, "Offer?"

Clifford continues, "We want you to come with us. I can hire you as a consultant."

Daniel, still rubbing his face asks, "Go where? What kind of consultant?"

Clifford sighs, "I will be completely honest with you. We're in trouble with some very dangerous people and we need to recruit help from some other dangerous people."

Daniel puts his hand out to stop Clifford, "Oh, hold up. I need some coffee first."

Clifford plugs in the single-serve coffee pot and starts brewing the crappy motel coffee while he and Sara start filling him in. After a few minutes, Sara hands Daniel a small cup of coffee. He nods while listening intently to everything they're saying.

They fill him in on everything from Bandoni, to Bailey, and even Tracy. They could see the concern on Daniel's face growing as they talk about Stacey and how dangerous and ruthless he is.

Daniel stops Clifford and asks, "So how did you get involved with this in the first place?"

Clifford stammers and turns to Sara. "Even you don't know this. In simple words—I took money from Bandoni to take care of a threat to his business."

Sara looks over at Clifford "Took care of a threat?"

Clifford looks a bit uneasy as Sara was putting the pieces together. Her mouth drops, "Are you a hitman?"

Clifford pauses and looks away.

"Oh My God, Dee! Why didn't you tell me you did that?"

Clifford looks back. "It's not something that you just bring up in casual conversation. Besides, I wasn't his regular hitman. I only did one other job like that. I am mostly an investigator or gather intel for him. I just took on a case that ended up where I needed to kill someone and then The Tye Brothers happened."

Sara Pauses. "Wait. Hold up. You were investigating the serial killers the cops are looking for?"

Clifford laughs nervously. "It's a bit more involved."

"Did you kill them?" Sara quips excitedly.

Clifford nervously nods.

"Oh My God! What? Nu-uh! That was national news. They're still looking for them," Sara continues.

Clifford stammers, "Yeah, well...hopefully they'll never find them."

Sara scoots to the edge of the bed, "You need to tell me all about this. I gotta know."

"No, stop. I'm not going into this right now. This is, uh, need to know, privileged, top-secret G-13 classified stuff and you don't need to know. I've already said way too much for my comfort level," Clifford says nervously.

Sara and Clifford both look over at Daniel. "Uh, so..." Clifford says uneasily. "This was probably too much information for you as well. You can not mention this to anyone, ever."

Daniel looked at Clifford dead in his eyes, "I'm in."

"You're what?" Clifford asks.

"I'm in. I'm coming with you. I want to help out. I'm in," Daniel repeats himself in a more sure tone.

"Oh okay. Great!" Clifford says, surprised at his unexpected willingness to jump right in.

Daniel continues. "I got nothing anymore. I don't have a home, it was foreclosed on. My parents are gone. I only have half of an engineering degree that I can't use. I need another starting point, and this sounds like it's the best thing I got right now."

Clifford relaxes. "Oh, okay. Well listen, If we get through this, I can hire you as a regular employee."

Daniel shakes his head, "No, teach me and make me a partner."

Clifford scoffs, "Partner? How about we work our way up to a partner. You have to learn first."

Daniel thinks a moment. "Sure, employee, but after I know as much as you, partner. Cool?"

Clifford smiles, "Sure."

––––––––––

Maggie, still damp and glistening from her shower, steps out of the bathroom, dressed in shorts and a t-shirt, with a towel around her hair.

"So, Chief. I guess you have some questions."

Bailey takes a deep breath, looks at her, and says, "Normally when a beautiful woman is in the room with all her glory on display, I tend not to ask anything. But, in this case, I am missing a few details on how I got into this particular situation, So yeah, would you mind filling in the blanks?"

Maggie smiled, "Ha! Okay. Well, I was hired to watch over you for a few days. My boss is Marlon."

Bailey shakes his head, "I don't know Marlon."

Maggie nods, "Well, technically Marlon's friend hired me. I think his name starts with D or something because they kept calling him D."

Bailey smiles. "Oh, Dee! As in D-E-E. It's his last name. I know Dee. He has saved my bacon a few times. Well, he should have, 'cause it's usually his fault, but he's a good dude."

"Okay," Maggie says, "Well, I'm glad you're awake because you were asleep for nearly two days. You took a bad beating."

"It feels like it," Bailey says. "Where is Dee now?"

Maggie jumps off the edge of the bed and exclaims, "Oh, right! That reminds me!" Bailey eyes her as she walks across to the other side of the room and pulls out a bag from the nightstand. "He says to give you this when you wake up."

She hands the bag over to Bailey.

Bailey opens the bag and pulls out a burner cell phone. "What am I supposed to do with this?" He asks.

"He says to hang onto it and lay low. We got this room for three more days, I assume he will be in contact with more instructions."

"Okay. "What do we do until then?" Bailey says in a slight flirtatious tone and gives a subtle smile.

Maggie smiles back and slowly starts to walk toward the bed, "Well, I can only think of one thing really," She says in her own flirtatious tone. She removes the towel from her hair and leans over Bailey, letting the slight brown curls of her damp hair, gently touch his skin. Bailey starts to smile as she gets closer to him when she reaches her arm around his side to grab the remote control.

"Here!" she says, handing him the remote, "You can watch TV. I just got outta work so I'm going to get some sleep."

"Funny!" Bailey says with a slight laugh. "Wait, you work nights? Looking like that? Someone did you wrong," He continues.

Maggie lets out a half-smile. "I'm paying my own way through Med School."

"Ohhhh," Bailey says. "You said Marlon, right? Is he the owner of that... Ohhhh. That makes a lot of sense now," Bailey continues, coming into realization.

"Yeah, like I said, I'm paying my own way. Now, let me get my beauty sleep," Maggie replies as she lays down on the bed next to his.

"Okie-Dokie" Bailey says as he points the remote toward the TV. "I guess I'll see what's on." Maggie pulls the covers over her head, "Okay, just try to keep it down over there."

Bailey looks over in disappointment and says, "Sure thing. Does this phone come with Angry Birds?"

Minutes turned to hours and Maggie was sleeping like the dead. Bailey struggles to quickly answer a ringing phone.

After a few seconds, he manages to answer it and whispers, "Hello?"

Clifford is on the other end, "Bailey! Hey."

Bailey continues to whisper "What's up, Dee?"

"Why are you whispering?" Clifford asks, confused.

Bailey leans into the phone, "There's a girl in my room."

Clifford chuckles, "Yeah, she's looking after you. Maggie, right?"

Still whispering, Bailey responds, "Yeah, Maggie. She's asleep. She worked last night."

Now Clifford begins to whisper, "Oh, makes sense."

Bailey pulls the phone away from his head and looks at it with confusion. "Dee, Why are you whispering?"

Clifford thinks about it for a second. "I don't know. 'Cause you are, I guess."

Bailey laughs, "You white people are weird.'

Clifford chuckles and says, "Hey buddy, I'm glad to hear that you're feeling better. We were all worried, but I need your help.

Bailey softly says, "Sure thing, whatcha need?"

"You have any inside jokes or stories with your cousin?" Clifford asks.

Chapter Thirty four

O **fficer Hall** walks into Martin's office with a packet and plops it onto his desk. "Hey Shaq, what's this?" Martin asks.

"I dunno, It was left at the front desk for you."

Martin picks it up and starts to open it as officer Hall continues on.

He pulls out a newspaper article that reads "**Local Athlete Receives Soccer Scholarship.**"

It's the same article his ex-wife sent him weeks ago.

He continues to glare at it and notices that some letters are underlined in the brief story about his daughter.

He begins to put those letters together.

F-O-R-G-E-T-S-T-A-C-E-Y

Martin lunges out of his seat and runs out to officer Hall. "Shaq, who left this?" He says as the paper trembles in his hand.

Martin, Hall, and a few other officers are scanning the camera footage near the front desk and are able to pick out a kid, no older than 14, walking into the station with the packet.

Martin slams his fist down on the table. "They got a kid to do it."

Officer Hall chimes in, "Want us to find him and bring him in?"

"No, it won't do any good," Martin says. "Besides, we know it was Bandoni. We just don't have the proof."

———————

Clifford asks Sara to stay with the car while he and Daniel walk the poorer neighborhoods of Chicago.

Daniel looks over to Clifford and says, "I think we're looking for needles in haystacks here."

Clifford nods and says, "Yeah, we should probably think of a better plan for this. Let's head back to the car."

Out of nowhere, four guys surround them. "You white boys lost?"

Clifford firmly says, "We're looking for JJ."

The guy asks, "What-chu want wit' JJ?"

Clifford puts his hands up and says. "We just want to talk, that's all."

"Nah, I don't think so," He says as they start walking toward them.

"Can you give her a message for me? If she doesn't want to talk, we'll just go," Clifford says.

The man motions to the others to stop. "What's the message?"

Clifford says. "Thank you for saying you broke Claudette's plate."

The guy puts a phone up to his ear and starts whispering into it.

Clifford overhears him say, "He sayin' thank you for taking the blame for a plate or somethin'."

"It was Claudette's plate. She said she broke it," Clifford says loud enough for the person on the other end of the phone to hear.

The man put his hand up toward Clifford.

"Yeah, he says Claudette. Somethin' about her plate. He wants to meet."

The man listens intently to the person on the other end and slowly lowers his hand away from Clifford.

"Yeah. okay. I will," The man confirms just before he hangs up the phone.

The man turns toward Clifford. "You got your meeting. Let's go."

Clifford follows the men down an alley and toward the street on the other side. They approach a car and open the door.

"Get in," The man says.

After a somewhat decent drive, they arrive at an apartment complex across town and pull into a small three-story parking garage across an alley to the side of the complex.

"We're here," the man says.

They open the door and escort Clifford and Daniel toward the stairwell of the garage and they enter a small, run-down shack in the alley. They walk completely through the building to the other side and back outside away from the apartments.

"We aren't going to the apartments?" Clifford asks.

"Why would we? JJ don't live there," the man continues, "The garage is free parking."

They enter a small public park and tell Clifford to sit on the park bench.

"Your boy here is coming with us," he says as he motions his friends to take Daniel with them.

Clifford watches as they walk completely out of sight in the direction that they came.

He turns his head to the left and sees three guys walking toward him. One of them stops and sits at a bench about ten feet away, facing him. The other two walk around him and sit on the other side, completely surrounding Clifford.

An extremely beautiful well-dressed woman with full features walks up directly in front of Clifford, escorted by men on either side. Her men stop short and she continues to the bench to greet Clifford.

Clifford starts to stand. "Stay seated," she says as she reaches the bench.

"My men don't spook easily and they are well trained, but they don't know you."

Clifford places his hands on his lap as she sits next to him.

"You mentioned my Auntie Claudette's plate..." With squinting eyes, JJ turns toward Clifford and continues, "There are only two other people that know that story. I spoke at the funeral for one of them and the other is missing and assumed dead, so, do you mind telling me who told you that story?"

Clifford looked at JJ, "My good friend Bailey told me that story. He says that he never thanked you."

JJ's eyes light up as she looks over to Clifford, "You know where Bailey is?"

Clifford lifts his hands and says, "I'm gonna reach into my pocket."

He can see the guards tighten in alertness and place hands on hidden guns.

Clifford slowly reaches into his jacket pocket and with two fingers pulls out a cell phone and places it on the bench between them.

"Speed dial one."

JJ picks up the phone, presses a button and it starts ringing.

"Yo Dee, that you?" Bailey says

JJ's eyes start to well up. "You're a little shit, you know that?"

"Oh Shit, JJ!" Bailey says. "Hey, girl!"

"I haven't seen or heard from you in forever and all you gotta say is, 'Hey Gurrl'?" JJ says as she lets out a little smile.

Bailey says, "Yeah, I meant to call, but I've been busy getting the shit beat out of me."

"Are you okay JayBee?" JJ asks.

Bailey says, "You know I hate when you call me that."

"I know, I worry about you. I promised your brother I'd make sure you were safe."

Bailey smiled, "Yeah. I know."

JJ looks over at Dee and asks Bailey, "This guy legit?"

"Dee? Yeah, he's my boy. He's taking care of me. He's cool, but don't tell him I said that, it'll go to his head."

JJ could feel Bailey smiling over the phone and it put her at ease. They continue to talk for a few more minutes before Bailey brings up Bandoni.

JJ's mood begins to shift. "You got beef with Bandoni? Shit. You know that guy is bad news. He's an Italian Mob piece of shit that organizes the hitmen for the whole region. The Chicago mob leans on him big time. This isn't good JayBee!"

Bailey asks, "Can you help?"

JJ stammers, "I, I guess I can talk to some people, but I don't know if we can get involved. We can't take on the entire Italian empire."

Bailey sighs. "He wants me dead. He's tried twice and Dee is the only thing that's stopped him."

"How does a nerd like you always find trouble like this?" JJ says.

Clifford mouths the word, "nerd" with confusion as she says it.

JJ continues, "You stay low and I'll talk to some people. I love you, Cuz."

After they say their goodbyes, JJ turns to Clifford and asks. "Is this trackable?"

Clifford shook his head, "No it's clean, it's a burner."

JJ shoves the phone into her front pocket, "I'm keepin' this."

Clifford says, "That's fine! It's yours," he continues, "You called him a nerd?"

She let out a slight laugh, "He is a big nerd! Always studying. He was my driver, I figured that it would be a safe job for him, but someone trying to take me out, shot at the car and hit him. After that, he couldn't drive so he'd spend his time studyin' and tryin' to hack shit. He was tryin' his hand at some white-collar crimes." She begins laughing at the idea. "He's much smarter than he lets on. Don't let him fool you," JJ continues.

Clifford smiles at the idea of Bailey being a nerdy tech geek.

JJ looks over at him as he smiles. "What?" she asks.

Clifford says, "Him being a nerd is a good thing."

The two continue to talk for several minutes until Clifford eventually tells JJ what he is planning.

"Bandoni won't stop until Bailey and I are dead. We want to take him out, or at least hurt him enough that it won't be worth killing us," Clifford says.

JJ shakes her head, "Like I told my cuz, we can't get involved like that. I have connections and the best I can do is talk to some people. I have the phone, and I'll be in touch."

Clifford knew that he was putting her in a difficult position. She was a rising star in the area, but she couldn't take on the empire of the Chicago Italian Mob. It would be suicide.

He nods, "Okay, good enough. Talk to your people. We'll wait to hear from you."

Chapter Thirty five

Martin sits on the sofa in the Captain's office with his head in his hands. The Captain walks in and shuts his blinds. He turns and sits next to Martin.

"I am taking you off of the Stacey case."

"Brian, NO! I want this guy," Martin says.

"It is way too much for you right now. He's threatening your family," the Captain says.

Martin shakes his head. "That is exactly why I want to bring his ass in and why I want to rake Bandoni over the coals."

The Captain looks over to Martin and says, "Listen, I get it, but you lost your family because of your decisions. I know you're determined, but we have to take these threats seriously. You need to understand that. This will not get your wife and kid back. Especially if something happens and they knew that you could have taken a back seat on this."

Martin listens intently and wipes his face with his hands. "I just..." He let out a huge sigh. "I know I fucked up my marriage and this isn't to try to bring her back to me. I don't want this guy to think he can threaten cops and they back off."

The Captain stands up and says, "I get it."

He walks over to his desk and grabs his cold cup of coffee. "I don't like this either, but this is protocol. We have to reassign it now that they're threatening civilian lives close to you."

He takes a swig of his coffee, grimaces over the cold temperature, and sets it back on his desk. "We can't have a pissed-off cop raging over this case because he's upset."

The Captain lowers his voice and walks back over to Martin.

"I know there are officers on Bandoni's payroll. I know he had his finger in the DA. I know exactly what he can do. This job will take finesse and I want you silently investigating this while another cop takes Stacey. Am I starting to make myself clear?"

Martin nods.

The Captain continues, "I wasn't sure about you, but since they're threatening your family, I know you're not dirty. That is typically a last resort tactic for them. I need your silence on this."

With that, the Captain stands up and loudly says, "And if you disobey this direct order, I will have your badge!"

He motions to Martin to leave. "Do I make myself clear?"

Martin stands up. "Yes sir! Perfectly." He shoots the Captain a half-smile as he walks to the door, and changes it to a scowl as he leaves. Several cops are glaring at Martin to gage him as he storms out of the office.

Clifford and Daniel are dropped off at the corner near his Jeep and walk back towards Sara.

She sees them in the side mirror walking toward the car and jumps out to greet them.

"Hey guys, how'd it go?" Sara asks.

Clifford shrugs his shoulders, "I'm not sure. She is concerned. Bandoni's a huge deal."

Daniel quietly looks on as they talk.

"We know he's a big deal, but how can we take him on without help?" Sara asks.

Clifford shakes his head. "Not sure, but we have to try because he won't stop until we're all dead."

"What?" Sara remarks.

"Well, I mean" Clifford continues. "They are going to look into it because he has ties back here. They are going to try to shake some feathers to see if they can get Bandoni to back off of us."

"I guess that's better than nothing," Sara says. "So do you know what Bandoni even does for the mob up here anyway?" She asks.

Clifford nods. "Yeah, I know exactly what Bandoni does for the mob up here. I used to work for him, remember?"

Clifford motions toward the car and the three of them get in.

"So?" Sara asks, "You gonna enlighten us?"

"In a nutshell?" Clifford says. "He's what they call a contract manager. He runs the books for Chicago, launders money, and also supplies hitmen for sensitive jobs."

"That sounds like important stuff for a mob," Sara says.

Clifford nods, "Sure is."

As the trio drive off Daniel chimes in. "I have a question. Well two, really."

Clifford asks, "What's up?"

"Well, first, where am I going to stay? And I was wondering how that Bandoni guy does his money laundering. I have always wondered how criminals did that."

Clifford smiles. "Let's focus on your living arrangements in a bit. Money Laundering isn't that tough. It's all about false assets with a monetary value. You associate the money with a fake asset, take your cut, have a bank process it, and the money is clean, with a paper trail."

Daniel nods, but is still confused. "Okay, I guess."

"He can stay with me," Sara says. "I have an extra room and a blow-up mattress. It's good enough for the time being."

Clifford agrees. "Yeah, that sounds like a good idea, but I don't think we should go back into town just yet. At least not in this Jeep. Stacey might be looking for us."

Daniel leans forward and says, "You really make this Stacey guy sound terrible."

"He is," Clifford responds.

Several hours later, Daniel walks around the corner and through the park in front of Clifford and Sara's building. He's carrying a small package and a clipboard.

He crosses the street and swiftly approaches the building. Two men notice and start to walk toward him.

When Daniel gets to the front steps he sits down on the stairs and starts to tie a loose shoelace.

When finished he gets up, looks at the package, and then the address of the building. He pulls out and checks his cell phone then shakes his head like he's lost. He shoves his phone back into his pocket then continues past the stairs and rounds the building.

The two men back off and change direction toward the park.

Daniel rounds the building and crosses the street then jogs toward an alleyway between two other buildings. He dips into the side street where Clifford and Sara are waiting.

"Your place is definitely being watched," Daniel says as he scoots into the car, a little out of breath.

"How many people?" Clifford asks.

"Two guys, at least. Maybe more," Catching his breath, Daniel continues. "They were packing, too. I saw a gun when one of the guys' jackets flew open while he was jogging across the street."

Clifford shakes his head and begins to rub his face in frustration. "If they're sitting on our place, we can't go home. Let's get Bailey and we'll figure out what to do next. Maybe, Marlon can help."

Liam Stacey drives a white panel van, dressed in a utility shirt from the local gas company. He parks next to the police station on top of the sewer entrance manhole. Opening a compartment in the van, he exposes the manhole.

He pries open the cover, climbs down with a bag strapped to his back, and starts to walk through the tunnels under the station, looking for the sewer main that leads up toward the police station. Once he finds it, he pulls out a small explosive device with a circuit board and connects it to an old burner cell phone and a small canister.

He duct-tapes it all to the outside of the piping and checks the cell phone bars to find the signal is too low. He pulls out a small signal amplifier, tapes it to a pipe next to the phone, and retreats back to the van.

On the underside of the manhole cover, he tapes a small box with an antenna that reads 'Signal grabber2000'. He attaches a coax cable to the rear of the device and drops the cables into the sewer. Gritting his teeth and tugging the cable, he pulls it until reaching the amplifier and plugs it in.

The phone beeps as it reaches four bars.

Liam climbs back out of the manhole into the van, packs up his gear, then drives off.

Chapter Thirty six

Marlon is unlocking the Dollhouse and starting to do his opening routine. From inside, he could hear a car pull up. He looks out and sees that it's Clifford.

He opens the door and strolls out. "Well, well, well. Look who rolled in. And almost rolling in," Marlon says as he moved his focus onto Bailey.

Bailey being helped into his chair by Sara says, "Hey, do not besmirch my ability! I can still kick your ass."

Marlon, confused, says, "Besmirch? Who says besmirch?"

Bailey narrows his eyes, "I do, that's who."

Marlon smiles, "Okay, we're going with besmirch."

Clifford walks up and slaps hands with Marlon, "Hey, you piece of shit, I just wanted to say thank you for helping Bailey."

Marlon says, "No worries, man. I'm glad to help."

Bailey rolls up toward Marlon and says, "So, you're Marlon?"

"The one and only," He returns.

Bailey extends his hand, "Thank you for helping us, especially me, out."

Marlon nods, "No problem. Glad you're looking better," he shakes Bailey's hand.

Clifford looks over to Marlon and says, "I'm glad you said that. I need one more favor."

There is a slight breeze and a cool nip in the crisp air. From the roof, the traffic below is almost silent, like watching a movie on mute. The police station can be seen through the scope of Liam's sniper rifle. He has a clear shot of the front, left, and right sides of the building. Only the back and few portions of the parking area are covered. He pulls out another old burner phone and hits the speed dial.

The phone rings the explosive device in the sewer and causes a small explosion. The explosion ruptures the gas lines to the police station. There is a slight tremor throughout the building and then a bigger explosion that shatters the glass in the windows and sends a large rumble through the building. Fire alarms are sounding and desks have been shaken. Ceiling tiles are falling to the floor and the emergency lights kick on. The fire sprinklers kick on and cause the people already in panic mode to slip and skid on the debris all over the floor.

Moments later Liam can see officers evacuating co-workers, civilians, and prisoners from the building.

Martin grabs a fallen officer with a head wound and helps her up. "Let's go, people. Evacuate!" he yells as she regains her footing. "Are you good?" He asks her.

"Yeah, thanks," she says as she starts toward the door.

Smoke is seen billowing out of some of the shattered windows. Martin heads to the door and makes his way outside into the blinding daylight. A junior officer walks in front of Martin and extends his hand to him in help as a bullet rips through his shoulder and explodes out of his back and lodges into the side of the brick building. Blood sprays across the face of Martin as he hears a faint gunshot in the distance.

"Shots Fired!" is heard, screamed by other officers.

"Officer down!" echoes through his ears as he can hear another faint shot in the distance.

Martin can feel slight pain and begins to look down. He sees blood pouring out of a hole, center mass in his chest. He drops to his knees as he hears another shot in the distance echo off of the buildings after seeing another officer get hit. On the ground, his vision slowly fades as he watches more officers fall to the ground moments before the sounds of gunshots reach his dying ears. The sounds of the chaos give way to the slowing sound of his heartbeat until suddenly he can hear or see nothing at all.

Hours later, Bandoni sits eating in his garden, he receives a call on his cellphone.

"Pronto," He says in a smug tone, as he always does.

His demeanor quickly changes when he realizes it's about the police station.

"Yes, I know," he says as he tries to get a few words in. "I will take care of th.." he tries to continue, but he's met with heated language spoken enraged with fire.

"I can still cost you and several of your men their jobs!" he shouts back, but the voice on the other end of the phone did not care.

"I am not done, I OWN YOU!" Bandoni begins to shout back as the phone goes silent.

He pulls the phone away from his ear, after realizing the call has ended. Hands trembling in frustration and anger he calls out to his man-servant.

"Bring Liam Stacey to me."

Clifford, Sara, Bailey, and Daniel leave the Dollhouse before it opens to the public. They decide to lay low for the night at the motel that Bailey is still staying in.

The guys are in one room and they were able to get an adjoining room for Sara.

Sara and Clifford are chatting when he gets a call on his cellphone from the police chief.

"Mr. Dee, It's the Chief. I know you were very close to Detective Martin DiPietro, so I wanted to tell you this myself."

Clifford nods and says very few words as the chief notifies him of the death of his friend and ally.

Clifford slowly walks away from the group as he listens to the Chief over the phone.

Bailey taps Sara and draws her attention to Clifford as he is intently listening.

The group stands up and focuses on Clifford as he turns away from them.

"Yes, sir. Thank you for letting me know. This is a horrible tragedy," Clifford says just before ending the call.

"Dee?" Sara asks, wanting to know what's going on.

Clifford turns around with grief in his eyes. "Martin Dipietro is dead."

Sara places her hand over her mouth. Bailey's eyes widen, "Oh shit, Dee. I'm so sorry."

Daniel takes in the emotion in the room and asks, "This was your detective friend right?"

Clifford nods.

Daniel continues, "I'm so sorry, man. How did he die?"

"Liam... fucking... Stacey!" Clifford says through clenched teeth.

Chapter Thirty seven

Two men stand on either side of Stacey as he is presented to Bandoni.

"Why?" Bandoni starts to ask, but out of frustration, squeezes his fists tightly, and changes his question. "What made you think I wanted you to shoot up the goddamn police station?" He asks with clenched teeth. Stacey begins to speak when Bandoini cuts him off. "Do you know what you have done?!"

Bandoni wrings his hands and begins pacing in his office. Stacey begins to speak up when Bandoni raises his hand to him and strikes him, backhanded, across his face.

"You lost my control over the police. You lost me the DA. You are costing me EVERYTHING!" He continues to shout, "I have a few angles I can play, but you are a liability."

Stacey blurts out, "I'm going to get Dee! DiPietro was just the first step."

Bandoni threw the back of his hand across the face of Stacey a second time. "It's not Detective DiPietro, you idiot. You shot several officers and one of them was the commissioner's son! He isn't going to be looking away anymore, you understand what that means?" Bandoni scoffs. "Of course not. You have no idea the politics involved in the business. You just fucking point and shoot."

Bandoni takes a calming breath. "When I was eight years old," he starts. "I grew up in a small village in Italy, outside the borders of San Marino. It was a simple time. My father brought home a puppy for my birthday. That pup never left my side. We ate together, slept together. He was my brother. One morning, we noticed a stir with the chickens. They were our livelihood, so any disruption would be devastating to our family. So, I sent out my dog. He saved the chickens from a hungry fox and officially became the guardian of the coop. Day after day, that hungry fox would try to steal a chicken, but my dog would stop him. One day the dog lay in the shade and the chicken coop was attacked. There were two foxes this time. My dog, confused, tried to chase both foxes and ended up destroying one of the coops and the chickens escaped. The foxes stole several chickens from the destroyed coop. We spent the entire evening rounding up chickens and repairing the coop. We lost many. So the next day, my father went to the market and bought two more dogs. He posted them outside of the coop and he shot my dog. Crying, I asked him why. He explained to me, once you have a liability, it will always be a liability no matter what."

Stacey chimes in, "This is a terrible story."

Bandoni scowls, "The point is, you were the guard dog trying to get the fox. You failed and cost me my coop. Now my chickens are getting away."

Stacey stands there with a scowl and blood dripping from his face from where Bandoni's ring struck him. "I will fix this," He mutters.

Bandoni grabs him by both cheeks, "There is only one way to fix this now."

He points at the guys on either side of Stacey and says, "Find this man a hole no one will find."

A tear rolls down Stacey's face as they grab him and walk him out of Bandoni's office.

"The explosion that shook three buildings in the downtown area today is still being investigated. Investigators believe the shootings that took place immediately afterward were tied as the explosion may have been a method to get the police station to evacuate into the open. Currently, there are eight dead and twenty others injured. No names have been released, but we do know that the majority of the deceased are officers and the majority of the injured were civilian bystanders."

Bailey uses the remote control to shut off the TV in Sara's room. He says, "I just can't watch anymore of this. I'm sorry."

Sara blinks and says, "No, I get it. I just don't know what to say. I'm numb."

Clifford sits in silence for a moment then says, "I just don't know why Bandoni would order this hit. It makes no sense."

Daniel looks over and asks, "What if it wasn't Bandoni?"

Clifford shakes his head and says, "He is the only one that could have. He...He" pausing for a moment to think.

Sara looks over, "What is it, Dee?" She asks.

Bailey says, "You got some wheels turning, bud, what's up?"

Clifford sits back in his chair. "Stacey has gone rogue."

Sara asks, "What makes you think that?"

Clifford runs his hand through his hair. "He is the only one I have seen skilled enough to make those shots. We know it was him. Bandoni would not order this out of the chance of losing the police. I mean, he already owns them, and Stacey doesn't care about collateral damage. Never has."

Sara looks over with a quivering lip, "I know too much about his collateral damage."

Chapter Thirty eight

S tacey looks skyward after the trunk of the car is popped open. Shielding his eyes from the blinding flashlight, he asks, "Jesus, Steve, you gonna blind me to death?"

"I'm Dave," He says as he pulls him from the trunk of the car and muscles him over to a hole in the ground. It's body length and about four feet deep. Stacey looks around and notices that he's at a construction site.

"Get in," Dave directs as he points to the hole with his gun. Steve walks away and starts up a dump truck filled with gravel. Stacey walks over to the hole and jumps in. The truck starts to back up as he motions Stacey to lay down in the hole.

With each backup warning beep from the truck, Stacey's heart beats a little harder. Dave points his gun and says, "In the hole. NOW!"

Stacey looks down and sees a rock. It's not a big rock, but not a pebble. He gently kicks it with his shoe and notices that it is loose from the ground. He looks back up at Dave and starts to crouch. Out of desperation he looks beyond him to one side and blurts out, "Who's that guy?"

Dave scoffs and says, "Nice try."

He cocks his head even more and squints his eyes. Out of a pure reaction, Dave starts to turn his head away from Stacey. His eyes begin to move away and focus more behind him to see that there is in fact nothing there.

He again scoffs at the piss poor attempt and turns his attention back toward Stacey. A rock smashes him directly in the center of his face. Stacey's aim was true. Blood pours out of Dave's nose and tears well up in his eyes. Blind, Dave begins shooting toward Stacey, but missing him with each shot. Stacey leaps out of the hole and scampers away, finding cover behind another construction vehicle.

Steve runs over to his partner, "What happened?"

"The fucker hit me with a rock. He broke my nose!"

"I got him," Steve says with a sigh as he pulls his gun from his waistband and runs away.

Stacey runs behind a stack of steel barrels and a forklift. He climbs inside the forklift and rummages through, but there aren't any keys. He hops down and lands on a three-foot-long piece of rebar. Steve hears him jumping from the forklift and walks over to investigate. Just as he rounds the barrels, Stacey jumps up from a crouching position shoving the rebar deep into his skull from under his neck. Blood flows out of his body onto Stacey like a fountain as he twists it deeper inside. Steve shook as life was draining from his body.

With tears in his eyes and blood still dripping from his nose, Dave calls out for his buddy to no answer. He slowly walks over to the barrels where he last heard any noises as his vision slowly starts to sharpen.

"Hey man. Are you okay? Did you get him?" He continues to blindly ask.

"Where are you?" he asks as he rounds the corner of the barrels.

His eyes focus, he can see his partner dead, propped up by the rebar in his head. The only word that he could muster out of his quivering mouth was, "Fuck."

Clifford's phone rings and it's a familiar number. He contemplates not answering but ends up answering it anyway out of curiosity.

"Dave! How's the family?" Clifford says as he answers the phone.

"Shut up, Dee, and listen. I'm only calling because we have a mutual interest to attend to," he says.

"Okay," Clifford says, "What is this mutual interest?"

Chapter Thirty nine

S tacey is out of breath as he shuffles into his doorway. It was a long trek from the construction site. He had to avoid being seen and take back roads and alleyways due to being covered with Steven's blood. That would have truly raised a few questions from someone.

He steps into his foyer and removes his shoes. He continues into his office and unbuttons his shirt, tossing it into his mesh office trash can.

Moments later Stacey tosses the bloodied clothing and shoes into his fireplace. He settles in a chair taking huge swigs of scotch from the bottle as he watches the flames dance across the fabric, turning the blood-soaked clothing into char. He knows he can relax for only a moment because he's sure it's only a matter of time before Bandoni finds out he's not dead.

Stacey takes another swig, but the scotch isn't taking the edge off. Frustrated, he tosses the bottle into the fireplace, sending the fire into a momentary blaze, as the bottle smashes to pieces against the brick. Assuming Dave would be close behind him, and needing a fix, he opens up a drawer in the coffee table and pulls out a small vial of white powder and examines it. He reaches over and picks up his phone as he starts to gather a few things. Stacey throws on a jacket and heads back to his bedroom to collect some clothes and slip on some shoes. He leaves out of the back of his house and walks down the alleyway to the street as he places a phone call.

"I need a score. I'm almost out," he tells the person who answers.

"Yeah, I have enough to last until tomorrow, we can meet then. What time?" Stacey asks.

"Okay, The Dollhouse? Yeah, I know it, the strip joint. I'll see you there," he confirms as he hangs up the phone.

———

"Some idiot threw a rock at a bird and it hit me in the face," Dave tells the nurse as she's popping gum while writing on a clipboard.

"Mmmkay," She says as she scribbles something down. "You'll probably need stitches, a splint and we're going to check you for a concussion, but you'll be able to go home soon."

Dave gives a half-smile and thumbs up as he pinches his nose with his other hand.

Just before dawn, Dave walks out of the hospital with two black eyes and stitches, and a taped-up nose, sucking on a lollipop. He reaches his car and tosses the stick on the ground. He climbs inside and drives off to find Stacey.

Chapter Forty

Bailey shouts over toward Sara's room to get the attention of the others, "Hey, turn on the news!" Clifford hurries to the door and says, "What's going on?"

"Come here!" Bailey says.

Clifford and Daniel walk over to the TV, with Sara following shortly after.

"...*again, the police have identified this man, Liam Nathaniel Stacey, as a person of interest in the bombing and shooting of the Broward Valley police department.*"

Clifford looks over to Bailey, "Stacey's going to be long gone now that the cops are after him, too."

Morning turns to afternoon, and then to evening. Stacey pulls up to the Dollhouse, and because the marquee is flashing, "Dollar Beer, Half Off Shots," he knew it would be busy. He finds a place to park and walks in. He spots his dealer friend and makes his way over to the booth.

"Jesus, Paul, Could you have picked a busier night?" Stacey says as he scoots in.

Paul smiles, "Yeah, I see you're famous now. Don't worry, no one's looking at any of the dudes here when there are so many beautiful tits out." he says as he looks around at the girls.

Stacey shakes his head, "What do you mean, famous?"

Paul continues, "You know, from the news. I saw you were wanted for questions or something, but don't worry man, no one's going to recognize you with that beard. The picture of you was all baby-faced."

Stacey pulls out his phone and scrolls to his news feed and sees the article with his picture in it. "Fuck!" he says and starts to panic. "I need to get outta here."

Paul looks over at Stacey, "But your stuff, man!" he exclaims as Stacey pushes his way out of the booth. A man from another booth points in his direction. "Hey, isn't that the guy from the news?"

Maggie nervously bites her fingers as Stacey is clearly spiraling out of control. She runs backstage to retrieve her cell phone from her locker to call Bailey.

He answers, "Hey, Maggie, what's up?"

Maggie says, "Remember that Stacey guy you told me about? The one on the news?"

Bailey says, "Yeah, um, why?"

Maggie replies, "He's at the Dollhouse, and people are recognizing him."

Stacey's head is spinning and people are starting to surround him. He pushes his way to the bar and the bartender presses the panic button to alert Marlon.

Marlon looks out from his office and hurries down to the bar.

The bartender walks up to Stacey and says, "Hey buddy, I don't know what you're doin', but you ain't doin' it here," and motions toward the door.

Just then another patron says, "Hey, that's the bomber from the news. Someone get him."

The bartender shouts "Hey!" as Stacey starts toward the door.

Stacey, surrounded by guys trying to impress the talent in the bar, gets pushed backward toward Marlon. He turns around and Marlon says, "Hey, buddy, why don't you come with us."

Josh and two other bouncers push into the entrance and make their way down toward Marlon, just when Dave walks into the bar with a rifle.

A stripper screams, "That guy has a gun!"

Stacey turns around to see Dave pointing the rifle at him.

The bartender shouts, "Hey boss!" as he tosses a shotgun toward Marlon.

People scramble away in fear when Dave begins to fire toward Stacey.

The first shot hit the side of the bar as Stacey dove to the ground. Marlon points his shotgun and shoots Dave right in the chest knocking him backward. Stacey jumps up to his feet as patrons begin to flee the bar. Marlon uses the butt of the shotgun to crack Stacey in the head, but strikes his shoulder, knocking him back to the ground.

People continue to push past Marlon in panic and knock him over. Marlon looks up to see Josh offering his hand. He takes his hand, gets helped to his feet, and notices that Stacey was gone through the panic of the crowd.

Clifford pulls up in his Jeep with Sara, Daniel, and Bailey in the back buckled in.

"You guys stay here!" Clifford says as people were running from the entrance of the club.

Sara shakes her head, "Hell no! We're right behind you," she says as she and Daniel both hop out of the car and run toward Clifford.

Bailey, in disbelief, "Okay guys, I guess I'll just stay here, ...to get kidnapped... again!"

The trio walks in and sees Marlon sitting at the bar on the phone.

He puts the phone down and says, "I called the cops. I had to."

Clifford looks back at the dead body he just climbed over at the entrance. "You shot Dave? Why'd you shoot Dave?"

Marlon looks over at Clifford, "That big motherfucker came in here slinging bullets, What the hell was I supposed to do?"

"Oh wow!" Clifford says, "That was just dumb."

The crowd is completely gone and Bailey watches the last patron flee in his car. His eyes narrow as he notices someone lurking in the shadows around the side of the building.

He could tell from the distance that it was Stacey by the way he walked toward his car parked on the side. Bailey unbuckles his belt and pulls himself out of the car. He draws his firearm and starts to crawl across the gravel to get a better shot. Stacey opens the car door when Bailey takes a few shots. He breaks the back side window and puts a hole in the side of the car. Stacey starts the car and throws it into reverse. Bailey continues to shoot at the car until the clip is empty, as Stacey drives off into the night.

Hearing the shots, the crew run outside finding Bailey face down in the gravel. "I saw him, Dee!" Bailey says.

Clifford and Sara help him up.

"Daniel, go get his chair," Clifford says.

"I couldn't get him. I had a shot, but couldn't take it because of my FUCKING LEGS, Man!" Bailey says in frustration. "I hate this shit. I could have ended it right here."

Clifford gives him a squeeze. "Hey man, it's okay. We'll get him."

Maggie walks up to Bailey and notices a tear running down his cheek. She takes her thumb and wipes it away. "Cheer up, Buttercup," She says, "You did good."

Marlon looks over and says, "Thanks, Sugar!"

Maggie sneers back at Marlon, "It's Maggie!"

Marlon replies, "You're still at work, so."

"I clocked out," she says as she walks away.

Clifford looks over to Marlon, "Do you need us to stay to make a statement?"

Marlon shakes his head, "Nah, you go. I got this."

Clifford pulls into the motel parking lot when he gets a call.

"Mr. Dee, are you still keeping my cousin safe?"

Clifford smiles, "Ask him yourself," he says as he hands Bailey the phone.

"Hello?" Bailey says, placing the phone to his ear.

"Fool, you better have more to say to me than that!" JJ says.

"JJ! Cuz, You better stop messin'!" Bailey says with a smile.

"Hey Cuz, I got some good news for you, but I'm gonna have to ask you and your friends for a huge favor?"

"What's up?" Bailey asks.

"I got out of a meeting this morning and I walked away with a promotion of sorts. But.."

"But, what?"

"Well, I need your help evicting someone from their office," JJ says.

"Girl, just come out and tell me, what's up?"

JJ pauses for a second. "The bosses gave me Bandoni's job and we need to take him out."

Bailey stops for a moment and says. "Oh, we need to meet."

Chapter Forty one

A golf ball flies through the air majestically for a few minutes just before plunging deep into the water trap.

"Dannazione!" Bandoni says looking on with the club in his hand.

"You pulled it, sir," His man-servant says.

Bandoni grimaces knowing he was right, but hated to admit even the smallest shortcomings.

"I pulled it," He says back to his man-servant, handing him his club.

A call came across the radio in the golf cart. "Sir? We have an uh, a situation."

Bandoni is driven by his servant to the front entrance where there are already a few guards with guns standing by the gate. He steps out of the cart and walks up behind his guards as they part, allowing him to approach.

At the gate stands JJ with two strapped guards.

"Nice pants!" She says in a cocky sarcastic tone. "Did I catch you at a bad time?"

"Who are you and what are you doing on my property?" Bandoni snaps.

JJ begins to reach into her jacket pocket when Bandoni's guards raise their guns toward her. She pauses just for a moment and looks over to the guy to her left. He raises his gun toward Bandoni's guards as two more of her men walk out from behind the van they arrived in. They point their guns toward Bandoni.

Bandoni waves off his guards. "Please, we do not want trouble here."

JJ cocks her head to the side and says, "Trouble is up to you and how you respond to this."

She then pulls out a letter from her inside pocket and hands it over to Bandoni.

"What is this?" He asks.

"Your eviction notice," JJ quips back.

Bandoni opens the letter and begins reading. He angrily folds the letter and starts to shove it back into the envelope.

"La Porcheria!" Bandoni exclaimes.

JJ raises her brow "Excuse me?"

"This is Horseshit!" Bandoni says, "You are horseshit!" He continues.

"Not horseshit, more like a coup' d'etat," JJ says.

He begins pacing back and forth in anger, cursing in Italian.

"No, I do not accept this," he says pointing his finger at JJ. "You need to leave now!"

JJ smiles, adjusts her jacket, and says, "I see you have to think this over. 24 hours."

"What?" Bandoni asks.

"You have 24 hours to vacate the property. This is a lease, owned by the corporation. If you decide to stay, you will be removed."

Bandoni walks back toward his golf cart and pulls a hand-gun from his golf bag.

He walks back toward JJ. "Remove me?" He questions as he raises his gun toward her. "Remove this!" he shouts.

"Think again, Mr. Bandoni!" JJ says as her guys raised guns toward him and his guards. The van door slides open and two more with AK47s cock their guns and step out.

From behind a tree, two men step out. One was smoking a cigar holding a rifle. He blows thick smoke from his mouth which highlights a laser scope coming from deep in the woods. Bandoni looks over at one of his guards to see a laser dot center mass. He looks down and sees one on his chest as well. After a moment, a few more appear on other guards.

Realizing they are seriously outmanned and outgunned, he lowers his gun and shoves it into the back of his pants.

"24 hours," JJ says, repeating herself as she backs away and climbs into the van. One by one her men climb inside the van.

"What are we going to do, Boss?"

Bandoni is left with a look of dismay on his face as he watches the van slowly drive down his driveway and pull onto the road. "I need to make a phone call."

Clifford, waiting by his phone, picks it up on the first ring. "How'd it go?"

"You were right," JJ says. "He is going to need a bit of convincing. Meet me at the Dollhouse in an hour."

Marlon is pacing the floor in frustration with Clifford. "Hell no, Dee! We are opening in two hours and I have to get things ready. It's our 5th anniversary of the club tonight. There is a lot to do. I can't have thugs from up north using this as home base right now!"

"Too late," JJ says as she walks into the club.

Marlon looks over at Josh who shrugs. "Sorry, boss. There are more of them than there are of me," he says as dozens of JJ's men walk through the door behind her.

JJ continues walking toward Marlon when Sara blurts out, "God, your beautiful," in awe.

"Keep it in your pants baby girl, that's my cousin," Bailey says, smirking.

Sara shrugs and says, "I call 'em as I see 'em, and I see her."

Bailey laughs and pats Sara on the back.

Marlon stands with his mouth open. "Uh-Marlon," he says nervously, trying to introduce himself.

"A fish?" JJ asks.

"No, uh, sorry. I'm Marlon," he repeats.

"Right. You own this place. I was told a lot about you," She says.

Marlon continues to nervously stare at JJ, taken by her beauty.

"Is everything okay?" JJ asks again, this time more irritated.

Marlon shakes the nerves from his head, "Uh yeah. Yeah. I'm sorry. It's just that I see beautiful women every day, but you are the first to completely take my breath away."

"That's sweet," JJ says, "You do realize who I am, don't you?"

"A goddess?" Marlon says laying it on thick.

JJ rolls her eyes and turns away toward Clifford with a little smile on her face, "How about you get control of your boy over here."

Clifford shakes his head and puts his hand over on Marlon, "Hey loverboy, let's get to business. We have a lot to talk about."

"Agreed," JJ says, "and, Mr. Fish…" she continues with a smirk on her face. "I think we need a space for my guys to set up operations. Do you have a spare room out of the way of your business?"

Marlon hated when people played with his name, but for JJ, it was more than okay. "Yes, ma'am, we have a big storage space in the basement that no one will be using tonight. No one goes down there except my guys and I can have them stay out of there tonight."

JJ looks back to her guys still bringing equipment into the club. "Great. Let's get to work."

Chapter Forty two

Minutes turned to hours and Marlon had to break away to start his duties. They moved their conversation to the basement just before the girls started showing up for work.

By the time night had fallen and the club was in full swing, they had a plan in place, and it started with Sara and Daniel.

Under the cover of darkness, Daniel and Sara quietly walk up through the woods to a chain-link fence stretching across a well-groomed lawn. Daniel pulls out a device and places it on the fence. The device has wires and cables coming out of the top. He takes out a matching device and places it on the fence feet away. He takes the wires and plugs them into the other device. He takes wire cutters and snips a hole into the fence in between the two devices.

They crawl through the hole in the fence and low-crawl toward a few bushes and stop for a moment.

Daniel hands Sara another smaller device and points to a conduit that leads up to security cameras on the roof of the building.

She sprints over to the conduit and then she mutters to herself the instructions on how to set it up as she goes through the steps. As she finishes and turns on the device, she hears Bailey say, "Great job, baby girl, we got eyes!" through the earpiece in her ear.

Meanwhile, Daniel is setting up another device connected to the phone lines. He plugs it in and connects to a utility phone. There's a dial tone, and he places a call.

Bailey's burner phone rings and he answers, "Daniel's pizzeria! We have an extra special deal on Italian dishes tonight."

Daniel laughs, "You have phones. You should be able to record every call they make. I'm also gonna set up a few bugs around the parameter, and then set up the birthday candles."

Bailey smiles, "Affirmative."

Clifford looks over toward JJ and says, "He is really in his element, isn't he?"

JJ laughed, "I told you he's a nerd. This guy could hack into anything."

Clifford asks, "If he can hack anything, why do we need to send Daniel and Sara in?"

Bailey swivels his chair around and says, "I was able to reach the exterior comms device of Bandoni's demarcation point, but he has encrypted firewalls on two points after that and his cameras are all CCTV, so no external access points. This also means that they should have internal, non-web connected servers to store the camera footage, but that really has nothing to do with it. Anyway, the point is, we needed to have a non-encrypted way to plug into their network before I can take over."

Clifford nods and looks over to JJ, "Ah. I see."

JJ looks over at Clifford and mouths, "Nerd."

Bailey sighs, "Yeah, okay. How's this? We could knock on the door with the hope they let us in and show us around orrrr we could just sneak in the window."

Clifford thinks a moment and nods, "Okay, that makes sense."

Bailey turns back around, hearing Sara talking over the mic.

"Sara, who are you talking to?" Bailey asks.

Sara continues to talk, but not to Bailey.

Clifford and JJ walk over to Bailey as he exclaims, "Jesus Christ, Sara's been caught!"

The Patrol guard says, "Again, who are you and what are you doing out here?"

She rolls her eyes as she hears Bailey tell her to flirt her way out of it. With her hands in the air, she slowly turns around and starts popping her gum. "I'm about to do the show."

The guard, looking confused asks, "What show?"

"What show?" Bailey says in Sara's ear.

"Oh, shut up!" she says, meant for Bailey. "You know what I mean," she quickly continues without skipping a beat, "Honey, y'all hired me. The show depends on the tips if you know what I'm sayin'."

The guard, not fazed, says, "No, I have no idea what you're saying."

In her ear, Bailey says, "You're losin' him."

"I'm the Stripper. I'm doing the GI Jane show. At least that's what y'all said you wanted me to do. Why else would I be wearing this camo and face paint?"

Thinking, the guard shakes his head. "I'm calling this in."

Sara clenching her hands is not sure what to do as the guard raises his mic to his mouth.

Bailey, still in her ear, says, "You just need to stall a few more minutes. Daniel is on his way to you now."

"Control, this is Armond, come back," he says into the walkie.

A lightbulb went off in Sara's head. "Oh wait, you're Armond? Well, shoot, honey."

Armond looks over, "What?"

"You're the guest of honor!" Sara says. "I was told to look for Armond and give him the special," she continues with a wink.

"This is control, go ahead, Armond," comes across his walkie.

"Don't tell them I ruined the surprise!" Sara says, "Isn't it your birthday soon? Right?"

Armond raises the walkie, hesitates, and then puts it back down. "It was last week. I thought they forgot."

"See!" Sara says.

A smile comes across his face. "Really? You're here for me?"

Sara steps closer, "mmm-hmm," she says as she puts her hand against his leg.

"I have plans to do things…with your….thingy," she says awkwardly as she has no idea how to flirt with a man.

"Do what witch-cha what?" Bailey says into her ear.

"Shut up!" Sara says.

Armond looks over "What?"

Sara says, "I was just telling myself to shut up. I don't want to ruin your special surprise!"

"Armond, this is control, are you there?" Came across the walkie.

Armond lifts the Walkie and says, "I just wanted to thank you, guys."

Control called back, "Uh, you're welcome? Weirdo."

Armond steps closer to Sara and leans down to put his lips on her neck. She starts to nervously tremble when he can see an earpiece in her ear.

Armond pulls back, "Wait a secon.."

Armond drops to his knees and rolls over to his back, unconscious after Daniel smashed a brick over his head.

"Jesus, Daniel, what took you so long?" Sara asks.

Daniel smiles, "I was actually standing there for a minute, I was kinda curious if you would have let him kiss you."

"Seriously?" Sara says in disbelief. "Unbelievable. You're on my shit list."

Daniel laughs and says, "I was just kidding. I'll get the wrists; you grab his ankles."

They drag Armond to a shed in the back by the garden. Leaving him tied and gagged inside.

They backtrack to the hole in the fence and climb through. They prop the cut portion of the fence up onto the hole to make it look undisturbed and place an orange flag next to it. Daniel ties a string to a tree by the wood line and walks it all the way toward the street. They jump into a car and make their way back to the Dollhouse.

Chapter Forty three

B ailey is surrounded by the crew in the basement of the booming nightclub.

"Thanks to these two," He says pointing over to Sara and Daniel, "We have total control of Bandoni's home network. We have his closed-circuit cameras, his security systems, the communications with his muscle, and we can even control his electricity."

JJ looks pleased. "Okay, if he doesn't leave, and I don't think he will, we should be able to clean this up nicely."

Clifford looks over to JJ's crew and says, "Okay, get some rest, we move out in a few hours."

The guys don't budge until JJ looks back and nods.

Bailey, clicking away on his keyboard says, "Oh shit! Dee, you're going to love this."

Bandoni's grounds are beautifully nestled between rolling hills and thick woods. It's great for privacy, but that privacy comes at the price of security. No one can see what anyone is doing on the property, but you also can't see who's coming to the property without the cameras;

The cameras which are now controlled by Mr. James Bailey in the basement of the Dollhouse.

Because of the vast lands, you must use radios and phones to communicate to all of your security staff; Radios and land phones which are also controlled by Mr. James Bailey in the basement of the Dollhouse.

Two guards sitting in the main gate are having a conversation about sex when a call comes over the radio. "Main gate, come in."

One of the guards picks up the radio, "This is the main gate."

"We're seeing something on the fence line over to your left about 100 feet, do you have eyes?"

The guard replies, "We'll take a look."

He motions to the other guard to check it out who grabs a shotgun and steps out into the cold dark morning. He pulls out a flashlight, turns it on, and heads down the path surrounding the fence line toward the area they mentioned.

With one guard in the shack, a dark car with no lights flies up the drive. The driveway cameras power off and the main control has no sight of what's happening. The guard in the shack can see the small driveway lights reflect off of the dark paint of the car which gives him the sense that something is approaching quickly.

"What the fuck?" He questions out loud to himself. He grabs a shotgun and pushes open the door and steps out. From behind the shack, a black man dressed in dark clothing steps out with a revolver and cocks the hammer behind the guard. He stands there with hands raised and the shotgun on the ground as the car approaches, skidding to a halt on the gravel drive.

The second guard hears the commotion and begins to head back.

Two men step out of the car. One walks in the direction of the other guard and the other opens the passenger door. JJ steps out of the car and walks over to the guard.

"I don't see any moving trucks. In fact, it doesn't seem like you guys are leaving at all. Is your boss home?"

The guard nods nervously.

JJ takes the guard's walkie and raises it to her mouth. "Attention to everyone who's listening. 21 hours ago, I gave you a full day to vacate the premises. Well, you can call me impatient, but I just can't wait to start my new job. Since I am a bit early, I'll leave you with two choices. One; lay down all your weapons and head to the front gate. Leave the property and don't even think about coming back. Now, I am a fair person and I wouldn't want any of you suffering in this job market, so you may apply for a job within MY organization at a later date after this transition is complete. Choice number two; stay here with your current employer, who is no longer being paid by the way, and fight alongside him to your death. You have five minutes to decide.

The guard looks over at JJ and says, "You expect to take over with only four men?"

JJ looks at the guard and says, "You are not very good at your job, are you?"

The guard looks around and begins to notice that there are a lot more men than he first counted. He notices movement behind trees and men walking up the driveway. He's now counting about thirty to forty men approaching.

He looks over to JJ and says, "I'll take option one."

She motions for him to leave.

He steps away just as one of JJ's guys stops him and pats him down. Afterward, he says, "You may go."

The guard swiftly walks down the driveway, passing many men walking toward the house. The second guard in the wood line sees him walking away and says, "Fucking coward!" He starts walking toward him and raises his shotgun.

One of JJ's crew members, Tyrel, sneaks up behind him and says, "I don't think so. Hand it over."

The guard turns slowly towards Tyrel and with one swift movement charges at him, knocking the rifle out of his hand. Tyrel falls to the ground and kicks the guard in the leg, knocking him down. Tyrel jumps up and kicks the shotgun away from him. He begins kicking the guard when he grabs Tyrel's foot, twisting it and forcing him away. Now both the guard and Tyrel are on their feet exchanging blows. Tyrel knocks the guard to the ground but on top of a hard stick. Tyrel tries to stomp on the guard but he rolls out of the way with the branch in his hand and with a swift move, jumps to his feet and hits Tyrel right across the face, knocking him headfirst into a tree. The guard walks up to him and jabs him in the ribs several times. He pins him against the tree and throws the full bodyweight of his knee into his stomach. He lifts up his blood-soaked face and pushes him back against the tree. The guard throws a huge haymaker punch, but Tyrel dodges causing the guard to smash his fist into a tree.

"FUCK!" the guard screams in pain as he cradles his freshly broken hand.

Holding his hand and grimacing in pain, the guard starts to walk over to a bloody and beat Tyrel crawling on the ground.

He sees him trying to reach the shotgun just a few feet away, and runs up and gives him a swift boot to the face, knocking him out.

The guard reaches down and tries to grab the shotgun, but cannot grasp it with his broken hand. He holds it with his left and props it up with his right and starts to head back to the gate.

Up at the house, one by one Bandoni's men are walking out to stand by the front of the house with rifles and shotguns held up over their heads. One man walks up with his hands up and goes straight toward the gate. He is accompanied by Bandoni's personal servant.

They approach JJ and the man says, "This is the personal servant for Mr. Bandoni. He has nothing to do with operations nor is he a militant, I trust that you will see to his safety."

JJ nods and motions for him to leave. "And you might be?" She asks.

"My name is Ricardo. I'm Chief of security and operations. This is not a surrender, but a plea for deliberation," Ricardo says.

"Unacceptable. I gave you time and that time is up. In fact, we're almost at the end of your five minutes," JJ says.

Ricardo looks over the dozens of men that JJ has backing her up and says, "We have three times the men you do, we are fortified in the home, and we have a stockpile of weapons. If you choose to go down this path, it will not turn out the way you hope."

JJ nods and looks down at her watch. She picks up the walkie and says, "Thirty seconds to start walking. Then we come in."

Ricardo looks at her. "Do you think I'm bluffing?"

JJ responds, "I hope you don't think I am." She stares into his face with death in her eyes. Ricardo swallows hard and says, "Well, I guess we're going to have a situation on our hands."

Shots can be heard from the woods out front of the property. The guard in the wood line thought he could get the jump on some of JJs men, but instead became surrounded.

The firefight between the guard and JJ's men startles Bandoni's men at the house. Ricardo shoves JJ to the ground and shouts to his men behind him.

"DEFEND TO THE DEATH!"

The men scramble from the front of the house and start firing toward the front gate.

Ricardo pulls a handgun from the back of his pants and draws on JJ. She taps her stiletto heel on the ground, which triggers a blade to emerge from the front of her shoe. She swiftly kicks the blade into the crotch of Ricardo. Screaming, Ricardo stumbles backward when a sniper in a tree fires, striking him directly in the chest. JJ jumps up and scrambles back toward the gate and into a van. Several of her men run up and fire assault rifles to provide cover as Bandoni's men run away from the bullets.

In the van, while strapping on guns, JJ calls out to Bailey on her radio to the dollhouse. "Hey cuz, you got the comms?"

Bailey says, "Yep, I'm about to direct traffic here in a minute."

With control of the camera, Bailey is able to blind the control room from seeing anything and use the cameras to direct JJs men toward the enemy. He hacks into the electricity and is able to power down all of the lights on the compound. At that point, Bandoni's men are deaf and blind. Quiet fills the land as JJ's crew starts to approach the home from all directions.

Inside, Bandoni's men are scrambling, trying to figure out what's happening with the lights. Over the radio, you can hear them calling to don night-vision goggles.

Bailey directs JJs men to each entrance of the house and tells them to hold their positions.

"Okay, men," Bailey can hear being called over the radio by Bandoni's crew, "everyone with NVGs head toward the entry points and report."

Bailey radios to his guys, "Alrighty crew, the mob have put on night vision goggles and are heading to the entry points. Remain unseen and prepare for lights."

Bailey starts a countdown. "Three.......Two......One." and with that, he mashes the enter key on the keyboard turning on every light in the Bandoni compound. All of

Bandoni's men at the entrance points screech in pain as they are blinded from the brightness of the light through the night vision goggles.

"Now!" Bailey says to the crew and they burst through the doors laying fire to Bandoni's men, killing them all.

After several seconds of light, Bailey cuts off the lights and allows only emergency lighting. JJ's crew begins sweeping the home and killing every single one of Bandoni's men.

Bandoni looks out from his bedroom window and sees JJ gun down one of his men and then stare back at him from the front lawn. Three of Bandoni's men burst into his room, pulling him from the window.

"Boss, we gotta go. They hacked into the system, shutting down our security measures. We need to get you to the helicopter."

Bandoni grabs a bag from his closet and throws on a hat and jacket and leaves the room.

He grabs one of the guards and says, "Destroy the servers!"

The guard radios down to men in the comms room and says, "Burn the server racks."

With that order, three men grab incendiary grenades and go into the server room. They set them on top of the server racks and pull the pins and vacate. The grenades catch as soon as they shut the door of the comms room and the glow of the fire can be seen from under the locked door.

Several of JJs men are being held off by Bandoni's men. "GO! GO! We can't hold them off for long." One of the men says, just before being shot dead. The three guards rush Bandoni toward an elevator in the back hallway. They press the button several times before the doors open. They push Bandoni inside as bullets whiz by their heads. Two guards climb in and one stays behind and screams, "GET HIM OUT NOW!"

He lays down fire and the doors begin to close. Several bullets dent the inside door of the elevator and the guard screams in pain as the elevator descends down away from the fire-fight. The doors open in the basement and the two guards pop out to sweep the area. They motion for Bandoni and climb into a golf cart and begin to speed away down a dark tunnel.

Bailey calls out to Clifford over the radio. "Yo Dee, the mouse is approaching the cheese. Prepare to light the birthday candles."

Clifford is laying down in a prone position about 50 yards away from the helicopter.

Bandoni and his two guards are seen approaching in the golf cart when Clifford pulls a remote from his pocket and presses a button. The helicopter explodes into a ball of light and fire. Bandoni's cart comes to a screeching halt as parts of the burning chopper are landing feet from them. The two guards pull their guns and start backing Bandoni away from the flames when a single shot rings out and strikes one of the guards, center mass. The other guard grabs Bandoni and screams, "Let's go!" and shoves him back into the cart. He runs over to the driver's side and begins to climb in when Clifford grabs him up and fires a single shot into his skull from a pistol.

Bandoni stumbles out of the cart onto the ground.

Clifford walks around and the fire shines a shimmering amber light onto his face.

"Oh, Mr. Dee!" Bandoni says as if he's a friend. "Thank goodness. Help me out of here."

Clifford smiles and says, "Hello, Mr. Bandoni."

"Dee, let's go together. You were always my top guy. We can start over in another city. Maybe somewhere warmer. I know a spot in Sicily we can go to with plenty of work to do." Bandoni pleads.

Clifford shakes his head. "You got it all wrong. I told you to let me leave, but instead, you wanted me killed. This," Clifford says, spreading his arms out to display the destruction around them, " is all me, Eustachio!"

Bandoni trembles for a moment as he looks over his beautiful estate in the soft glow of the dawn's first light, being torn apart in the distance.

He turns back to Clifford and says, "Fine, kill me if you must, but there will always be someone looking to hunt you down!"

Clifford smiles and says, "I have something better in mind for you," as he holds up a pair of handcuffs.

"Arrest me?" Bandoni says with a laugh. "You have no proof of any laws I broke. I will be sipping Espresso from my villa by Tuesday." He continues to lightly chuckle to himself.

"Yeah, I heard you burnt your servers. That was really smart." Clifford says.

Bandoni gives a very smug look just before Clifford strikes him in the head with his rifle, knocking him out.

Chapter Forty four

Sara sits in a coffee shop downtown with a vanilla chai latte and her laptop. She eyes a very professional-looking man walk up to the counter and order a cup of coffee and wait. After a few minutes, he receives his coffee from the barista and proceeds to add artificial sweetener and non-dairy creamer then stirs it with a wooden stick.

As he proceeds to leave the establishment, she calls out on a mic to Daniel, "Headed your way, Baby Bear."

On the corner, Daniel is sitting with a newspaper, "I got eyes on him." Watching as the man, an FBI agent, is heading over toward the FBI field office. Just as he enters the front door, Daniel says, "Now."

A van pulls out from an alleyway as Sara places a call from a burner phone.

The van pulls up and a man with cuffed hands and a pillowcase on his head is forced out onto the sidewalk. Daniel walks up to the man and sits him on the fourth step of the building and places an FBI Lanyard around his neck and tapes a note to his chest.

Daniel says, "Be careful, you're on a lot of steps."

The agent's phone rings just as he reaches the elevators. He answers, "Agent Forrester."

Sara speaks just one phrase. "You should go back outside."

Forrester shakes his head and turns away. He walks back to the entrance of the building where he sees a white van speed away and a handcuffed man with a pillowcase on his head slowly stands up and then plops back down.

He runs down the steps and helps the man to his feet. The note on his chest reads, "Attn: Agent Forrester." He looks down at the lanyard and sees a USB drive attached. He lifts the pillowcase, embroidered with the initials 'EIB', from the man's head. "Holy shit!" Forrester says.

Sara looks on as Forrester pockets the USB and walks Mr. Bandoni up the stairs into the building. "Payload delivered," she says, into her mic and finishes her tea.

Climbing into Clifford's Jeep on the corner she nods at a car full of JJ's men and everyone drives away in different directions.

Sara is the last to arrive at the Dollhouse. She walks in and everyone raises their drinks and yells, "Sara!"

She laughs and says, "Woo! Someone get me a drank!"

Bailey points to a seat next to him and says, "We already poured you a bourbon, Baby Girl."

"You know the secret to my heart!" she says in excitement as she joins the crew at a table.

As everyone was settling into their glasses, Clifford stands and says, "I would like everyone to raise a glass."

Everyone gets quiet and eyes turn toward him. "I want to take this moment to remember those who have fallen. Especially Martin DiPietro. He had our backs from day one and was murdered for doing so." He looks over at Sara, "And to Tracy. An innocent person who just wanted to help a neighbor out."

Quietly everyone raises their glass and takes a swig.

A moment later Clifford gets a phone call on his cellphone. He looks at the caller ID.

"Hey, I think I should take this," and he excuses himself.

"Hello?" Clifford says as he walks away.

"Long time no hear, Sergeant," the voice on the other end of the phone says. "You guys must be celebrating."

Clifford turns and looks at everyone at the table laughing and smiling. "Yeah. We are. How've you been?" He says with a grin.

JJ walks over and stands behind Bailey and raises a glass. "Hey, everyone. I just want to thank my nerdy cousin here. Because of him, this transition went over a hell of a lot better than I thought."

Everyone laughs and cheers as she continues. "We only lost 4 men today and no one was seriously injured. So, here's to Bailey, the super nerd!"

With drinks raised, everyone shouts, "Super Nerd!"

Bailey shakes his head. He looks back at JJ and says, "You know that's going to stick now, right?"

She leans down and kisses him on his cheek, "Love you, Cuz" she says as she gives him a hug.

Daniel stands up and says, "I have a toast as well!" Everyone looks over and gets quiet.

He continues, "This is to Sara!"

"Aww," Sara says as she places her hands over her heart.

"I couldn't have asked for a better teammate to get stealthy with when we were setting up the coms. I still want to know what things she was planning to do with his, 'thingy'!"

Everyone bursts out in laughter as Sara grabs a stale pretzel and tosses it at Daniel. "Ass!" she says smiling.

JJ throws back the rest of her beer and says, "Okay guys, I have to cut and run." The group makes their disappointment known with a collective, "Awwwwww."

She continues, "I've already called a construction crew to clean up the mess we made of my new home."

Everyone looks excited as she speaks. "Yeah, I'm moving my entire operation down here. I just need to redecorate all of that gaudy Italian décor in that house."

"You should keep some of it as memorabilia," Clifford says as he rejoins the group.

JJ looks over and gives him a hug and mouths, "Thank you." She pulls away and says, "Nah, it's all goin'."

The group laughs and JJ thanks all of them again. She walks past Marlon and softly swipes her hand across his back. "Later, Guppy!" She says as she walks away.

"Ha-Ha!" Marlon says in a sarcastic tone and turns to everyone sitting wide-eyed.

"She likes giving nick-names, doesn't she?" he says with reddened cheeks.

Clifford chimes in, "So, I have some news."

The group gets quiet for a moment as he continues, "The call I just got was from my former Army Captain when I was in the war. Apparently, he rose through the ranks, retired, and now works for the Federal Government in D.C."

Everyone was listening intently.

"He offered me a job."

Bailey spoke up, "What kind of job?" he asks.

Clifford smiles and says, "It is a civilian consultant job to his office directly at some Alphabet soup agency. He wouldn't tell me which one as it would be classified."

"So are you leaving?" Sara asks him.

Clifford folded his arms. "Well, I told him that I would think about it because it all depends on if my team is interested. Because I get to build my own team."

They all started to look around.

"I'm saying I won't go without you guys. Are you in?"

Daniel nods, "Yeah, I am going wherever you go, Dee!"

"Heck yeah!" Sara says, "Let's go to D.C.!"

Bailey smiles and says, "Yeah Boss, we're family. I got your back, always!"

Everyone looks over toward Marlon. "Hell NO!" He says folding his arms. "I have a business to run here. And besides, someone has to be here for JJ!"

Bailey chimes in, "Yeah, I think she can handle her own, there buddy."

A sheepish grin forms across Marlon's face for a moment, "She called me, 'Guppy'."

Clifford sighs, "Oh Jesus, man. You're pathetic."

Marlon says, "You guys have one more hour. I have to open soon."

In unison, the group utters, "Aww, Guppy!"

Marlon shook his head, "I knew that would come back to bite me."

Chapter Forty five

It's been quiet but the news is still running the same stories on the TV. *"Weeks after the bombing and shooting at the metro police station, the police still have no leads to the whereabouts of their main suspect Liam Stacey,"* The news reporter says as they are still plastering the same old mugshot of Stacey on the screen, but have added some cell footage of his night at the Dollhouse. Thankfully, the footage was before any shots were fired.

Sara turns off the TV and unplugs it as the movers are removing her couch to load it onto a truck.

Clifford, dodging boxes and movers walks in and says, "I can't believe that you're not done packing. You had over a week."

Sara says, "Yeah, I know. I had to sort through a lot of Tracy's things. It was hard."

Clifford wraps his arms around Sara and gives her a light squeeze. "I miss her so much," she says.

"I know," Clifford responds. "I know."

Sara pulls away and says, "Let's have the guys over for pizza and beer?"

Clifford laughs and says, "Sure, but let me help you get packed so the truck can get out of here."

"Deal!" Sara says.

Later that night Daniel knocks on Sara's door with a huge paper bag.

As Sara answers the door he says, "I got champagne. To celebrate."

Sara takes the bag from his hands and says, "Daniel, we packed the glassware! It's pizza and beer for a reason."

Daniel says, "I brought four, we can just drink from the bottle!"

"Brilliant!" Sara says. Her face changed as she came to a realization. "Wait, you're only Twenty!"

Daniel grins and says, "Fake ID."

The pizza delivery guy arrives a bit later. Daniel and Bailey were already a few beers in. Sara takes the pizza and Clifford slips the delivery guy a hundred, telling him to keep the change. The four pop the champagne at the same time and take huge swigs from the flowing bottles. Music is being played from a cell phone, and Sara and Daniel start dancing in the empty living room.

Bailey starts to wheel out of the room and meets Clifford in the hallway.

"How ya feeling, buddy?" Clifford asks his friend.

"I'm floatin'. I gotta rock a piss," Bailey says.

"Ah, damn. I was about to go. You go ahead, I can hold it a little bit longer," he says.

Bailey smiles, "Thanks, brother."

Clifford walks back into the living room and leans against a pillar, watching as Sara and Daniel dance to "Groove is in the Heart," by Deee-lite. Sara dances over to Clifford and motions for him to join them. He waves her off, but she insists.

Clifford dances awkwardly as he really is not a good dancer. He finally says. "I have to pee. Bailey's in yours; I'll go over to my place."

Sara nods and Clifford says, "I'll be right back."

Sara watches Clifford as he leaves the condo. She turns to the phone and shouts, "Oh no no no, change this!" as the music changes to "All out of Love," by Air Supply.

Daniel grabs his phone and shuts off the music. "Sorry, Sara, I had it on shuffle."

Sara sighs.

"Was that-"Daniel stammers, "Was that a special song or something?"

Sara looks over and says, "No! It was Air Supply."

Daniel laughs and says, "Let's grab some more pizza."

Sara throws a slice on a paper plate, grabs her bottle of bubbly, and says, "Who knew pizza and champagne were so good together?"

Daniel chuckles with a bite of pizza in his mouth. "Apparently, I did," he says with his mouth full.

"Ugh, Chew-swallow-then speak," Sara says.

"Sorry!" Daniel says, still with a mouth full of pizza.

Sara rolls her eyes as she takes another swig out of the bottle. She walks over to the bathroom and knocks.

"Occupied!" Bailey says.

Sara says, "Hurry up, I have to go, too, and Dee is already in his."

Bailey says, "Don't rush me wumman!"

Sara laughs and says, "I am not beneath hitting a cripple!"

Bailey says, "Well, It's going to be another minute. Number one turned into number two."

"UGH!" Sara says. "I'll go over to Dee's. He'll probably finish first."

Sara walks away and turns to Daniel, "I will kill that guy if he stinks up my bathroom."

She takes another swig of champagne as she heads out of the condo and into the hallway. She notices that Clifford's door is slightly open and can hear a bit of commotion.

She pushes the door open as Clifford is knocked across the foyer floor from the hallway inside his condo. Sara hides briefly in the hallway next to the door as she sees Stacey walk toward Clifford.

"I lost everything because of you Dee," Stacey says, drawing a pistol from his waistband.

Clifford leans up and props his weight onto one elbow as Stacey continues. "I just couldn't skip town without saying goodbye," he says pointing the pistol.

Before Stacey could pull the trigger, Sara bursts into the foyer and breaks the champagne bottle over his head.

His eyes roll to the back of his head as he drops to his knees and falls awkwardly to his side.

Seeing Stacey on the ground, she lets out a huge primal scream and jumps on top of him, and begins throwing punch after punch until his entire body is a limp bloody mess. Blood sprayed across Sara's shirt from splitting his lip and breaking his nose.

Clifford is able to push himself up off the floor and pulls a now sobbing Sara off of Stacey. She lets out a guttural sob and Clifford cradles her head into his chest.

"You got him, Sara. It's over. You got him," he says to her, trying to catch his own breath, "Thank you for saving me."

Daniel, hearing the commotion, hurries into the room, "What's go-OH my God!" He exclaims as he sees a bloodied Clifford and a bloodier Stacey on the floor. He rushes over to check if Stacey is still breathing.

"Daniel, get something to tie him up," Clifford says with a mouth full of blood.

"I'm on it!" he says already on the way to Sara's condo.

Bailey wheels past Daniel and asks, "What the hell is going on?"

Daniel is rummaging through the packing materials and says, "I need to find something to tie that guy up."

Wheeling faster away Bailey questions, "What guy?"

Sara throws Clifford's arm around her and helps him as he limps out of the condo and into the hallway.

Bailey wheels towards them with a concerned look on his face.

Sara looks at him and says, "It's Stacey!"

Sara's eyes widen as she sees Bailey reach into a side pocket of his chair and pull out a small handgun and point it at them.

"Get down!" Bailey demands as Stacey slides out of Clifford's condo with a gun trained on them.

Sara pulls Clifford down and the two fall, giving Bailey a clean shot.

Three shots echo through the hallway of the building as the rounds hit Stacey in the chest. Clifford and Sara, looking back, watch as Stacey falls to the ground, blood pouring from his wounds.

Bailey looks over at Sara and Clifford on the floor and asks, "We can't get to D.C. fast enough?"

Daniel runs into the hallway with packing tape in his hand and looks over at Stacey as he bleeds out in the hallway.

The three look up at Daniel as he holds up the packing tape and he asks, "Do you think we still need to restrain him? No?"

(jdr)